STOP IN THE NAME OF LOVE

NINA BRUHNS

Entangled Publishing, LLC
2614 South Timberline Road
Suite 109
Fort Collins, CO 80525
Visit our website at www.entangledpublishing.com.

Ignite is an imprint of Entangled Publishing, LLC.

Edited by Liz Pelletier
Cover design by Louisa Maggio
Cover art from iStock

Manufactured in the United States of America

First Edition November 2015

ignite

For Beverly, and all my friends at SMCNS. Thanks for teaching me all about kids.

Prologue

Where the hell had *he* come from?

Pasadena Police Detective Sergeant Russell Bridger straightened and peered through his binoculars in annoyance at the young bicycle patrolman who came wheeling into the alley where Bridge's vice squad team had set up today's sting—the culmination of two months of risky undercover work and careful planning. This was not good. The targeted meth dealer was due to turn up any second now, along with the buyer, complete with heavily armed entourages. According to the team's CI, today's meet was supposed to be a major buy. And both parties had nasty reputations for shooting first and asking questions never.

This kid was going to get in the way.

Shit.

"Who the fuck is that?" Jose's growl came over Bridge's earbud, along with the colorful curses of four other team members.

Jesus, could he look any more out of place in this rough neighborhood, with his new bike, shiny badge, and summer uniform of neat navy-blue shorts, crisp short-sleeved shirt, and APD baseball cap? Hell, he barely looked old enough to shave. Had he graduated from the academy last week, or what?

"Hold your positions," Bridge murmured into his com. "Hopefully the kid's just taking a shortcut."

Or not.

Bridge gave a mental groan when the rookie glided to a stop, dismounted his bike, and approached a homeless guy sleeping against the dirty brick wall. A homeless guy who was actually Chen, one of the team.

Right about that same time, a trio of trailer trash ninjas appeared in the mouth of the alley. The one in the middle was carrying an incongruously nice aluminum briefcase, filled with money no doubt, and the two flanking him were armed to the teeth.

Fuck.

"We got movement, Sarge," Flip reported from his position on the roof. "Target's vehicle approaching from the east.

Holy hell. "Chen, get that kid out of here, *now*," Bridge ordered. "Light a goddamn fire."

There was another round of curses in his ear as a sleek white Mercedes halted at the other end of the alley, blocking it off. Three bad guys emerged from the car with noticeable bulges under their fancy suits.

Effectively making the kid a bicycle rookie sandwich from hell.

Fucking *damn* it.

Bridge didn't even stop to think. He threw the binoculars at Jones, touched the Glock 21 tucked under his ratty, oversized T-shirt, and stumbled from his concealed doorway out into the alley, singing a loud, wheeling, drunken version of *O Danny Boy*. It was the first tune that popped into his mind. Possibly from too many gleefully boisterous renditions by his dad upon every single solitary festive occasion in his whole damned life.

Bridge almost smiled. But that would have blown his cover.

Chen said something sharply to the rookie, who proceeded to frown, then look up and down the alley like a fucking navy-blue neon sign that screamed HEY BAD GUYS! POLICE SET-UP!

A feeling of absolute impending disaster swept over Bridge nanoseconds before the hail of bullets started flying. He started to run.

And lunged for the kid.

Chapter One

Mary Alice Cathryn Flannery did *not* make mad, passionate love to men on the hood of her car.

Didn't matter how hunky the guy from the road construction site down the street from her Sierra Madre Canyon cottage was. She had no plans to ask him out on a date when he stopped her vehicle on the way to work—or even flirt with him—and she definitely would not be having monkey sex with him on the hood of her SUV.

Which made it somewhat mortifying that he'd invaded her dreams all night, doing just that.

She, who hadn't so much as looked at a man in three years, was suddenly having erotic dreams about the muscle-bound brain trust holding up a freaking stop sign on a road crew.

She was losing it. No doubt about it.

She bent down and swooped up the shards of her favorite

coffee mug, flinging them into the kitchen rubbish bin—right on top of the remains of the half dozen eggs she'd splattered across the floor a few minutes earlier.

Seriously. They should make him put on a shirt. Every single female driver had her eyes glued to that ripped, tanned, hair-sprinkled chest. The man could cause an accident.

Sure, he was handsome enough to stir any woman's blood—yeah, even hers. His body was hard and lean without an ounce to spare under those loose-hipped jeans. And the come-hither way he crooked his finger at her when he spun his sign from stop to slow, motioning her through the pitted construction site? Well, no wonder he induced snooze-button abusing dreams.

Still. It didn't matter how provocative the sight of the man's bare, muscular torso. Or how sexy the hint of spicy cologne, honest sweat, and canyon dust that drifted off that wide expanse of male flesh when he stood next to her open car window. Though granted, it was pretty darn sexy.

It was ironic, really. The first guy to get her engine going in three years, and his job was to hold up a stop sign.

Gawd. Was the universe trying to tell her something?

She yanked her flannel robe tighter over her breasts and groaned. The plastic noses of her Snoopy slippers clicked furiously on the hardwood floor as she marched to the bedroom and flung open the closet door. When she pulled a neat cotton blouse off its hanger, the top button sailed across the room, ricocheted off the vanity mirror, and landed smack in the middle of the unmade brass bed. She allowed one succinct expletive to escape.

Enough, already!

Gritting her teeth, she glanced at the clock. With the long trail of distracted disasters this morning, she was running super late. Quickly, she shrugged on a loose, shapeless T-shirt dress over an equally shapeless sports bra—her usual garb for her job as a nursery school teacher. Frumpy? Maybe. But it was comfortable and bleachable. That's what counted.

She hurriedly ran a comb through her long red hair. Lord, it just got redder and redder every summer. Only May, and already the sun had turned it bright enough to stop traffic. With a grimace, she gave it a final swipe and wound it into a twist.

There was nothing about her appearance that would attract the attention of a certain broad-shouldered Adonis. Definitely nothing to make him pin her to the hood of a car, lift her skirt, and—

Good lord.

How on earth would she ever face him this morning—the raven-haired man who'd had the starring role in dreams that even now left her knees weak and her body aching?

She gave herself a stern mental shake, slipped her feet into clogs, and clattered down the hall. She grabbed the oversized canvas bag that doubled as her purse on workdays and sailed out the front door. When she reached the SUV, she squeezed her eyes shut, barely resisting the urge to lay a hand on the hood.

"Hey there, Mary Alice!"

Her eyes sprang open and she spotted her neighbor, Charlie Watson, waving to her. His huge contemporary home towered over her miniature craftsman cottage. Charlie stood on the edge of his beloved water lily pond pulling out dead leaves and fussing with the buds and blooms, as he did every morning before leaving for work. For a bachelor, the man was a bit obsessive about his water lilies. Of course, she didn't blame him. She was the same way about her treasured roses.

"Hi, Charlie."

"Looks like it's going to be another hot one," he called over in a friendly voice.

She looked up at the sky, barely seeing it. She smiled and

waved back. "Nice breeze, though."

Charlie was a good neighbor—always keeping a protective eye out for her. His frequent parties were first class, if somewhat disorderly. And it was fun teasing him about his silly water lilies. He actually thought they were prettier than her roses.

With another wave, she turned back to her car. And frowned. There was a folded piece of paper fluttering under the windshield wiper. She pulled it out then gave a small gasp as she noticed the time on her watch. She'd barely make it to school before the kids got there at eight-thirty. Even worse than keeping the kids and parents waiting, she'd be forced to endure one of her boss Lucinda's lectures on the virtues of punctuality.

Cramming the paper hastily into her pocket, she slid into the car, adjusted the seat-back straight up, and reversed out of the driveway, praying the stupid road construction wouldn't delay her. Maybe they—meaning *he*—would be taking the day off.

The way her day was going? She should be so lucky.

Chapter Two

A *nother fucking day in paradise.*

Bridger leaned his butt on the treads of a big yellow construction Caterpillar, stuck his grimy stop sign up in the air, and caught sight of a familiar blue SUV as it approached. The corner of his mouth twitched upward as the attractive female driver looked everywhere but at him.

Ah, the lovely Miss Flannery. Finally.

He straightened a bit and deliberately flexed the muscles in his sign arm. Oh, yeah. She was peeking. She just didn't want to admit it.

Cute. Most of the women driving by made no secret they were ogling him. He grinned. He felt so objectified.

When Chief Trujillo had told him last week he'd been loaned out to the FBI to serve on the Charlie Watson joint task force, Bridge had protested long and loud. The feebs were so damn stuffy. Rule-followers. They wore *suits* to work. Then insult was added to injury when his assignment turned out to be this lame undercover stakeout gig in the sleepiest damn 'burb in the entire San Gabriel Valley, spending eight hours a day playing traffic cop along a dusty road-construction detour in the quaint and trendy Sierra Madre Canyon. Just to keep an eye on their suspect Charlie Watson's house…on the off chance he took his treasonous activities home with him. Which, so far, he hadn't. Naturally.

Okay, okay. There were a hell of a lot worse ways of spending one's day than basking in the warm California sunshine with your T-shirt hanging out of the back pocket of your jeans, watching the ladies gawk at your bare chest. And Bridge had done most all of those worse things. Being in Pasadena Police Department's Special Investigations Section—i.e. the vice squad—pretty much guaranteed there would be blood, drugs, prostitutes, gunplay, or all of the above, as part of your day. And Bridge loved every minute of it.

He was pretty sure the chief had put the feebs up to choosing him for this plum assignment. Bridge was on Trujillo's shit list because, although he had made the promotion list three years in a row now, he steadfastly refused to give up his wild and woolly job in SIS for a lieutenant's badge and a desk. *Hells* no. Bridge liked his life exactly as it was. Exciting, never the same, no ties, and no responsibilities beyond himself and the job he loved. Well, and his dad, of course. But Dad was Dad, and quite capable of taking care of himself.

Still, Bridge had to admit the gig had its upsides, FBI or no. Beat the hell out of sweltering in a sardine can on wheels sucking down hot coffee just to stay awake, which is what he normally did on stakeout duty.

Okay. Maybe the chief wasn't as pissed at him as he'd thought….

The blue SUV crunched to a halt several yards in front of him and Ms. Flannery made a big show of fussing with something on the seat beside her.

Bridge pushed himself off the big Cat, tucked his sign under his arm, and sauntered up to her car. According to her file, she wasn't much younger than he was, but she came across that way. There were freckles sprinkled on her nose, and yesterday there'd been a little smudge of green paint on her cheek when she came home.

Very cute.

Not that he had any interest in cute. Absolutely not his speed.

Even so, a strand of long, reddish-gold hair had fallen out of her ugly bun, and he had to make a conscious effort not to reach over and tuck it back in.

Or maybe tug out a little more.

Once he'd recognized her as Charlie Watson's neighbor, he'd made sure he stopped her car at the front of the line so he could begin flirting with her, casually starting up an acquaintance that might be useful to him in the stakeout.

Draping an arm across the bottom of her open window, he looked in at her and smiled. "Mornin', ma'am."

"Oh!" A pair of sunglasses flew from her hand onto the vehicle's floor.

He pushed his hard-hat up with a forefinger and peered down at the shades, his gaze lingering for a moment on her fine, shapely legs. Instinctively, his gaze was drawn to the ring finger of her left hand resting nervously on the steering wheel—even though her background check had already told him what he'd find. *Nada.*

Okay, so maybe she had piqued his interest. Just a little.

He gave her a slow, easy grin. "Sorry to delay you, ma'am. Just have to radio ahead and make sure none of the trucks are heading this way."

She smiled back uncertainly. "*Um.* Sure."

Damn, she was sweet.

Straightening, he folded his arms across the edge of her car roof, deliberately letting her get up-close and personal with his chest. In his imagination, he could see her cheeks flood with rosy color, as they had morning and afternoon for the past three days, every time he spoke with her.

He chuckled. He hadn't thought women actually blushed anymore. Judging by her increasingly flustered reaction to him, his campaign to attract her attention was working.

Stifling a grin, he spoke into his walkie-talkie. "Deke, we got anything coming our way?"

The radio squawked back, "You're clear, Bridge."

"Thanks, bro." He bent back into her window. Yep, her cheeks were red as sweet, ripe strawberries, so real he could even smell them. This assignment was definitely growing on him. "Okay, ma'am. You're all set."

Stepping back, he spun his sign from STOP to SLOW, and as a parting shot, he gave her a wink.

Her eyes widened and her foot hit the accelerator, sending the SUV forward with a lurch. After the hard-bitten, burnt-out females he normally encountered as a cop, and the fast, glitzy women he usually dated, this woman was like a breath of fresh air.

Yes, ma'am. Fresh, sweet, strawberry-scented air.

Chapter Three

Somehow, Mary Alice managed to make it through her day at the Sierra Bonita Parent Co-op Nursery School. It was a quarter to four, and the sixteen three-year-olds in her Toddler Group had all been picked up. One thing about being a nursery school teacher, the curriculum wasn't all that demanding. If the parents working in her class thought she was unusually absentminded today, they hadn't said anything.

Thank God.

How could she possibly explain that she was distracted because her sleep had been plagued the whole night by dreams of a sweaty, half-naked, midnight-haired construction worker doing unspeakable things to her on the hood of her car? Not to mention fretting over the way he'd flirted with her this morning. As if he'd *known* about her dreams.

Of course, that was ridiculous. How could he? Aside from which, he could flirt all he wanted, and it wouldn't do him any good. Finding a man was one of the very *last* items on her Master Plan for a Perfect Life. There were at least a dozen things she wanted to check off the list before she even considered that one.

"Mary Alice Cathryn! What are you *doing*?"

She glanced at the container of perfectly good red paint she was pouring down the sink, then looked up horrified into the face of her best friend, Nancy, who taught the Pre-K Group of four-year-olds, then back to the sink…and groaned.

"Don't you dare tell the dragon lady."

Nancy smirked. "Won't have to. Lucinda measures them at night."

Mary Alice snickered then looked around quickly. "*Shh!*"

Nancy regarded her, amusement in her eyes. "And what has Miss Frugality so rattled today that she's dumping out school supplies?"

Setting her mouth in a line, Mary Alice shook her head. No way was she going to tell Nancy the truth. "I, *um*…got a letter from the Pasadena Heritage Rose Society yesterday. They've set my interview for Thursday."

Well, that much was true, at least.

"Mac, that's terrific! I know how much it means to you, getting into the Society."

Roses were a big deal in Pasadena, and it was a real honor to be a member.

"Well, it's the only way my roses will be officially recognized and registered. I feel I owe that much to old Mrs. Trent. She nurtured them for seventy years before selling that cottage to me last year."

Nancy smiled sagaciously. "And I'm sure nearly completing one more item on your five-year Master Plan makes you very happy."

Mary Alice put the lid on the paint with a snap. It was an old discussion, and she didn't feel like once again debating the merits of setting sensible life goals versus randomly falling in love with any guy who came along and drifting into an uncertain future. Especially after a disturbing night of sexy car-hood dreams that just might sway her way of thinking. She really did miss—

Good lord.

"Yes. It does feel good to cross another accomplishment off my list," she affirmed proudly. Lots of people made resolutions, but few actually met them.

"You really are determined to keep your ridiculous timetable on track, aren't you?"

She set her jaw and placed the paint on a shelf. She knew Nancy wasn't being critical. They just had very different philosophies on life and love.

After Mary Alice's fiancé Jack's death three years ago, her father's murder a month later—and her favorite uncle being gunned down when she was a child—she had made a choice to create a fulfilling life for herself without the presence of a man in it. Loving the men in her life always seemed to bring her profound loss and heartache in the end, leaving her broken and grieving when their lives were ripped away much too soon.

But with time, the pain had dulled and her common sense had prevailed. Losing her fiancé, father, and uncle had been horrible, but she realized it shouldn't make her reject the idea of falling in love altogether. The men in her family had all been police officers. Therefore, she just needed to avoid relationships with men who were cops, or in equally risky professions.

When she was ready for marriage and family, that is.

Which she wasn't. Not yet. It had only been three years since she lost Jack…and there were too many things left on her Master List to do before she could even consider falling in love and settling down.

Nancy didn't agree with her decision to forego love in favor of other priorities. But then, Nancy was a diehard optimist and an incurable romantic.

"It feels good to have order in my life and accomplish the goals I've set for myself," Mary Alice said, firmly deflecting the melancholy that threatened, sending it down to the far corners of her heart. She did want to have a husband and kids someday. *Someday.* "What's so bad about that?"

Nancy gave her a sad smile. "Nothing, sweetie. Unless it takes over and makes you push aside everything else. Such as falling in love, or even just having a little fun once in a while."

"I have lots of fun," Mary Alice protested. "With my students, in my garden, with Mom." She lifted her chin when Nancy rolled her eyes, but couldn't help a wry smile. "All right, maybe not with Mom. But what about Charlie's parties? I always go to those."

Nancy made a face. "Yeah. I suppose you could meet someone there. Though, if his friends are anything like him... God. Those stupid water lilies."

Mary Alice grinned, and noticed for the first time that Nancy had changed into a fancy dress. She poked a finger at it. "Hey! Speaking of parties, what are you up to today?"

"Picking up Ben for a night on the town. He's going in tomorrow to have that series of tests at the hospital. You know what a baby he is, so I promised him steak and lobster and a dirty movie tonight." She waggled her eyebrows lasciviously.

Mary Alice giggled. "You two are unbelievable. I thought you were supposed to lose interest in that sort of thing after six years of marriage."

"Are you kidding?" Nancy got up and headed for the door. "We're just getting warmed up. You should find yourself a man and try it." Grinning, she disappeared with a finger wave.

Try what? Being married for six years...or *that sort of thing*? Nancy knew how Mary Alice felt about the first, but the second...? With a groan of frustration, she jammed her hands in her pockets. Those damn obnoxious erotic dreams!

Feeling something crinkle under her fingers, she suddenly remembered the paper from under the windshield wiper that she'd stuck in her pocket that morning. She pulled it out and opened it to find a note handwritten in a quick scrawl.

Ma'am, Since the crew will be working on the street directly in front of your driveway starting tomorrow, please see me this afternoon about where you can park your car overnight so you're not blocked in. Russell Bridger

Great. Just what she needed.

Suddenly, she looked more closely at the name. Surely, it couldn't be *him*?

What was the name she'd heard over the walkie-talkie? Brad? Brett? *Hmm*. Not Russell, anyway. *Thank God*. It had been bad enough making eye contact with him that morning. She didn't think she could stand face-to-face with the man, trying to carry on a normal conversation. Not with her mind flooded with visions of his bronze, callused hands on her body, his warm tongue delving into her mouth, his hard—

Ho-boy.

Grabbing her canvas tote bag, she rushed out the classroom door, barely managing to lock it, and hurried to her car. Her heart galloped and her cheeks burned as she fumbled with the ignition. Lord above, somehow she had to find a way to exorcise those damn dreams from her mind.

Along with the all-too-sexy man who dominated them.

Chapter Four

Bridge glanced at his watch. Five minutes to quitting time, and still no Mary Alice Flannery. For three days in a row she had driven up at exactly eight-thirty a.m. leaving for work, and at four p.m. on the dot coming home. But now it was nearly four-thirty. He slapped his stop sign against his thigh and let out an impatient curse. Why today, of all days?

Had he pushed his flirtation too far? Scared her off?

He leaned his butt against a muddy backhoe and slung the sole of his boot onto the running board. *Damn.*

It had been a lucky break for him—an attractive, single woman living next door to Charlie Watson. At least, Bridge had hoped it would be a lucky break. He'd figured he could ask her out on a date or two, use his well-honed charm to schmooze as much information out of her as he could about her rich neighbor. Ask if she'd been to any of Watson's rumored parties.

Inquire if she wanted to go to one of Bridge's own.

He felt a pleasant tightening below his zipper. Yeah, a wild party just for two.

He blew out a breath. *Down, boy*. Her background file listed her occupation as nursery school teacher. One look at the woman's hair and clothes said she was the sweet and proper type of woman. He had to remember that, especially when his libido got sidetracked by her cute freckles and long, curvy legs. She wasn't his speed. Not by a long shot. He didn't do sweet, and he certainly didn't do proper.

He'd made a promise to his late mother on her deathbed, and he'd lived by that promise all his adult life. He'd sworn that as long as he worked as a police officer, he wouldn't marry some fragile and sensitive woman and send her to an early grave worrying about whether or not he'd come home alive every night. As his mom had worried about his dad.

Bridge had been too young to understand the danger, so he hadn't worried about his cop father so much as despaired over his delicate mother's slow decline. In that sense, as a child he had been just as affected by the situation. One more good reason to avoid serious relationships—no kids to mess up.

He'd had no problem keeping his promise to his mother. Being a cop in this town was a hazardous profession. Officers died every year. He'd seen growing up what the endless worry had done to his mom's nerves, and how that had impacted his own life. No way did he want to be the cause of that for anyone he loved.

Besides, avoiding meaningful relationships suited his footloose lifestyle.

Sure, he'd break his rule against sweet and innocent and ask Ms. Nursery School Teacher out a couple of times—but only for the sake of the case. He'd probably be bored stiff, anyway. What could they possibly have in common to talk about?

The construction foreman blew the whistle, and Bridge gave one last irritated look down the road then headed for his truck. He tossed his hard-hat on the bench behind the driver's seat. Today *would* be the one day she veered off her clockwork pattern. Hadn't she gotten his note? He frowned. Or was she deliberately blowing him off?

Hell. He'd just have to come back and talk to her later. Whether she liked it or not.

Chapter Five

With a self-satisfied sigh, Mary Alice pulled off her clothes and headed for the shower. Take that, Mr. Sex-on-a-Stick. By coming home an hour later than usual, she'd managed to avoid seeing him for another fifteen hours. Maybe she'd get really lucky and it would be his day off tomorrow.

Hopefully, the respite would allow her to squelch the low thrum of desire that pulsed through her at the mere thought of seeing him…and to tame the crazy impulse to lean out her car window and run her tongue up his tempting bare chest.

Because despite her unruly hormones throwing tantrums at being denied the man's buff body, she was *not* interested in him. For crying out loud, he held up a stop sign for a living! The sex might be incredible, but what would they talk about afterward? Clearly, the man was a California sun bum with no real ambition in life. Somehow, she couldn't imagine discussing James Joyce with him…or even Steven Hawking.

She groaned at the foolishness of her body, and turned on the shower faucets full blast. The first man she'd been attracted to in three years, and *this* was the one her sadly misguided libido picked. She stepped under the warm water and picked up the soap.

Though, admittedly, it could have been worse. Construction work was a safe, honest profession. And he wasn't a cop.

When she was done with her shower, she pulled a brush through her damp hair and went to her closet. She hesitated, then chose an old, rose-colored satin slip from the thirties that she'd picked up at an antique shop. It could pass for a summer sundress today, and felt deliciously cool and comfortable over her bare skin with its simple lines and slippery fabric. The perfect antidote to not having air conditioning.

She'd just settled on the couch with a bowl of pre-dinner lime sherbet and a good book when a knock came at the front door. Probably a friend or neighbor dropping by to say hi. Sierra Madre was one of the safest towns in the country, so she didn't hesitate to open the door wide.

Regret came instantly.

It was *him*! Mr. Heart-Stopper himself.

"Oh!"

Shocked, she let the book tumble to the floor. The sherbet bowl started to slip from her fingers as she stepped back and stumbled over the rug.

In a flash, he reached out and grabbed the bowl with one hand and her waist with the other, reeling her tight up against him. His tall, hard body pressed intimately into hers. She regained her footing but was thrown way off balance in another, much more elemental way.

Wow, he felt good.

She looked up into his eyes and was instantly captured by the invitation she saw in the hot, searing look he gave her.

She couldn't move.

Thankfully, he could. He released her waist and wordlessly offered her the bowl. Lifting a shaky hand, she took it.

Slowly, he raised his thumb and licked off a dollop of sherbet that had stuck to it. She swallowed along with him.

Holy. Crap.

His gaze wandered down her body, then up again. "Ma'am."

Sizzling hot awareness zinged from the top of her head all the way to her toes. Her verbal skills regressed to the level of her toddlers. She doubted she could utter a single coherent sentence if her life depended on it.

She just stood there like an idiot, flushed and suddenly freezing, clutching the bowl in both hands.

"You get my note?" he asked, his dark eyes searching hers.

Huh? He was standing so close she could feel the heat from his skin. Or maybe it was from her own cheeks.

"*Um…*n—" She cleared her throat and tried again. "Note?"

He turned slightly and jerked his chin toward her car. "About the driveway being blocked tomorrow morning?"

"Oh." *Duh.* She nodded dazedly. "Yeah. I…*um*…got home late."

His lips tilted in a knowing smile. "So I noticed."

Her mental capability gradually started trickling back. *The note.* Which meant he must be— "Russell Bridger?"

The smile widened. "My friends call me Bridge." He looked at her expectantly.

Relief hit her that he wasn't here on a more personal mission…possibly involving hoods of cars. She retreated another step. "You came all the way back to show me where to park my car, Mr. Bridger?"

"Bridge. Miss…?"

"Miss?" She blinked. "Flannery. Mary Alice Flannery." God, could she sound like a bigger moron?

He shifted on his feet a little. "Well, Miss Flannery, we

start work pretty early, and I wouldn't want to have to wake you up from a sound sleep tomorrow morning just to move your car."

His gaze raked over her, making her wonder what he *would* like to wake her up for. The traitorous thought crept into her mind that it might be interesting to find out.

"*Um*. That's very nice of you, Mr. Bridger."

"Bridge. I'd be happy to move it for you."

She stared at him. "Now?"

"No charge." He gave her a devilish grin, and her heart did a backward two-and-a-half with a twist and landed somewhere in the vicinity of his feet.

She felt herself blush at her body's unfamiliar reaction to him. "Oh. Okay. Thanks." Or maybe it was from the memory of those dreams…

After several more seconds of staring at him and he at her, she smiled uncertainly. "*Um*…"

His grin widened. "Keys?"

God.

What was she, like, thirteen?

She shook her mind into gear. "Of course. I'll get them."

After all, what harm was there in letting him move her car? It wasn't as if he was here to ask her to dinner. Or… anything else.

Right?

Chapter Six

Bridge's amusement drifted to rapture as he watched Mary Alice turn and walk into the house. Her hips swayed gracefully; the soft wisp of a dress she wore clung to every curve like a silk glove. Tendrils of strawberry blond formed a halo about her head and bare shoulders. It was a sight that could make a grown man get down on his knees and beg.

He took a deep breath and landed nose-first in the lingering scent of strawberries. With a muffled moan, he speared his fingers through his hair.

Damn, she was sexy.

He could tell she was attracted to him. She had an adorably transparent reaction to his flirtatious teasing, as though she didn't usually let herself respond to a man's sexual advances, but couldn't help herself around him. Hell, it was enough to inflate a man's ego.

Among other things.

His plan was to coax information out of her about Watson. But the sight of her ripe, sensual body had Bridge instantly thinking of coaxing other things out of her. Things that had nothing to do with her neighbor's comings and goings and everything to do with her own.

Oh, baby. He wanted to look down on her long, sexy hair spilling all over his pillow and to taste the sweet promise of her full lips. To watch her going over the edge, and make her call his name, coming in his arms.

He squeezed his eyes shut in frustration.

Get a grip, Bridger.

Mary Alice wasn't the type of woman to be interested in a casual toss in the sack with a jaded vice cop. And that was all he had to offer. He wanted her, absolutely. But on *his* terms. Which meant *short* term.

No strings, no attachments, no regrets.

His job came first, and he didn't want any woman to do battle with the nerves and anxiety of being with a man who put his life on the line every day.

Like his mom.

Nope. That scene was so not for him. Bridge had made his mother a promise, and he meant to keep it. For his own sake, as much as for the women he was protecting by leaving them be.

Watching pretty Mary Alice float toward him in that flimsy excuse for a dress, he straightened his shoulders and plastered on his most charming smile. He took the car keys from her and strode purposefully to the SUV in the driveway.

Business, Bridger. Remember, this is strictly business.

Chapter Seven

M ary Alice stepped outside the house and gripped the porch rail nervously as she watched Bridge amble down the driveway and slide behind the wheel of her SUV. What had gotten into her? Nearly swooning at the man's feet.

Unfortunately, she knew exactly what had gotten into her—totally inappropriate thoughts. Her face heated just thinking about them.

He parked her car in a shallow cutout scooped into the hillside a bit down the winding street. She hugged her arms across her breasts, acutely aware of their hard tips through the satin fabric of the old slip. The way his gaze had stroked over her body moments ago had made her feel as if she'd been standing there naked. Which she practically was. She hadn't bothered with a bra or panties after her shower because of the heat.

Steadfastly ignoring the goose bumps on her arms, she forced herself to smile as he strolled back through the front gate. He paused at one of the rose bushes along the adjoining picket fence. "Damask?"

Surprised, she nodded, then walked down the front steps to join him. "Kazanlik."

He raised a brow. "I'm impressed."

She let her astonishment show. "So am I." He wasn't the type she'd expect to identify different types of roses.

He tossed her a lopsided grin and lifted a shoulder. "My mom had roses."

"Had?" She saw something raw flash through his eyes, and instantly regretted her nosy question.

"She passed on years ago," he said, his smile returning. "But her roses live on. I do what I can, but I'm afraid Dad sorely neglects them. Too bad. They're beautiful."

She touched a delicate flower with the tip of her finger, admiring the lush pink petals. "Yes, they are. What a lovely legacy she left for you."

His gaze lingered for a moment on her, then jumped to the next rose bush down the row. "And this would be Maiden's Blush, I presume?"

The man was full of surprises. "Mr. Bridger, you put me to shame."

"Bridge, please. How's that?"

"Before I bought this house I might have been able to tell you this was a rose, but that would be about all."

He chuckled, moved past her, and stooped to smell a yellow blossom further along the fence. "Growing up, I spent a lot of time pulling weeds with Mom. Couldn't help picking up a thing or two besides crabgrass."

She watched him bend over and sniff another blossom, his eyes crinkling in enjoyment. What a man of contrasts! She tipped her head and studied his starkly masculine body. His broad shoulders all but eclipsed the rose bush he squatted next to, and the muscles in his thighs and backside were pleasingly contoured under his snug jeans. She thought she detected a hint of some Native ancestor in the tough ranginess in his body and sharp facial features.

He looked up and caught her staring.

She snapped her mouth shut. Her heartbeat kicked up and her cheeks flamed, but she couldn't tear her gaze away to save her life.

Holding her prisoner with those endlessly deep eyes, he slowly straightened and took a step toward her. "Have dinner with me?"

Shock made her take a step back. "D-dinner?"

He glanced at his watch, his expression at once boyishly innocent. "It's getting late, and I owe you for that bowl of sherbet. It's probably well beyond salvaging by now. That wasn't dessert, was it?"

She almost choked. "Well, kind of."

"*Ah*. You've eaten already." He looked endearingly crushed.

Embarrassed, she gazed down at her bare feet, toeing a leaf from the grass into the flower bed. "No. I like to eat dessert first."

His eyes widened and he gave a bark of laughter. "Is that a streak of the rebel in our prim and proper Miss Flannery?"

She lifted her chin in defiance. "I'm not."

"Rebellious?"

"Prim and proper."

His mouth split into a saucy grin, and he reached out and tapped the end of her nose with a finger. "I'm delighted to hear that." He led the way back toward the house with a lazy, confident gait. "Go slip on some sexy shoes, and let's find us a couple of steaks."

Mortified, she hurried after him, rubbing her nose. "I didn't mean—"

"I know you didn't," he said, still chuckling. He propped himself against the column holding up the porch roof. He winked. "Shoes."

She honestly didn't remember accepting his invitation, but she was too busy putting out the fires in her blood from that wink to notice. In a daze, she mounted the steps and reached for the screen door.

"And Miss Flannery," he called in a low voice.

She peeked over her shoulder, brushing her hair aside to look at him. "Yes?"

His eyes glittered like black jewels under a slash of dark brow. "Don't even *think* about changing that dress."

Chapter Eight

The screen door smacked behind the delectable Miss Flannery, leaving Bridge grinning into the twilight. This was going way better than expected. Catching her with her hair down—both literally and figuratively—had surely tumbled her to him faster than any smooth pick-up line he could possibly have come up with. And that kept things nicely uncomplicated.

Now, if he could just keep his mind on business long enough to ferret out some useful information on her neighbor.

When she came out five minutes later, he nearly groaned in disappointment. Back to the old Mary Alice. Her hair was tucked into her usual hands-off up-do, and she'd encased that gorgeous, slinky dress in a boxy jacket made from some stiff, scratchy-looking material.

He took her key and locked the door for her, giving it a hard push to double-check it was secure. *Ah, well.* He really shouldn't be noticing her dress, anyway.

He still wanted to rip off the jacket and yank the pins from that monstrosity confining her pretty red curls...but it was kind of nice that she put up a little resistance to his unsubtle come-on. More than nice. In fact, it made him feel something he hadn't felt in longer than he could remember.

Anticipation.

Returning her key, he deliberately brushed his palm over hers. It was warm and soft, like her smile, and sent a stroke of longing through his whole body.

What would it feel like to have her soft hands warm him all over?

He smacked himself mentally and waited while she deposited the key in her tiny handbag, then settled her purse strap neatly on her shoulder.

Sticking to business was proving to be a real pain.

"Ready?"

She nodded.

He walked her to his truck and opened the door. He took her arm, and she turned to climb up into the cab.

Nope. He just could not stop himself.

Instead of helping her up, he tugged her gently into his arms. He needed to taste her. Now.

She stared wide-eyed at his lips as he lowered them slowly toward her.

Soft as the sigh that escaped her, he settled his mouth on hers. Unhurried and undemanding, he allowed himself to savor the feel of her moist lips moving lightly under his. When he reached the corner of her mouth, he flicked his tongue over the seam. Her body trembled in response.

For a split second, desire threatened to claw through his restraint.

God*damn* it.

He pulled away.

A strand of hair spilled from her neat bun and feathered down her temple. Rooted to the spot, she gazed up at him, confusion running riot over her face.

Fucking hell. Now what had he gone and done?

Winding the stray lock of hair between his fingers, he concentrated on not thinking about how good she'd tasted, and instead on coming up with an acceptable excuse for kissing her.

In the end, he resorted to the tried and true. He winked, and said, "Just thought we'd get that over with."

Chapter Nine

What had just happened?

Mary Alice's lips still tingled where Bridge's had traveled over them. Her pulse skyrocketed. Was this the way the dreams had started?

"Now we can relax and not be distracted all evening thinking about it," he said.

"About…?" Her tongue went to the corner of her mouth and caught a taste of him.

"Our first kiss."

"Oh." Her mind snagged hard on the middle word. "I…" *Wow.* "I guess that's…sensible."

Sensible?

Sensible? Who was she kidding? She'd count herself fortunate if she could think a single lucid thought all night, after that kiss.

"Wanna go for a second?"

She came to with a start and backed away. "I don't think—" She caught the amusement in his face. "You're teasing me."

He reached out and touched the collar of her jacket,

running his fingers down the lapel. "Do you mind?"

She let out a breath in consternation. "Not nearly as much as I should." She tipped her head in mock reproof, feeling oddly comfortable with a man she'd known less than an hour. Maybe there was something to that kiss theory, after all. "I fear you're a rake, Russell Bridger."

"A rake?" He grinned. "You mean one of those long, hard things with—"

"No!" He was seriously misbehaving, but she couldn't help grinning. "I mean a rogue and a rascal, the kind of man my mama is always warning me about."

With a devilish laugh, he swept her up off the ground. "Lucky for me you never listen to your mama."

"And you would know that how?" she squeaked as his strong hands deposited her on the bench seat of the truck.

"Care to deny it, Ms. Dessert-Before-Dinner?"

Barely suppressing her laughter, she gave him her most indignant face and straightened her dress primly. "I most certainly do. I'll have you know she thinks I'm a perfect angel."

A slow, easy smile slid across his face. "Can't argue with that."

Her mouth dropped open as the truck door slammed.

Good lord. She could almost feel her halo slip.

Chapter Ten

The restaurant Bridge chose was a rambling rustic affair with a spangled sign boasting of the best steaks, ribs, and live country music west of San Bernardino. She'd heard about The Blue Palomino often from Nancy when her friend would come to work the next morning with a big smile, sore feet, and a slight drawl. Mary Alice wasn't sure where the drawl came from, but she was feeling slightly alarmed at the prospect of finding out.

"You're not a vegetarian, are you?" Bridge asked.

She snapped out of her thoughts and shook her head at him over the menu. Before she had a chance to say a word, he'd ordered for both of them—deluxe combo platters and salad bar, along with two goldfish bowl-sized margaritas.

"Salt?" he asked, his only uncertainty about the order.

She shook her head again, and regarded him with a frown after the waiter had left. "Do you always order your date's meal?"

He looked up and smiled blandly. "Always."

"What if she doesn't like what you pick for her?"

"I make it my business to know what she likes."

Mary Alice leaned her elbows on the table and rested her chin on her laced fingers, undecided as to how annoyed she should be. "How?" she asked.

He leaned back in his seat and accepted his margarita—with salt—from the waiter. He took a sip. "Are you really interested, or are you only after ammunition to blast me with for being a hopelessly old-fashioned male chauvinist?"

She arched a brow. "Both?"

He chuckled. "Forget it, angel. I'm not about to load both barrels and hand over the shotgun. You'll just have to tell me how I do."

"Well, I have to admit, you're doing pretty well so far. I love margaritas." She lifted her glass and frowned, wondering why it seemed to dwarf her completely while his fairly disappeared into the geography of his large hands and broad chest.

He waved his hand dismissively. "A gimme."

"Oh?"

"Your lime sherbet."

She pursed her lips. Okay. Point to him. "Does anything ever get by you?"

"Only if I let it." He gave her a predatory look that made her insides shiver in delighted panic.

For the first time in her life she felt singled out. Like a female cut from the herd for closer investigation by a dangerous male.

Her late fiancé didn't count, of course. She and Jack had practically grown up in each other's pockets. And if anyone had done any singling out it had been her father. Jack had always been like a son to her dad. She'd loved Jack for his goodness and unflagging loyalty and how he'd always seemed to know how to make her smile. But, despite being a cop, Jack had been the least dangerous man she'd ever known.

Not so, Russell Bridger. One look in those dark, beckoning eyes, and a woman knew she didn't stand a chance against his bad boy appeal. Not that she would want anything he might be offering. She had her Master List all carefully planned, and starting a relationship was way down around number twenty-five. A one-night-stand? Not even on it.

"Shall we get our salads?" he suggested.

The buffet was huge, and with Bridge's advice on the best selections, she loaded her plate with a sample of every imaginable concoction, from carrot salad to caviar. Then, as they ate, she told him of her job at the nursery school, and they laughed over stories about the antics of her kids.

"Sounds like a great job," he said, chuckling.

"It is. I love it."

"But I'm wondering why some lucky guy hasn't married you and given you a dozen kids of your own by now."

She toyed with her fork for a moment, testing the feelings his question aroused. *Sadness. Regret. Still a little anger.* But surprisingly, not the misery and longing she had felt for so long after Jack's death. Those terrible emotions which had kept her alone and hiding out with just her job and her roses for company, steadfastly ticking off items on her Master List, for fear of repeating the hurt with someone else.

"My fiancé was killed three years ago," she said quietly.

He winced. "Damn. I'm sorry. Didn't mean to bring up something unpleasant."

She shook her head. "It's okay. He was a police officer, gunned down in the line of duty. It was rough, but I've gotten through it." She studied her fork. "In any case, I won't make that mistake again."

"What's that?" he asked.

She glanced up, surprised. Had she spoken out loud? He had a puzzled look on his face, so she lifted a shoulder. "Loving a cop. Dating a cop. Ever looking at a cop again. Take your pick."

A stab of shock flashed through his eyes, but his expression was back in neutral so fast she thought she must have been mistaken.

"A wise decision, I'm sure," he said.

She paused while the waiter exchanged empty salad plates for sizzling platters. "So, what about you?"

"What about me?" He avoided eye contact as he dug into his meal.

She almost laughed at his valiant attempt to hide his discomfort at the direction of their conversation. She was pretty sure this must be where most women Bridge dated got all starry-eyed about marriage and family and how he must surely want one. And where he ran for the hills. Little did he know, between the two of them *she'd* be running the fastest.

Nabbing a grilled shrimp by the tail, she bit it off and savored the delicious tang. "Why don't *you* have a wife and a dozen kids?" She paused, suddenly alarmed. *Oh, shit.* "Or maybe you do?"

He held up both hands. "Nope. Not me. Not a wife and kids kind of guy."

Ah. There it was, just as predicted.

She should be glad. Getting involved was definitely not what she wanted. She should be greatly relieved they were on the same page.

So, where had that sudden stab of disappointment come from?

"I see," she said.

He cut her a look, as if to gauge how she'd taken it. "I don't have much to offer a family in the way of security. My job—" His words halted abruptly. Then he shrugged. "No woman should have to put up with my lifestyle."

"Construction?" she said dryly. "I'd think that would be fairly stable."

For a moment he looked nonplussed. Then he shrugged again. "I just hold the stop sign. No building skills involved. Not exactly recession-proof," he finally said, turning back to his dinner.

Could anyone really be that devoid of ambition? He didn't exactly look like the typical California surfer dude… but looks could be deceiving, she supposed.

"Why do you do it, then?" She waved a cherry tomato on her fork. "Holding up a stop sign doesn't really seem like the kind of job a man of your intelligence would choose." He was obviously no idiot, and she hoped she hadn't offended him.

"It's sort of temporary," he said around a mouthful of barbecued rib.

She picked up her margarita. "Oh? Did you get laid off?"

His eyes met hers, and the corner of his mouth twitched. "Not recently." He waggled his brows mischievously.

She took a sip of her drink and shook a bemused finger at him. "I might have to get out the soap for that kind of talk, young man."

"Yeah? I can think of a lot more developmentally appropriate uses for that soap," he dared, his eyes sparkling.

She hiked a brow at his use of the term she'd used in their earlier conversation about her work at the nursery school. "Oh, really?"

"Yep. I could let you soap me up in more appropriate places, and see what develops."

She tried desperately not to blush or giggle, but lost on both counts. "Bridge!"

The smile he gave her was bad boy naughty. "Time out?"

"Definitely."

"Okay, how about on the dance floor?"

She glanced in consternation at the small stage where a four-man band had begun to play without her even noticing. "*Um*. I'm not the world's best dancer…"

"I'll show you the steps. Come on, angel. Live dangerously."

Like she needed more encouragement.

He rose and offered his arm, and a guilty thrill of excitement zinged up her spine. Hesitantly, she curled her fingers around the roped muscles of his forearm. And prayed the heat from his skin wouldn't melt her common sense quite as easily as it was dissolving her knees.

Chapter Eleven

As Bridge led Mary Alice onto the wooden floor, the band launched into a typical country tune about some poor guy having loved and lost. He pulled her close to his chest, and at first she resisted his tug. He could tell she'd planned to keep a proper distance between them. But he smiled when, after a few moments, she slipped into his arms and sighed out loud, nestling close against his body.

He really had to get hold of his rampaging hormones, or before he knew it, he'd be trying to talk her into things he shouldn't.

Still. She was awfully nice. And she smelled so incredibly —

"How do you like living in the Canyon?" he asked, forcing himself out of his inappropriate musings.

Sierra Madre Canyon was a narrow, winding alcove crammed with one-way streets and every type of home imaginable. The old neighborhood had been renowned for its quirky, artistic bent — and lack of parking — since the fifties. Somehow, it suited her.

"I love it. So quiet and peaceful. And I couldn't ask for

better neighbors."

Jesus.

He stumbled over his own feet at the reminder.

"Something wrong?" she asked when he cursed.

"Damn. Sorry!" He'd completely lost the rhythm of the dance.

He'd gotten so wrapped up in enjoying himself that he'd totally forgotten this date was *not* a date.

Strictly business.

"We can sit down if you're tired," she said, about to step away from him.

"Hell, no." He pulled her back. "Go on. You were saying something about your neighbors?" He swayed them into the dance again.

"Oh, just that everyone is so friendly."

He forced his mind back on track. "I gotta say, that guy who lives next door to you seems a little strange."

"Charlie? Strange?" she said, startled, then shook her head. "No, not at all."

"Charlie?" he said pointedly, leaning backward to look into her face. "You know him pretty well, I take it?"

She glanced at his frown, and her brows flickered. "Not really. Just in the usual neighbor kinds of ways."

"Such as?" he asked, unable to prevent the edge that crept into his voice.

Thankfully, she didn't seem to notice. "Oh, you know, he keeps an eye out for suspicious characters lurking about, and such. He's a really nice guy. He has this lily pond he's always fussing over." She rolled her eyes with a grin. "It drives his gardeners batty. He constantly makes Jose and Enrico wade in and pull out the yucky dead lily pads." Her eyes twinkled. "On the other hand, every Friday he sends them over to do my lawn, so I can't complain."

"Mighty generous." Bridge wondered what she was

expected to do in return.

"You haven't seen my attempts with a lawn mower," she muttered as he led her back to the table when the song ended.

"Call me next time, and I'll come watch," he drawled, and held her chair for her. "So, I hear ol' Charlie throws some wild parties."

She grinned. "Once a month, like clockwork."

"Doesn't the noise bother you?"

"Nope. He always invites me."

He choked on a gulp of margarita and stared at her. *Well, well.* The pretty nursery school teacher certainly could come out of left field. Definitely more layers to her than he'd have guessed. That prim, angelic image was beginning to tarnish big-time.

Perhaps he should do some re-evaluating of his strictly business angle.

As they finished eating, Bridge wondered what other surprises he might uncover if he dug deep enough. Good ones or bad?

He wasn't sure he was up to finding out. He'd be sorely disappointed if Mary Alice was even remotely involved with a scumbag like Charlie Watson.

Though, he didn't think that was possible.

He hoped to hell it wasn't.

Either way, her impish innocence might just be Bridge's own downfall. He was already way too attracted to this woman for his own good. He needed to be careful.

Even setting aside his promise to his mom, he wasn't cut out for serious relationships. Mary Alice was absolutely right. Cops were terrible husband material. His parents' marriage had proven that in spades.

His mother had been so young, and she'd loved his father so much. But every time Dad was late from work, Mama had withdrawn from them both a little more. As a boy, Bridge couldn't understand the debilitating stress she'd felt from not knowing if something had happened to Daddy out on the mean streets of L.A. Slowly, bit by bit, her nerves had deteriorated. In the end, the anxiety became too much for her to cope with.

Dad's job as a cop had killed her just as surely as Mary Alice's fiancé had been gunned down in the line of duty.

He glanced over at the sweet woman sitting across from him.

And yet, could any man with a pulse possibly resist Mary Alice's cute freckles and the prospect of holding her enticing, satin-covered curves close to his body?

He sighed ruefully. *Not this man*.

The band returned from a break, and the first riff of a lively two-step came over the speakers.

"Come on, let's work off some of all this food," he suggested.

When she rose, she discretely wiped a bead of perspiration from her brow.

"Why don't you take off that jacket?"

"Oh, I don't think—"

"What's the matter? Shy?" he challenged.

Her chin went up, just as he'd known it would. "Of course not." She shrugged off the jacket. "It did get a little warm out there last time."

He let his gaze glide down the smooth, slippery fabric of her barely-there dress, and back up again. *Damn*. It was likely to get downright scorching out there this time.

Oh, yeah. Definitely time to re-evaluate.

The band played a Cotton-eyed Joe after a couple of two-steps, and then a country swing number. He couldn't remember having so much fun in ages, teaching her the steps and feeling her become more and more confident whirling in and out of his arms. When the last strains of the swing tune faded, they were laughing like a couple of teenagers.

She reached up, attempting to put right the French twist their dancing had loosened. Her mass of red hair curved upward, wild and loose, to the twist, tendrils curling about her temples, like a sensual model in some old-fashioned painting.

"Lord, you're good on your feet," she said with a grin, catching her breath.

He chuckled. "And on my knees, and lying down..." He hardly recognized his own voice, it had suddenly turned so deep and suggestive.

She froze on the dance floor, and a deep blush started at the apples of her cheeks and spread outward. Mesmerized, his gaze dipped and followed the rosy stain as it fanned across the exposed swell of her breasts.

He met her eyes and slowly reached for her. "My God, you're beautiful," he murmured as she melted into his arms.

The next dance was slow and romantic, and the woman he held was warm and soft. He wrapped himself around her and surrendered to the moment, drowning in the feel of her silky body under his hands, her curves pressing enticingly into him, surrounded by the intoxicating scent of strawberries and desire.

And found himself wanting more of it all.

Damn, he wanted *her*. In the worst way.

He knew he was treading on dangerous ground. He'd never been drawn to a woman like her before. He knew she'd want more from him than just hot sex. A lot more.

And for the first time ever, he was suddenly afraid he might want to give it to her—to try a normal relationship with a real woman, not a quick fling with a superficial groupie who was only attracted to his badge or his overrated charm.

No, Mary Alice was different. She was genuine and honest and pure. Her quiet grace and innate goodness reminded him a lot of his mama. That alone should scare the hell out of him.

Not to mention the fact that Mary Alice hated cops with a passion.

Which meant that either Bridge could never, ever be honest with her, or that she'd bolt as soon as he told her who he really was.

How ironic was *that*?

Hell, no, it would never work. *They* would never work. Everything was stacked against them. Bridge had no business toying with her.

But dammit, he was only a man.

And there was just something about this woman that called out to him, to the part of him he kept carefully hidden, to the loneliness in his soul.

Once, just once in his life, he'd like to touch a woman who turned his hard, harsh world to wonderfully tender mush, and eased the aching in his heart.

When the song ended, he whispered in her ear, "It's getting late. Shall we go?"

The only question was...did he dare?

Chapter Twelve

Mary Alice was sure Bridge would kiss her right there on the dance floor.

When he turned away, she didn't know whether to be disappointed or immensely grateful. The memory of their earlier get-it-out-of-the-way kiss lingered in her blood, trying to obliterate what was left of her good sense.

Under no circumstances should she let him kiss her again. He was a laid-back charmer and an obvious player. He would love her and leave her. Not the kind of man she should take a chance on—especially the first chance she'd even dared contemplate since Jack.

She'd had all the misery she could take in the love department and had no intention of setting herself up for more. Not if she could prevent it by being smart. The three most important men in her life had been cruelly taken from her, and she couldn't stand it if she fell for another man, only to have her heart ripped to shreds once again. Which was sure to happen with a man like Bridge. Better by far to leave the whole thing alone before it ever got started.

And if for some crazy reason Bridge felt differently, she could just point out his own words. He wasn't really interested in her. Not for anything serious. He'd said as much plain as day just moments ago—he wasn't the marrying kind of man. But she wasn't the meaningless affair kind of woman.

Still…she couldn't help but wish for just one more lingering taste of Russell Bridger's talented lips before she said good-bye. He had the most uncanny way of disarming her defenses with his hard, masculine body, and making her long for things she hadn't let herself think about in three years.

By the time he'd driven her home and parked his truck in front of her house, her pulse had doubled. He set the brake, killed the engine, and looked over at her.

"I had a wonderful evening, Bridge," she said, reaching for her purse. "Thanks so much."

"My pleasure." After releasing his own seat belt, he squeezed the button to free hers. His eyes followed the belt as it glided up and over her breasts to the roll-up casing. "I hope we can do it again soon."

She fiddled with her purse strap. "I'm not sure that's a good idea."

His surprised gaze sought hers. "No?"

"It's not that I don't like you," she rushed to explain. "I do. You're very attractive and…" She cleared her throat. "But, well, I'm just not—" She looked up, helpless to get the words out.

He turned to lean his back against the truck door, searching her face contemplatively. "Not that kind of girl?"

"Let's just say I'm not in the market for a…casual relationship."

"*Mm-hmm.*" He moved his arm up and rested it along the back of the bench seat, running a finger over the shoulder of her jacket. "It sure would be a shame to waste it, though."

She was almost afraid to ask. "Waste what?"

"All the incredible electricity we're generating with each other."

Oh, no. Now she was in trouble. "Sorry. I'm not into flying kites in the rain." She smiled feebly. "Too dangerous."

His finger left her shoulder and strayed onto her neck, and he lightly drew his fingernail along the bare skin of her nape. Lightning streaked down her spine. She could practically hear the rumble of hormonal thunderheads gathering in the cab.

He pursed his lips. "So, you prefer the more domestic variety of electricity, *eh*? Flip a switch in the comfort of your own home and, *voila*, a safe, predictable turn-on."

She tried not to be offended as she struggled to ignore his nail softly scoring her neck. "There's something wrong with wanting safe?"

"No, not at all. If you're…that kind of woman."

She scooted a little closer to her own door, away from him. "Which works out well, because I *am* that kind of woman."

He slid after her. "Are you?"

Gently, he caressed the back of her neck. His thumb and forefinger were callused, she noted absently, not just from the rigors of stop sign turning, but the pads roughened from hard, physical work.

Fighting a losing battle not to enjoy his touch, she tried to focus. "I'm a nursery school teacher," she said a little breathlessly. "I raise roses on the weekends and read romance novels in the evenings. And until tonight I hadn't had a date in three years. I'd say that's about as safe as it gets."

He tipped his head. "Makes me wonder what you're hiding from."

It was a real effort not to let him see just how near the mark he'd hit. "Why would I be hiding?"

His brow went up. "So, you're not?"

"No."

"Prove it. Come here."

He leaned in at the same time he pulled her closer, bringing her face to within inches of his. "Let me see the tip of your tongue."

Losing her nerve completely, she shook her head, keeping her lips firmly closed.

"Who are you afraid of, Mary Alice? Me…or yourself?"

She swallowed heavily. "Don't be ridiculous. Neither."

"Show me."

There had to be something basically illogical about proving she didn't want to hook up by letting him kiss her — if in fact that was what he was going to do. But she couldn't have come up with a counter-argument if her life and future depended on it.

And she had a sinking feeling they just might.

"Fine," she said, desperate to prove they were both wrong.

His hooded gaze traced her mouth for a moment before locking onto her eyes. Her cheeks burning, she hesitantly poked her tongue out between her teeth.

His grip on her neck tightened. She watched with a madly tripping heart as his face came closer and his own tongue emerged, stopping a hair's breadth from hers. She wanted to close her eyes, but his hypnotic gaze held her paralyzed.

He lowered a fraction and she tasted him. Warm and spicy, with a hint of lime. Then he proceeded to torture her. Teasing her senses with the very tip of his tongue, not allowing more contact than the size of the rounded end of a well-used crayon.

Oh. My. God.

She thought she'd pass out from the sheer eroticism of the act.

Very gradually, he increased the area of contact, skimming his tongue back and forth along the edge of hers, then over the top and around in a circle. Every molecule in her body throbbed. Feelings and sensations she'd never known she was capable of surged through her, carried on the incredible power of the sensual current he'd created between them.

She wanted more. But his firm grip on her neck prevented her from moving closer.

Finally, in frustration, she stretched her tongue as far as it went, trying to capture his quicksilver touch.

His thumb skimmed around and found her chin, urging it down. Suddenly, they were mouth to mouth, deep inside each other, his tongue thrusting, claiming her, marking her with his profoundly male taste. Coaxing and teasing. Seducing her with heavy hints of sensual pleasures she'd only dreamed of. Pleasures she *had* dreamed of. Like…last night.

Of their own volition, her fingers sought his shoulders, his hair. She wanted to touch him, to pull his body to her. Wanted to abandon herself to his mad, sensual dance, and allow him to discover the secret yearnings she'd kept hidden so deep inside for so long. So very long.

Abruptly, she stilled.

Oh, Lord, what was she thinking?

She jerked back, and he let her slip away just far enough to elude him.

"You have fantasies about sweaty men on road crews," he whispered into her ear. "You eat your dessert before your dinner, and you let a man you barely know kiss you to within an inch of your life. But you want me to believe you like things *safe*? I don't think so, Mary Alice."

"I do!" Frantically, she twisted and pulled at the truck's door handle.

"Run away if you like, angel. But you can't escape what just happened. Let me show you how good it is to dance out here in the eye of the storm."

"No."

She jumped out of the truck and ran to the door of her cottage. As she struggled with shaking hands to fit the key into the lock, Bridge came up and took it from her.

"Here." He opened the door and reached around the jamb for the light switch. After giving the room a quick visual check, he turned to her. He smiled down tenderly, as if he knew the chaos he'd created within her, then he reached up to touch the wild strands that had fallen from her twist. "Just think about it, that's all I ask."

She doubted if she'd be able to think about anything else for a month. But it wouldn't make any difference. She didn't want to get involved with him. With anyone right now.

He stuck his hands in his pockets and jogged down the steps.

She leaned against the doorjamb and let out the breath that was choking her. She *wasn't* hiding. She just liked her safe, secure life exactly as she was building it. Honestly, she did. She had her Master Plan to complete, and when she'd checked off all the items, her life would be perfect. Her days would be filled with her cozy house, her satisfying job, her cherished roses, her close friends, and a brand new pet. Only then would she be ready to take a chance on love.

"Bridge!" When he turned, she had no idea what she wanted to say. "I—"

He flashed her a roguish wink. "See you tomorrow, angel."

Chapter Thirteen

"That is it, Mary Alice Cathryn," declared Nancy the next morning. They had met early at school to cut out construction paper shapes for the day's art projects. "I can't believe it. You're *drawling*." Nancy speared her with a look worthy of Sister Benedict back at Immaculate Conception.

Mary Alice nearly groaned out loud at the name of her elementary school alma mater and the mental image it conjured up. Why did *everything* remind her of sex this morning? "I am *not* drawling," she insisted.

"Where were you last night?" Nancy demanded. "I called you three times."

"What happened to the dirty movie?" Mary Alice asked, concentrating on not snipping off her finger along with bits of paper. Blood spatter made bad glue.

"It was great. We only made it halfway through. And don't change the subject."

She avoided her friend's laser-like gaze. "I was out."

Nancy tilted her head, eyes narrowing. "Spill."

Mary Alice took a deep breath and let it out. "If you must

know, I went to the Blue Palomino with one of the guys from the road crew."

Nancy froze, her eyes going wide as beach balls. "You're dating a musician?"

Mary Alice let out a nervous laugh. "Not that kind of road crew. One of the construction workers fixing the road in front of my house."

Nancy just stared.

"You might want to pick your jaw up off the floor before one of the kids trips over it," Mary Alice muttered.

"I— You— That's— Wow."

"Why thank you, Nancy. As a matter of fact, I did have a wonderful time. And, yes, he's intelligent, incredibly good looking, and a great dancer, too. Did I mention his kisses could scorch paint off the walls?"

"Mary *Alice*!" A slow grin crept over her friend's stunned face. "Scorch paint? Really?"

Mary Alice stifled the urge to touch the tip of her tongue. "Down to the primer."

Nancy let out a low, sultry laugh. "Maybe I was wrong. Maybe you weren't drawling but *drooling*."

"Ha ha."

"When do I get to meet him?"

Mary Alice glanced at the clock and calmly started gathering up the mess. "It was just one date. I'm not seeing him again."

Incredulous, Nancy folded her arms across her chest. "Why not? Worried about your paint job?"

Mary Alice shot her friend a withering look. "He's a confirmed bachelor. He doesn't want a real relationship—he's just looking for someone to keep his bed warm and lively."

"And this is a bad thing because…?"

"Oh, Nan. You know me better than that."

"Yeah. I know what you want everyone to believe—all

that prim and proper stuff. And I know how you've convinced yourself that buying a house, having the right job, getting into the proper service clubs, and volunteering with the correct organizations will make your life fulfilling."

"Which they will," she said firmly.

Nancy propped her chin on a hand. "Bullshit. I've seen the longing in your eyes when I talk about Ben and me. What you really need is someone to love. And someone to love you back."

Mary Alice looked away, wishing she could summon a lie and deny it. She resorted to her Master Plan. "I'm getting a dog as soon as I can research appropriate breeds."

"Dog schmog. Listen to yourself, Mac! It's been three years since Jack died. You need to move on with your life. But you're running as fast as you can in the other direction because you're afraid you might like what you find in the arms of a man you're actually attracted to."

"There's a big difference between love and attraction," Mary Alice pointed out.

"What's wrong with both? Honey, you can't bottle yourself up forever. Eventually, you have to let yourself feel again, or you'll go crazy. You have so much love inside you it's just bursting to come out. Does this guy want to see you again?"

Crossing her arms tightly over her chest, Mary Alice reluctantly nodded.

"So, go! Give yourself a chance to live! You might even change his mind about the relationship part." Nancy peered at her calculatingly. "And if you have a little fun along the way, what's the harm? You're over twenty-one."

"That's part of the problem," she said, blocking out the part of her that was actually listening to her friend's advice. "I'm old enough to know the consequences—"

Suddenly, the door to the playroom opened, and she

looked up, infinitely relieved at the timely interruption. She smiled at the tiny newcomer. "Ivy! Hi, sweetie."

Ivy was one of the kids in her Toddler Class. The towheaded girl shyly buried her cheek in her foster mother's skirt as she was led through the door.

"Thanks so much for letting me bring her in a few minutes early today, Mary Alice. You have no idea what a help it is."

She smiled. "No problem, Heather. Ivy, would you like to help carry the construction paper into the art area?"

Nodding, the little girl gave her mother a big hug and kiss good-bye, and came to stand next to Mary Alice. As Heather turned to go, she blew a kiss to the three-year-old and sent a silent, grateful smile to Mary Alice. They had worked hard all year to get Ivy to the point where she trusted her teachers enough to willingly leave the protective shield of her foster mother's arms. She still didn't talk, not a word, but she loved playing with the other children. As long as Mary Alice was in sight, she did fine.

It was adults Ivy had trouble with, and all of the nursery school staff was involved in rebuilding her trust.

"Can I come with you?" Nancy asked gently.

With serious eyes, Ivy looked up at Mary Alice, who smiled and nodded encouragingly. The little girl glanced hesitantly at Nancy, then tugged at Mary Alice's hand, dismissing the other teacher. She and Nancy exchanged a look of understanding.

"That's okay. I should be getting up to my classroom, anyway," Nancy said.

"See you after school?" Mary Alice asked.

Her friend shook her head. "Gotta go pick up Ben at the hospital." She grinned. "Assuming he lives through the tests."

Mary Alice chuckled. She admired her friend for being so calm in the face of her husband's mysterious symptoms. She would have been a wreck, even if it was just tests. "I'll give you a call later to see how it went."

"You do that. We can finish our conversation."

Mary Alice made a face. "Come on, Ivy. Let's get this art project set up, shall we?"

But for that whole day at school, Mary Alice couldn't shake her friend's advice.

Give yourself a chance to live.

Was she fooling herself to think she could stick to the strict timeline she was so carefully following? She *did* have a lot of love to give. Up until now, she'd believed showering it on her tiny students and buying a dog would be enough to keep her happy until she was truly ready to risk falling in love again. But she had to admit, Nancy had touched a nerve. Would Mary Alice ever *not* be terrified to take that leap? Maybe her friend was right about moving on sooner—just taking a chance, and jumping into the deep end.

Mary Alice longed for children of her own. And to make that happen she'd have to overcome her fear of getting close to a man emotionally. Because purely physical closeness would feel wrong without the emotional part, too.

She lightly touched her lips. Well. At least, she'd thought it would. But apparently there was something to be said for purely physical pleasures.

Who knew?

Even so, Russell Bridger was the absolute worst possible man to test her sexual wings with. He was footloose and fancy-free. He wasn't interested in a real relationship. And as tempting as it was to just go for the temporary fun, she knew herself well enough to know she wouldn't settle for the kind of no-strings sex he was offering.

The possibility of having a real family—husband and children—would be the only reason she'd risk putting her heart on the line again. She wasn't ready for anything else.

Hell, she wasn't even ready for *that*.

Letting out a sigh, she chided herself for even going there.

Marriage and kids? Seriously? Talk about getting ahead of herself. Agreeing to a date or two was only the smallest first step toward the possibility of a relationship. Who said it would go any further with Bridge, even if he were the ideal guy? They weren't talking instant picket fences, here.

And maybe, after giving dating a try, she'd realize she really *wasn't* ready to take that step yet. Better the man didn't have any expectations, in that case. Better a man who wouldn't be hurt if she felt she had to leave him.

Better a man like Bridge.

Mindless sex wasn't intrinsically a bad thing. Lots of people did it. Men *and* women. But she had been the living definition of prim and proper for so long, she didn't know if she could make such a drastic a change in her lifestyle. Especially on her first true venture into the dating world since losing her fiancé. Mindless sex was definitely not an item on her Master List.

On the other hand, she would never know if she even wanted to *try* mindless sex with Bridge unless she saw him again.

God, this was so confusing.

And heaven help her, she was actually beginning to take Nancy's suggestion seriously.

Chapter Fourteen

Later that afternoon, Mary Alice did her best to concentrate on the flowers as she groomed the rose garden in front of her cottage in preparation for the Historic Rose Society membership committee's visit the next day. But it was impossible. The whole time, she just continued to debate with herself.

She could see Bridge now, working out on the street in front of Charlie's house, all flexing muscle and bronzed skin under his bright orange construction vest. The sexy planes and angled cheekbones behind his mirrored sunglasses were enough to take any woman's breath away.

If she had even a lick of sense, she wouldn't let herself get within a hundred yards of a man who so blatantly exuded masculine temptation. She needed to peel her eyes off that sexy body before she gave her rose bush a Mohawk by accident.

If only she could talk her eyes into moving.

She and Bridge hadn't spoken since he dropped her off last night. He'd been busy directing a long line of traffic when she'd walked by that morning to get to her car, and when she parked it after school, he'd been talking with his foreman.

She realized with a start that, despite her mental flip-flopping about sleeping with him, she'd missed his usual sexy flirting. Missed the way he looked at her—like she was a beautiful, desirable woman.

He glanced up and waved when he saw her studying him from under the brim of her gardening hat. Knowing she was playing with fire, but unable to help herself, she sat back on her heels and smiled, raising a gloved hand in greeting.

Girl, you are in such big trouble.

A short time later the crew packed it in for the day, and she spotted Bridge heading her way. On her knees, she brushed at the dirt covering her jeans and T-shirt, only succeeding in making the mess worse.

"Hi. Doing some gardening?"

She smiled up at him. "Wow. You should be a detective."

For a split second, he froze. Then he cleared his throat. "They coming today for your interview?"

"Tomorrow." She'd told him last night about her quest to join the Historic Rose Society and have a couple of Mrs. Trent's old roses listed in their registry. "Must have the yard looking its best."

"Well, it looks great to me." He tossed his hard hat onto the grass and lowered himself down beside it. "They're bound to be impressed."

"Thanks." She looked around. It was pretty, she had to admit. The lush, English-style garden was one of the things that had sold her on the cottage the minute she'd laid eyes on it. The plants had been wild and rampant, neglected due to Mrs. Trent's failing health, but in the two years since Mary Alice bought the place, she'd gotten the gardens into picture-perfect condition.

The ideal setting for a spinster teacher-lady hiding out

from life, Nancy had said.

Mary Alice frowned. "The lawn really should be mowed, but it's getting dark now, and I won't have time tomorrow after school."

Bridge lay back, propping himself up on an elbow, looking absurdly handsome. "I'll knock off early tomorrow and mow it for you, if you like. You have a mower?"

"Yeah," she said hesitantly. "That's very nice, but you really shouldn't—"

"I'd like to do it. I live in an apartment, and I miss putzin' around in a yard." He broke off a long grass stalk and chewed on it. "Besides, I'd want something in exchange."

She pulled off her gardening gloves and regarded him suspiciously. "Forget it, Bridger. It can stay long."

He let out a low chuckle. "What are we talkin' about here? The grass or my—"

"Both!"

"—face," he finished with a twinkle in his eye. "*Ow!*" He laughed when she smacked him on the shoulder with her dirty gloves. He grabbed them, pulled, and rolled onto his back, bringing her down on his chest when she didn't let go soon enough.

"*Oof!*" Her breath whooshed out when she met that solid wall of muscle.

Not that she wouldn't have lost it anyway.

She clutched his shoulders to keep from squishing into him. Unfortunately, that just gave her a better view.

A layer of road dust covered his face around the clean mask left by his sunglasses. It clung to a sexy five o'clock shadow. His vest had slipped aside, revealing tantalizingly defined pecs and a set of flat, brown nipples. A decorative but modest sprinkle of black hair curled down his chest, the funnel disappearing under her where she lay across him. Through the soft cotton of her T-shirt and sports bra, the tips of her breasts grazed his body, instantly pebbling at the contact.

That little fact had obviously not escaped his attention, because the expression on his face as he gazed up at them resembled a hungry wolf shocked to suddenly find a spring lamb napping in his lap.

"You haven't heard my proposition yet," the wolf said.

"Oh, I've heard it loud and clear." She tried to escape, but his fingers caught her around the ribs and held fast.

He winked. "I'll mow your lawn if you come to an engagement party with me tomorrow."

She stopped wrestling long enough to hike a brow. He'd managed to surprise her again.

"A couple kids from the road crew decided to get married."

"Kids?"

He shrugged, grinning. "With age comes wisdom. You wouldn't let the wise old bachelor go alone, would you?"

She should, of course. That wisdom crack made her want nothing more than to challenge his über-chauvinistic attitude. But the way he held her suspended above him, his chest subtly caressing the tips of her breasts with each breath, completely obliterated the will to refuse.

"You're insufferable, you know that?" she gritted out.

His grin went lopsided. "One of my more endearing traits."

A chorus of hoots and whistles suddenly rose from the street. "*Yeow!* Bridge!"

"Doin' a little public relations work on the side?"

Mary Alice blanched, then squirmed to get out of his grip. Bridge groaned, and she was fairly certain it wasn't because he was embarrassed. Her leg had been thrown over his thigh when she fell, and she could feel his growing arousal pressing intimately into her. Her face blazed.

"Got a wild one there, Bridge!"

"Think she likes you!"

Mary Alice scampered up with as much dignity as she could muster. Ignoring the teasing men—*all* of them—she gathered her gardening tools and walked coolly and calmly toward the backyard.

"Better ask her to the party before she gets away!"

"Mary Alice!" She heard Bridge follow her to the small wooden shed where she determinedly busied herself cleaning and putting away her tools. He peeked in and she saw him grimace at the old hand mower leaning against the wall.

"Sorry about that." He propped himself against the open door, a grin easing onto his face.

"So, there really is a party." *Shocker.*

He bristled in mock offense. "What? You doubted the sincerity of my motives?"

She rolled her eyes.

"So, do we have a deal? Though, I should charge double because of that antique mower," he grumbled.

She tried to keep a serious face. She wanted so badly to poke that cocky, impudent self-confidence of his and turn down his—party or no—ridiculously transparent bargain. But against her will, laughter bubbled up instead of the snappy rejection he deserved.

What a sight they must have been, both covered in dirt, panting on the front lawn like a couple of hormonal teenagers. She clapped a hand across her mouth and giggled. "Oh, Bridge. What am I going to do with you?"

His eyes filled with mischief. "I could give you a suggestion or two…" He unpropped himself and approached her.

And heaven help her, if he kept looking at her like that she was totally in danger of taking him up on them. She attempted a stern frown, but his smile was so winning she couldn't help but fall even further under its spell. Damn the man.

She shook her head in amused resignation. "I won't change my mind, I want you to know that."

"Maybe." He shrugged. "Maybe not." He put his hands lightly on her shoulders. "Come to the party and give me a fighting chance."

"No assumptions?"

He shook his head and crossed his heart. "No assumptions."

She took a deep breath and prayed she wasn't making the biggest mistake of her life. "The Historic Rose ladies will be here at four-thirty. I'll leave the shed unlocked so you can get to the mower."

Chapter Fifteen

Bridge walked into the station house an hour later still half aroused. Even a punishing cold shower hadn't doused the flames Mary Alice had ignited in his cock. The memory of her breasts skimming over his bare skin sent him running for the water cooler even before he hit his desk.

Damn, he had to get it together.

But he couldn't help giving himself a congratulatory pat on the back at getting her to agree to another date. And he didn't harbor any illusions about it being for business purposes, either.

A prick of guilt at deceiving her about his profession made him crush the paper cup in his hand and fire it into the waste basket. He'd have to find out just how deep this aversion to cops she'd mentioned really ran. Maybe someone at the station would know what had happened to her fiancé to make her hate his profession so much. He was heading for his desk when someone yelled out that Sam Grayson, the FBI Special Agent in Charge of the Charlie Watson task force, wanted to see him up in Captain Trujillo's office.

Grayson was competent, if nothing else. And helping the FBI with the case against Watson was turning out to be far more interesting than Bridge had thought at first. Charlie Watson worked for one of the big computer software companies contracted by the federal government, Conrex Data Systems, as a vice president—emphasis on vice. He was known to be stealing top-secret technology from the company and selling it to China for some major bucks. The FBI had a certain amount of evidence against Watson, but they wanted rock-solid proof, as well as the identities of the Chinese spies involved so they could also be tried, or at least flagged and deported.

Sam Grayson was a young, good-looking hotshot. And full of himself, as were most FBI SACs Bridge had met over the course of several past joint operations.

This should be fun.

He grabbed the Watson file and went upstairs.

"We did a deeper background on the Flannery woman," Special Agent Grayson informed him, "and she still came up clean. You find anything to think otherwise?"

"No," Bridge muttered, wondering where this was going. Naturally, they'd investigated Mary Alice's background before the op, but did this mean the FBI actually suspected her of being involved in Charlie's treason?

"How close have you gotten to her?" Grayson asked.

Bridge stiffened at the man's insinuating tone. A few days ago he'd mentioned his plans to ask her out and pump her for information about her neighbor. Now he regretted his big mouth. "Barely past small talk," he said.

"No chance of you spending a few nights with her?"

Fighting the urge to smash the guy's pretty-boy face in, he kept his own impassive. "Highly doubtful."

"Too bad." Grayson looked up from the file he'd been perusing. "Watson's made the night shift. He reported them to the Sierra Madre PD as suspicious loiterers. Having anyone posted out on that narrow street is too damned conspicuous." He sighed. "You'll just have to tell her about the operation and pray she doesn't blow us out of the water."

Bridge scowled. "Wait. What are you saying?"

"We want you in her house, Bridger, every night, starting tomorrow, babysitting Watson."

"Are you kidding me? That could be dangerous for her. She's a civilian."

"Her property is the only one with a good view of his whole place. It would just be a staging area for the stakeout. No danger involved. It is imperative we find out who Watson's Chinese handler is. It's critical to our whole case. Flash your badge and fix it with the Flannery woman. Use the obvious cover to avoid Watson suspecting something."

Obvious? What the hell?

Ignoring the quick kick of excitement that hit his gut at the possibilities implied in what Grayson suggested, Bridge shook his head. "No dice. She won't do it."

Captain Trujillo, who had been sitting quietly, spoke up. "Why not?"

"She's a bit old-fashioned about that kind of thing."

The cap's brows shot up.

"Besides, she hates cops," Bridge added, realizing his mistake too late.

"That's quite an analysis for barely past small talk," Grayson commented dryly, a knowing look settling on his disgustingly GQ features.

"Stuff it, Grayson," Bridge snapped, making the cap's brows furrow.

"I take it you didn't tell her you're on the job," Grayson said, ignoring the insult.

"Didn't want to break cover." He glanced guiltily at the captain, who was now staring down at his hands, neatly folded on his desk. He obviously knew something Bridge didn't. "Do you know what happened to her fiancé, Cap?"

The older man sighed, and nodded. "Her father, Officer Seamus Flannery, was a good friend of mine. We came up through the ranks together until I made lieutenant. He was a good man and a better friend. But he chose to stay in uniform rather than trade it in for a suit and a promotion. He was a bit like you, Bridger." Trujillo shot him a humorless smile and continued. "Anyway, the fiancé, Jack Maxwell, went out on a robbery-in-progress call. Got caught in the crossfire. DOA." The cap looked up. "They'd known each other since they were kids. Seamus had always thought of Jack as the son he never had."

"Jesus," Bridge muttered.

"A month later, Seamus was shot down in an alley behind some greasy spoon. Couple of punk teenagers. Totally senseless and unnecessary. Mary Alice took both deaths hard. Real hard, especially coming right on top of each other like they did."

Bridge frowned, his heart stalling. "Shit. Her father was killed, too?"

The cap nodded. "It was her father's death that really pushed her over the edge. You see, Seamus's brother was also killed in the line of duty, out in Boston, when Mary Alice was a teenager. Her favorite uncle, and all. She'd never really gotten over that, and it made her worry about her old man. Used to call the station here every day to make sure Seamus was safe. Every day for ten years. Till the day he died."

Bridge slumped back in his chair, blowing out a long breath. *Fuck.* It was worse than he'd ever imagined. No wonder Mary Alice avoided getting involved with cops. When she found out what he did for a living, she'd never speak to him again, let alone—

"Well, that's all very touching," Grayson cut in, "but we

still need her cooperation. We can cover tonight by hiding someone in the bushes, but that won't work long-term. I don't care how you manage it, but I want you in her house by tomorrow night, Bridger." The feeb stood, gathering his papers. "That's an order."

Shit. Shit, shit, shit.

"Who've you got to take over on the road crew?" Bridge asked, swallowing his instinct to tell the guy where to stuff it.

"You, Detective Sergeant. Just until we can get Jason Deane set up in a day or two."

"When the hell am I supposed to sleep?" he asked incredulously.

"While Watson's at work tomorrow we'll install motion detectors around his property that will set off an alarm on your laptop if anyone's approaching. We're already monitoring his phones. You'll really just need to watch the monitors, do an occasional perimeter check, and investigate anything that looks or sounds suspicious. Plenty of time for sleeping." He shot Bridge a smug leer before exiting the room. "Or, you know, whatever."

When he was gone, the cap scrubbed his face with his hands. "God, what a—"

"Do I really have to do this?" Bridge demanded, irritated as hell at not being able to tell Mary Alice about himself on his own timetable.

"Sorry, Bridge. My hands are tied. That new head honcho at the FBI's L.A. field office is from out East and used to lots of cooperation from local jurisdictions." He paused and lasered him a look. "Listen, you aren't hustling Mary Alice are you?"

Bridge didn't bother to be offended. The captain was more than familiar with his exploits with the opposite sex. But Bridge had never let his activities interfere with the job. The captain knew he could rely on that. "She's awfully sweet," he hedged.

"Yeah. That's right. Not your type at all," the cap said firmly. "Leave her alone, Bridger. Work this from a different angle. *That* is an order, too. If she gets hurt, I'll bust your butt to meter maid instead of promoting you to lieutenant."

Bridge looked up, surprised. "I'm not in the business of hurting women. You know that, Cap. They just…like me. What can I say?"

"This one's not the same as the others. Hands off—on pain of Traffic duty."

Biting back an argument, Bridge walked out. What he did on his own time was none of the captain's business. Besides, he was on the FBI's ticket now, and Grayson had just ordered him to move in with the woman and pretend to be her boyfriend.

He shot a hand through his hair. The fact that the cap was right just made him angrier.

Hell, she was too good for the likes of Bridge. He lived hard and loved harder, never tying himself down to one woman. He'd made a promise to his mama and he intended to honor it until the day he died. Besides, if he hadn't known it before, the minute Trujillo had related Mary Alice's full story, Bridge understood for certain he'd never stand a chance in hell with her, once she knew the truth about him.

So what was he thinking, even *considering* putting moves on her while undercover? It was damn certain he'd never be able to offer her even a tenth of what she deserved. And she deserved the best.

The problem was, he liked her. *Really* liked her. He was at such peace with himself when he was with her. Inner peace was something he'd had damned little of in his lifetime. And she was so soft and sexy, the tug of longing in his belly nearly threatened to overwhelm him every time he looked at her.

He should leave her the hell alone. For her sake. For his

own damn good.

But how could he stay away when he was supposed to move into her house, where they'd be together every day?

And every night.

This whole thing was nothing but a disaster waiting to happen.

He jetted out a breath and dropped into his desk chair. But orders were orders.

So what the hell was he supposed to do?

Chapter Sixteen

Bridge leaned against the long handle of the push mower and swiped his bandanna over his sweaty forehead. He stifled a sneeze from the pungent scent of freshly mowed grass and tucked the soaked fabric back into his pocket. He wanted a shower bad. *Real* bad.

He looked toward the bungalow.

Mary Alice had barely glanced up as she'd hurried past him into the house an hour ago, tossing him a quick wave of the hand. Nor had she cast him a glance through the kitchen window since.

Boy, those ladies from the historic rose club really had her in a meltdown. Even from here he could tell she was rattled.

She probably wouldn't even notice if he slipped into her house and took a quick shower. After a day of working on the dusty road crew, and an hour of wrangling grass with the stubborn, primitive mower, he didn't feel like driving home and then coming right back to get her for Gary's engagement party…

A shower would take him two minutes flat. In and out.

Then maybe he'd sneak over to Watson's and snoop around for a bit while she was being interviewed.

Yep. Sounded like a plan.

He stowed the mower back in the shed, fetched his gym bag with fresh clothes from the truck, and bounded up the front steps.

"Mary Alice?"

"In the kitchen."

A wall of delicious smells hit him as he slid out of his boots on the porch and stepped into the living room, smelling his way to the kitchen. "*Mmm.* What's baking?"

"Tea cakes."

She'd changed into the prettiest summer dress he'd ever seen. It was all slinky and ivory lace and satin, and her hair flowed wild and free about her shoulders. He almost forgot to breathe. "Jesus, you look beautiful."

She glanced up and gave him a flustered smile. "Oh. Thank you."

He tore his eyes from her and looked around the small, serviceable kitchen. Every available surface was covered with home-baked goodies and teacups. "Holy shit. How'd you manage all this in an hour?"

"I made most everything last night. I just have to get it all presentable today. I'm going crazy."

"Don't worry, you'll knock 'em dead." He helped himself to a cookie. "Can I borrow your shower? Hate to go all the way home, and all…"

"I'm never going to get all this ready in fifteen minutes!" she lamented, turned, and pulled a pan of cinnamon cakes out of the oven. "What did you need? I'm sure you'll find it in the shed."

He chuckled and hoisted his bag. "No worries. I'll be done in a flash." No sense distracting her even more.

"Okay," she said, already oblivious to his presence. She

glanced at the wall clock and started counting off on her fingers all the things still left to do.

He'd been in dozens of these old Craftsman cottages, so he knew exactly where to find the shower. He'd just shed his clothes onto the floor and was reaching for the faucet handle when he heard the doorbell.

Uh-oh.

"Damn, they're early," he murmured solemnly to his reflection in the mirror.

Slowly, it grinned back.

Chapter Seventeen

When the doorbell sounded for the second time, Mary Alice stared at her watch in abject horror. Oh, no! They were ten whole minutes early. In dismay, she looked around the kitchen and out into the living room.

Well, nothing to do about it now.

Everything would be fine.

After turning up the flame under the teakettle, she went to answer the door. A formidable trio of women stood facing her.

"Miss Flannery?" The tall, bird-like woman didn't wait for an answer, but announced loudly, "This is Mrs. Wyeth, Miss Beadle, and I am Mrs. Underwood. We are the committee from the Historical Rose Society."

Mary Alice opened the door wider. "Yes, won't you please come in?"

Mrs. Underwood's gaze swept haughtily over a pair of muddy black construction boots that stood casually on the porch next to the welcome mat. Mary Alice scowled. What on earth were they doing there?

The intimidating ladies sailed into the house, their eyes taking in every single detail. Quickly forgetting the boots, Mary Alice nervously motioned them into the antique sofa and chairs arranged in front of the brick fireplace. "Please, have a seat."

Sitting tidily on the edge of the sofa, the steel-haired Mrs. Underwood pulled a fat, leather-bound notebook from her purse. "The interview will proceed in the following manner," she began.

Mary Alice lowered herself nervously onto the chair opposite.

"First we will ascertain if you have the proper knowledge to be admitted as an apprentice docent. If you pass that part of the test, we will proceed to—"

"A tour of your lovely garden," Miss Beadle interjected, smiling kindly at her. "My, what a darling cottage you have here! Is that the kitchen?" she asked, casting a covetous glance toward the open pocket door. Miss Beadle was the opposite of Mrs. Underwood in most everything Mary Alice could see. She was short, plump, and had wildly frizzy hair dyed an interesting shade of henna red.

"Thank you, yes, it—"

"As Mrs. Underwood was saying," the third woman, Mrs. Wyeth, cut in, "we'll evaluate your roses and determine if any are worthy of note in our—" She halted as the unexpected sound of running water floated from the hall into the room. She turned her large, bespectacled eyes toward the source of the disturbance. "What's that?"

Mary Alice peered in consternation toward the bathroom. "I can't imagine…" It sounded oddly like— "Oh!"

Suddenly, she put together the boots on the porch and Bridge's appearance in her kitchen a few minutes earlier toting a gym bag. *Oh my God*. He was in her house. *Taking a shower.*

"It's nothing," she assured them uneasily. "Do go on." Good grief. What would she do if he suddenly appeared, dripping wet and asking where the towels were? She nearly choked. "*Um…* You were saying, if there are any roses worthy of note…?"

"We will make a recommendation, and the full board will come out to view the specimens. Upon approval, photos will be taken, and you'll be given instructions for harvesting seeds."

"I had no idea it was such an involved process." Mary Alice surreptitiously glanced toward the hall.

"We are very selective in choosing both our new docents and the roses for our registry," Mrs. Underwood stated, and squared her shoulders. "They must be worthy of the honor, in all respects."

Mary Alice pulled in a steadying breath and sat up straight. *She could do this*. It was important to become a docent, part of her Master Plan. And she would happily face any number of snobbish society matrons for Mrs. Trent, to see the look on the old woman's face when she could walk into the retirement home and show her the page in the Pasadena Historic Registry describing her beloved roses. She just had to concentrate, that's all. She would prove she was just as worthy as any one of their uppity members.

Mary Alice had studied the culture of old roses in her spare time for two whole years, but still their questions were difficult. She was hesitating in panic over her answer to one involving the history of the Tudor Rose, when a deep, masculine voice behind her nearly startled her out of her chair.

"Ah, the York and Lancaster, named for the feuding families in the War of the Roses. Truly the essence of the old garden roses, don't you think? Beauty *and* history."

The three elderly ladies sat transfixed on the sofa, staring past her, mouths agape. Miss Beadle's eyes had widened like cabbage roses in full bloom, and an appropriately rosy color had crept into her cheeks. Filled with foreboding, Mary Alice gripped the chair arms and turned.

Bridge stood there, naked from the waist up, still misty and gleaming from his shower, a hand towel draped casually around his neck.

She was going to kill him.

Just as soon as she recovered from the paralyzing shock of seeing him stroll across her living room floor in nothing but low-slung jeans, acting as if he belonged there. And then having the audacity to lean down and kiss her on the cheek!

"Darling, I believe I hear the water boiling. Shall I make you ladies some tea?"

She narrowed her eyes at him in warning.

"Well, I never!" Mrs. Underwood declared, and snapped her mouth shut.

"Me, neither!" said Miss Beadle with a distinct sigh, her awestruck gaze riveted to the sight of Bridge padding away across the hardwood floor.

"Would you prefer jasmine or rose hip?" he called from the kitchen. He stuck his head out. "Or perhaps you'd like to try something more decadent, like peppermint mango? *Hmm?*" He winked at Mrs. Wyeth, who turned as scarlet as a Chrysler Imperial in July.

Miss Beadle actually giggled. "Oh, decadent, absolutely, please!"

Mary Alice sank back in her chair and covered her eyes.

"Who *is* that man?" Mrs. Underwood demanded, flipping quickly through her notebook with a frown.

"Tea cakes, ladies?"

Mary Alice peeked out from between her fingers. The towel from his neck was now draped over his arm in the best maître-d form. Bridge had loaded her silver serving tray with the fruits of her baking efforts and was offering them to Mrs. Underwood. Miss Beadle looked from the tray to Bridge's chest and back, apparently unable to decide which she'd rather sample.

"Mary Alice, sweetheart, aren't you going to introduce me to your charming guests?"

She dropped her hands, glared savagely at him, then plastered a smile on her lips as she made the introductions one by one. "And this is Russell Bridger. He's a… He's my…" She stuttered to a stop, flustered beyond rational thought.

"Fiancé," he supplied smoothly, without blinking an eye.

It was all she could do not to jump up and wring his tanned, corded neck.

Mrs. Underwood flipped madly through her notebook. "This is most irregular. In your application for membership you make no mention of—"

"It was all rather sudden," Bridge supplied with a grin. "In fact, there is an engagement party tonight."

"Russell Bridger!" Mary Alice sputtered. "You are—"

"Half naked, it seems." He cut her off, waggling his eyebrows. "Excuse me a moment, ladies." He stuck the tray in her hands and absconded into the bedroom.

Of all the impossible—

"How delightful," Miss Beadle crowed, piling her plate high with an assortment of cakes and trifles from the tray Mary Alice was white-knuckling. "Congratulations to you both. Such a handsome young man your fiancé is, and he obviously knows a thing or two about roses, too."

Mary Alice opened her mouth to give a scathing reply and correct the outrageous notion that she was in any way involved with the reprobate.

But before she could utter a word, he'd returned. "Yes, Mary Alice has been teaching me all she knows." He smiled guilelessly. "About roses."

His smile flashed brilliant in the sunlight pouring through the mullioned windows, breaking her train of thought with its heated undercurrents. Tucking in a polo shirt, he went back to the kitchen for the tea things.

Speechless, she watched him seat himself and pour for them, chatting all the while, until even Mrs. Underwood's stodgy attitude had melted under the warmth of his attention.

Good lord, the man was dangerous. *More* than dangerous. If he was capable of worming his way into the enthusiastic approval of even these lofty ladies, what possible chance did *she* stand against such a formidable arsenal of charm and attraction? She swallowed, her knees feeling weaker already.

"Well, shall we get these questions over with, Mary Alice?" Mrs. Wyeth said.

She snapped her attention back to the interview.

Mrs. Wyeth smiled at Bridge over the wire rims of her bifocals. "Just a formality, you know."

He nodded graciously and leaned back in her best chair, resting his bare foot on the comfortably worn knee of his jeans. Sitting there, sipping tea from a delicate porcelain cup, he looked the height of tamed, tethered, and domesticated male.

Ha.

Appearances had never been so deceiving.

The rest of the interview flew by. Bridge hardly uttered a word, only tossing in an occasional distracting comment when she found herself faltering over an answer. She could feel his support in his every nod and smile. By the time the group wandered out into the garden, it seemed the most natural thing in the world to have his arm slip around her waist.

"*Fiancé?*" she asked in a fierce whisper to hide the excitement that shot up her spine at his touch.

"Just thinking of your reputation, angel," he whispered back. "Of course, I could always tell them the truth—"

"Don't you dare!" She squirmed out of his grasp.

"I must say," Mrs. Wyeth declared from the middle of the garden, turning in a circle for one last look. "I'm well pleased with everything I see."

It was all Mary Alice could do not to kick Bridge in the shins when he casually skimmed his gaze over her breasts and murmured with a grin, "Me, too."

When the tour was concluded, Mrs. Underwood made a final entry in her notebook with a flourish. "Two of these varieties I don't believe I've ever seen before. You can be sure our report will be favorable."

Miss Beadle beamed. "Oh, yes. We'll *so* be looking forward to seeing both of you when the full board visits."

The old lady nearly swooned when Bridge bent to brush a quick kiss good-bye over her cheek, then did the same for the others.

"Oh, my!" They were still fussing and exclaiming when they piled into Mrs. Underwood's sedan.

The man was a genuine menace.

He caused the kind of thrillingly guilty reaction only a true bad boy could bring out in a woman, young or old.

When their car had safely departed, Mary Alice turned to him and rolled her eyes. "You are a brazen gigolo," she scolded, only half joking. "You ought to be ashamed."

"Who, me?" He batted his dark eyelashes innocently.

"You." She poked him in the chest. "Dazzling them with your gorgeous body so they wouldn't notice I had no idea how to answer half those questions."

A brow quirked along with his grin. "You think my body's gorgeous?"

She slammed her eyes shut. *Open mouth, insert foot.* Like she wasn't in enough trouble without giving him any more encouragement. She cleared her throat and opened her eyes, startled when he was standing right in front of her.

His other brow went up expectantly, waiting for an answer.

She huffed out a breath. "Fine. Yes. I do." Slipping past him, she strode into the house. She could almost see the smug expression settling on his face. She grabbed the tea tray and started cleaning up, determined not to get into *that* discussion.

He took the tray from her and stood patiently as she loaded it with dirty cups and plates. She didn't dare look at him. Or his gorgeous body.

"I'm glad you like it," he said, following her into the kitchen, where he set the tray down on the counter. "I like yours, too."

"Bridge, please." She didn't want to hear this. She was having enough trouble ignoring how adorable and likable he was without muddling her thoughts even further with his obvious physical merits. *Dangerous*, she reminded herself.

"Just stating facts. Look, my hands are in my pockets."

"Then take them out and pass me those dishes."

He was subtle, she had to give him credit. As they loaded the dishwasher and wiped tables, he brushed her arm just a couple of times, and only once did he stand too close behind her—when he was reaching past her at the sink to grab the sponge. For a fleeting moment his hand settled on her hip, his whole torso pressing against her back. But before she had a chance to fully savor the feeling, he was gone.

Damn the man. He knew exactly what he was doing.

Driving her to distraction.

Chapter Eighteen

Mary Alice was glad Bridge had urged her to change out of the modest dress she'd worn for the interview, because it was way too nice-girl for the boisterous, hole-in-the-wall Cuban restaurant where the engagement party was held.

He'd also stopped her from pulling her hair into a neat braid as she'd planned and made her wear it loose. But she'd put her foot down at the mini-skirt he'd dredged up from somewhere in the back of her closet—the result of a momentary lapse in fashion judgment several years ago in an effort to spice things up with Jack. The slouchy cropped top Bridge had chosen for her was already pushing her out of her comfort zone. She still wasn't sure how he'd gotten the idea he could tell her how to dress. It had just sort of happened in the confusion of hurrying to get ready.

She glanced around the bar, tugging unconsciously at the hem of the top. Her jaw dropped when he came back from the bar carrying one of those huge concoctions in a coconut shell, complete with umbrellas—and two straws. But he looked so cute thinking he was being clever, she could only laugh.

She didn't know if it was the relief of having the interview over, and therefore two years of pursuing a major goal were well on the way to paying off, or if it was Nancy's words that had suddenly come back to haunt Mary Alice. Whatever it was, she was feeling comfortable…and yeah, a bit reckless.

Bridge sat down beside her and pushed one of the two straws toward her. "Don't look at me like that or I'll make you share mine."

The thought had definite possibilities.

She let herself relax and had a great time getting to know Bridge's friends from the road crew and their dates. The food was heavenly, and after dinner Bridge led her to the dance floor and showed her the steps to a hot Cuban salsa. After three songs, she followed him back to the table, exhausted.

Laughing and still tingling from his hands on her, she took a long pull on their half-empty drink. "Is there any dance you don't know?"

He snaked his arm around her shoulders. "I'm better at some than others," he teased. "Interested in lessons?"

Licking the straw in her hand, she slanted him a glance. "Don't think so. You're too fast on your feet for me."

He took the straw from her fingers and dipped it back in the drink, then put his lips to it and sucked. Her throat tightened when he swallowed and gave the straw's tip a little flick with his tongue.

"I don't know," he murmured in her ear. "You've been following pretty well, so far."

Mercifully—at least for her badly wavering willpower— just then the future bride and groom, Gary and Denise, jumped up and announced the start of the traditional party games.

Mary Alice groaned inwardly at the news that they would all be playing as couples, then almost groaned aloud when she saw the first game. It was a list of anagrams each competing couple had to unscramble.

TWENTY THINGS YOU'RE LIKELY TO FIND ON A HONEYMOON.

Chapter Nineteen

"Garter" and "condom" were easy.

Bridge quickly scanned the paper in Mary Alice's hand and stifled a grin. *Ooh, baby.* Gary and Denise had taken no prisoners when they'd composed the list of anagrams for this silly party game. Bridge pressed close to Mary Alice and draped his arm over her far shoulder, pretending to hold up one side of the paper so he could see better.

He pointed to it and whispered a few more suggestions, enjoying how an enchanting blush crept up her neck to her earlobes. Her handwriting wavered badly when she wrote the naughty words next to the scrambled letters. The point of her pencil snapped when he murmured, "Hard-on," in her ear.

Damn, he was having a good time.

Too bad it was all going to come to a crashing halt when he told her he was a cop...and had gotten orders to move in with her.

He sighed into her hair, then breathed deeply of its strawberry scent. Of the many women he'd dated through the years, he couldn't remember ever feeling like this with anyone. Amused and relaxed, tense and horny, all at the same time. He loved what she did to him—his pretty, red-haired angel.

If he'd been looking, he couldn't have found a more perfect candidate for serious companionship. She was smart and fun, sweet and sexy, all wrapped up in a feminine package that made his dick constantly stand up and take notice.

It was a real shame he wasn't looking for serious companionship.

He leaned over and stole a kiss before whispering to her, "Orgasm."

They ended up coming in last place because every time he guessed at a new word, testing the outer limits of his vocabulary and imagination, she started to giggle and couldn't write.

The next two games didn't go much better. They were having too much fun flirting with each other to concentrate on the task.

For the final competition of the party, everyone was herded onto the dance floor. Bridge cocked his head wryly at the life-sized cardboard cutout of a popular male actor that Gary proceeded to set up.

When Denise whipped out a black satin blindfold and a handful of small foil packets and pushpins, Bridge laughed out loud.

Mary Alice sank back against him in horror. "Tell me this isn't what I think it is."

Still laughing, he slipped his arms around her, savoring the feel of her firm backside curving into his thighs. "'Fraid so, angel."

"Ever play pin the tail on the jackass?" Gary asked with a snicker.

"I can't do this," she groaned into her hands.

When her turn came, Bridge tied the blindfold over her

eyes, spun her around, and watched in amusement as she fumbled with the packet, unrolled the contents inside out, and poked the pushpin through the wrong end. But he managed to outshout the competition, giving her directions to the target. She hit it dead-on.

A dozen male voices yowled as the pin drove home.

Completely embarrassed, she gingerly chose their first prize from among the gaily wrapped packages and thrust it into his hands.

"You open it," she said, slipping behind him to hide in mortification.

He yanked the ribbon off and pulled the paper from the package. He felt a truly devilish grin creep across his face.

Mary Alice peeked around his shoulder into the box and gasped. "Oh my God."

Chapter Twenty

"Glow-in-the-Dark, Black Mamba, *Heavy Duty*—?" Mary Alice read the labels on their overflowing first-prize box aloud, then looked up at Bridge, mystified, as he turned into her driveway after the party was over.

Damn, she was an innocent. How had she managed to graduate from college without learning about this stuff? A horrible thought struck him. Surely, she wasn't— Then he remembered her fiancé. Right. She'd probably been on the pill.

He cleared his throat with a grin, then shrugged, feigning modesty. "Sometimes you just need a little extra…you know. When things get wild."

She rolled her eyes and continued to leaf through the box of assorted condoms while he killed the truck's engine and pulled the brake.

"Super Silky, Swedish Tickler—" She frowned. "What on earth is that?"

Bridge squirmed in his seat, his pants suddenly way too tight. "Mary Alice, I don't think I can have this conversation wearing clothes."

Alarm flashed across her face. "You understand, I'm curious from a strictly informational standpoint." She edged away from him. "I'm a teacher, and it appears I need to broaden my education."

Seriously? He snapped off his seat belt and did the same for hers. "If it's broadening you want, baby, I'm more than ready to oblige."

Her eyes skittered down to the obvious ridge of his arousal beneath his jeans, which he did nothing to hide. The woman was playing with fire. No one was *that* innocent.

"But I'm more of a 'show' than a 'tell' kind of guy," he added.

Her gaze jumped back to his and she swallowed heavily. "No assumptions, Bridge. Remember?"

"If I were entertaining assumptions, I'd have that Swedish Tickler on and be halfway into you by now." He leaned back in agony and regarded her.

"You are so bad." She squeezed her eyes shut, and he could see both desire and fear flit across her face.

Desire he didn't dare take advantage of. He would only hurt her if he laid even one finger on her before admitting who—what—he was. *Damn.*

"Unfortunately, not bad enough," he said with an exhale. He hooked his forefinger around hers where it lay on the bench between them. "Do I at least get a kiss good night?" Surely, a simple kiss or two couldn't hurt before he lowered the boom. Because he sure as hell wasn't getting any afterward.

She looked up at him through her long lashes and blinked uncertainly.

"Please?" Jesus, when had he ever begged for a kiss? But he wanted one that badly.

To his relief, she nodded. "I'd like that."

"Thank God." Stifling the overwhelming, desperate urge

to flatten her under him on the bench seat, he slid closer, circling her with his arms. "So...how about a couple?" he suggested, his voice going husky.

She gave him a "nice try, buddy" look. But said, "Okay. But just two."

"Right."

As if.

He buried his fingers in her hair, tugging her head backward, then gave her two gentle brushes across her lips. He drew back and gazed into her sparkling eyes. She looked slightly disappointed at his withdrawal. *Ha.* "More?" he queried innocently.

"Well..." Her hands skimmed up his chest. "A few more might be nice. But just a few."

Gratified, he lowered his lips to hers and kissed her softly, then kissed her again. He touched the corner of her mouth with his tongue and skipped it lightly along her bottom lip. A quick suck on its plumpness and he withdrew once more, savoring the taste of her.

"Few enough? Or too few?"

Dreamily, she gazed up at him from under sleepy lids. "Can you count to a hundred, Bridge?"

"I'll give it a try," he murmured, pulling her tight against his chest. "But I might lose track..."

He felt her arms slide around his neck.

"Then you'll just have to start over"—she shivered when he angled his face over hers so they nearly touched—"until you get it right."

With a soft moan he pressed his lips to hers, gently demanding entry. He wanted to consume her, to fill his senses with the taste and feel and smell of her. To touch her everywhere, and rock himself in the cradle of her warm, welcoming body.

But he held back, feeding his overwhelming need with

the sweet succor of her mouth. His hand fisted in her hair, and he held her fast as he plumbed her velvety depths.

Her response was dazzling. Her body writhed against his with every wet dip of his tongue. Her fingers pulled at his hair and dug into the back of his neck, kneading his flesh to the rhythm of his strokes.

He kissed her senseless, kissed himself witless, kissed her until the only thought in his head was how hot and good she tasted and felt in his arms.

"Come here, angel."

Pulling her thigh over his, he set her straddling his lap, one folded leg on either side of him, face-to-face. Her skirt bunched up around her hips, and he could feel hot satin glide over burning denim where his body ached to join hers. He was near to bursting.

He met her lips again while he massaged her back, his fingers testing for sensitive places on her shoulders, her ribs, her waist. He felt his way down her leg, then slid his hand up under her skirt. A little moan escaped her as he gripped her bare thigh.

When his fingers touched satin, she pulled her mouth from his. "Bridge," she panted, a reluctant warning.

He leaned back against the seat and grappled for control, rubbing his hand up and down her thigh. She reached up to tenderly push a lock of his hair back from his brow, and he lost it all over again.

He gulped down several breaths, let his head drop backward to rest on the seat back.

"Oh, baby. I'm pretty sure I lost count somewhere around four or five," he murmured.

Smiling, she snuggled against him, her legs hugging his thighs, her arms lining his shoulders, her warm breasts nestled into his chest. He cuddled her close, feeling as though he'd landed somewhere just this side of heaven.

Oh, what the woman did to him.

He nearly groaned.

From pleasure.

From guilt.

She must have sucked out every brain cell he possessed through that delectable mouth of hers. What the hell did he think he was doing? What would happen now when he told her he was a cop? And worse, that he was supposed to move in with her?

Hell, he needed to tell her—*right now*—or he'd lose her before he'd even had a chance.

And suddenly, nothing was more important than having a chance with this surprise-filled woman who had him scrambling like mad to recall exactly why he wasn't interested in a serious relationship.

Stroking her hair, he gathered his courage and opened his mouth to speak.

She trailed her finger across his lower lip. "Well…"

The confession caught in his throat. *Coward.* "Yeah, babe?"

"You know what I always tell my kids?"

"No, what?"

"Practice makes perfect."

He tried vainly to dislodge his mind from his dilemma… and his cock. "*Uh*, practicing what, angel?"

She lifted her head from his shoulder and gazed at him with languid, smudged eyes. Her wide, kiss-stung lips pouted sensually.

Oh, God. One look at her and he knew he'd do anything she asked. Anything.

"Counting to a hundred."

He looked at those lips again and felt dizzy.

Piece of cake.

He bent toward her. Hell, this time he might even make it to six.

Chapter Twenty-One

Mary Alice melted against the heat of Bridge's skin. She poured herself into the moist cavern of his mouth and disintegrated from the caress of his rough hands. She leaned into him, seeking…something…desperately.

She wanted him. She knew it was stupid, stupid, stupid. The feeling would pass when she put some distance between them and regained some part of her ability to think rationally. But right now, in his embrace, she wanted only to lose herself in the passion of the moment.

She had never, ever felt like this before. This insane craving. Not even with Jack. And that scared her to death. But she wouldn't stop Bridge's kisses for anything in the world.

She could feel the callused pads of his fingers rake her skin, under her top. How had they gotten there? Shivering in pleasure, she arched her body against his, throwing back her head as he kissed his way down her throat.

His thumbs passed over her breasts, deliberately stroking the quickened tips, and she cried out in blissful pleasure.

"Let me touch you," he coaxed, tugging her closer when

she should have pulled away. "Just touch you."

The assault of his lips and his hands were too much to resist. It felt too good. "Yes," she whispered into his mouth. "Please touch me."

He lifted her top and quickly undid the front hook of her bra. His large hands covered her breasts, enveloping them completely. She squirmed, her body instantly heating. She could feel the barely leashed urgency in his motions, and a part of her wished he would just let loose and take control. She moaned and rode his lap as he stoked her, moving in a slow circle, center to center. A low growl sounded from his chest that sent a thrill straight to her core.

He must have sensed her compliance for he pushed her gently backward, and she went willingly, suspended in the safe web of his fingers and arms. His mouth closed over a breast and the breath left her body.

She gripped his hair, holding his head. "Oh, God, Bridge." The tip of his tongue found her nipple and she moaned, dragging him closer. "Yes. *Mmm*, that feels so good."

With a noise of gratification, he suckled deeply, his mouth moving expertly over her breasts. She twisted and turned in his grasp, tangled up in his arms and his fingers and his tongue. He drove her wild. She ground her hips against his, pulsing to the beat of her frantically pounding heart.

She felt wild and free. Never had anyone unleashed such passion in her. In this man's arms she became the woman she'd always kept hidden. The woman she suddenly longed to let loose and become.

"Baby," he half-moaned. "Honey, hold still."

Dazed, she pulled herself upright. His fingers dug into her arms as his lips covered her face with kisses. His breath came in gasps and a thin film of sweat covered his face. The truck's windows were fogged, and the cab was filled with the scent of desire.

"Angel," he rasped, "you're either going to have to hand me that box by your knee and slip off your panties, or dump a bucket of water over my head before I embarrass us both." He groaned out loud when she shifted on his lap. "But for the love of God, don't move until you decide which."

"I'm sorry," she whispered, trying not to move a muscle, mortified at her loss of control. "I had no idea what I was doing."

He choked, smiling through his obvious discomfort. "Oh, I disagree. I'd give you an A-plus in knowing what you're doing." As he leaned his head back against the seat, his eyes drifted shut. The little crinkles at the corners that she'd grown to adore popped into definition when he smiled. "A definite A-plus."

Her gaze strayed to the box of condoms on the bench by her knee. She bit her lip. For the first time in her life she honestly didn't know which path she should take.

Safe or risky?

She'd made love with Jack, but it had never, ever, *ever*, felt like this. This urgent, gotta-have-him-*now*-or-I'll-die feeling. The hot, molten lava at her center, aching to erupt at his every touch, or leave her paralyzed with disappointment if he slipped from her embrace. She hesitantly lifted her hand from his shoulder, still unsure whether she would reach for the box or not.

His hand snaked up and caught her fingers. He brought them to his lips, kissed them one by one, then pressed a kiss to the center of her palm. "God, I want you," he whispered.

When he lifted his eyes to hers, she was shocked by the range of emotions she saw there. Raw, savage desire stirred in them, the likes of which she'd never seen. But also guilt, regret, and…was that a pinch of bitterness?

Her stomach cramped. Instinctively, she knew she wouldn't like what he was about to say.

"In my whole life I've never wanted any woman as much

as I want you right now." The confession seemed torn from him, reluctantly. And, yes, maybe even a bit resentfully. "I'm ready to explode from needing you."

"I, *um*—"

"*Shhh*," he urged, putting his finger over her lips. "Before you say anything, I need you to do one thing for me."

She nodded, giving his finger a little lick of reassurance. She didn't understand the change in her, couldn't analyze what had happened to make her want to do anything this man asked of her. It felt so dangerous, so frightening. She had suddenly lost control of her body and her emotions, and she wanted nothing more than to jump out of the truck and run as fast as she could to get away from this awesome, desirable, and totally unsuitable man.

But she knew she wouldn't.

She couldn't.

He scooted forward a bit and brought her hand around to the back of his jeans. "Reach into my back pocket and get out my wallet."

She hesitated, suddenly struck by a strong feeling of foreboding. Obviously, he wasn't after a condom. And there was nothing in his wallet that she wanted to see right now. Her heart murmured in protest while her mind raced through the possibilities—pictures of kids...or a wife. Lab results from Ancestry.com saying they were first cousins. Whatever it was surely added up to massive hurt and disappointment.

Wow. That was quick.

No! It wasn't fair. This wonderful lightness in her heart was too new to be crushed already.

He must have seen the fear in her eyes, but he just nodded. "Go ahead."

Her hand began to shake but she dipped her fingers into his pocket and extracted the leather wallet.

He exhaled, refastened her bra, and pulled her top back

down over her breasts. "Open it."

Dread swirled through her. Blood pounded in her throat as she flipped up the cover, then froze in her veins at what she saw.

It was a badge. A police badge. A Pasadena PD badge.

A Pasadena PD badge with an ID above that said DETECTIVE SERGEANT RUSSELL BRIDGER.

She gasped, dropping the hated symbol, feeling as if her fingers had been stung by touching it. She clapped her hands to her mouth in horror and stared into his chillingly calm eyes in patent disbelief.

It couldn't be true. It just couldn't.

But the proof was right there.

Hurt, betrayal, and anger roared through her. *He'd deliberately lied.* She'd told him about her fiancé, about her feelings regarding his profession, and still he'd relentlessly pursued her. All the while masquerading as something he wasn't. Some*one* he wasn't.

"You're a cop! A *cop!*" she choked out.

He nodded. "Undercover."

"You *bastard!* You *lied* to me."

He didn't even flinch at her words. "Baby, give me a chance to —"

"No!" She was suddenly aware of his fingers gripping her thighs. She swatted his hands away, trying to scramble off his lap. She didn't want him touching her. Ever again. "I am *not* your baby."

"Mary Alice, please listen to me." He grasped her arms, attempting to calm her flailing.

"You selfish bastard! You know how I feel about cops! How could you do this to me?"

"I'll admit things got a little out of hand tonight, but I did have some help getting them there."

She stopped struggling and stared hard at him, hating that

he was right. "Let. Me. Go," she gritted out.

He released her and she launched herself out of the steamy atmosphere of the truck into the chill of the night. She bolted up the path to her front door, but he was right behind her.

"Mary Alice, we need to talk."

"I don't talk to cops," she muttered. *Or betrayers. Or men she thought she could love someday.*

This was a painful reminder of exactly why she wasn't ready to date.

"You'll have to talk to me," he said. "One way or another." He took her key and unlocked the door for her.

She shoved past him. "Good luck making that happen."

Nancy was so wrong. This was the last time she'd ever veer off her Master List. This was why she *had* the Master Plan. She was cured forever from experimenting.

His voice was strong at her back, uncompromising. "I'm on a case. I need your cooperation."

She spun around, trying to make sense of what he'd just said. "You're delusional. I'm not involved in anything a cop could possibly be interes—"

Suddenly, the implication of his words slapped her in the face. She gasped and threw her purse onto the sofa. "Wait. You asked me out just to get my cooperation on a case?" For some reason, that hurt more than anything else about this mortifying situation.

He didn't say a word in response, but the guilty look on his face was answer enough.

Wow, he really hadn't been kidding about not wanting a relationship.

"Get out. *Now*."

Instead of obeying, he shut the door behind him and leaned against it. "Your friend Charlie Watson works for Conrex Data Systems. We're certain he's selling top secret computer technology to the Chinese."

She clamped her jaw. "Even if I believed that, it has nothing to do with me."

"We need hard evidence to put Watson away, and we have to find out who his Chinese contact is. We've got Watson under a microscope, from his email to his financials, to his physical movements, and everything in-between. My assignment is to watch for activity at his house."

She scowled, not believing any of this. No way was Charlie a spy for the Chinese. A traitor to his country. Aside from which… "Since when is the Pasadena PD involved in federal crimes?"

"I'm part of an inter-agency task force. FBI, PPD, and Homeland Security."

She crossed her arms over her chest, the kettle of hurt and betrayal within her boiling over into irrational accusation. "And what? You thought you'd seduce me into trusting you, so I'd tell you all of Charlie's dirty little secrets?"

His eyes narrowed. "If I thought you knew any of Watson's dirty little secrets, I wouldn't be standing here." He pinioned her with a look. "And if I'd been trying to seduce you, sweetheart, I'd be in your bed right now with you naked and under me."

He didn't move. He didn't even blink. She could feel the power emanating from him. He was like a magnet wrapping his carnal attraction around her, making it impossible to escape. She stood rooted to the spot, unable to deny his bald statement, praying he wouldn't choose to prove that, despite everything, it was still true.

"I want you out of my house."

"Not till I get what I came for."

Her pulse went into hyperdrive and the hairs prickled on her neck. She backed up a step. "And what is that, Detective Sergeant Bridger?"

"I want to move in with you."

Chapter Twenty-Two

For sheer audacity, Bridge had to hand it to himself. He'd certainly gotten her attention.

Mary Alice's response to his outlandish proposal was stunned disbelief. He watched her work past her instinctive assumption that it was sexually motivated, then reject that explanation as too outrageous even for him. He saw the exact moment when all the puzzle pieces fell into place.

That's when she really got angry.

"Really, Detective Sergeant? A honey trap?"

He winced at the formal venom in her voice. She shook her head and started backing away from him.

"So what was the plan? Couple of dates, a bit of flattery, and the pathetic little nursery school teacher will be so grateful she won't notice you watching Watson's place from her bed? Oh, and be sure to tell her you're not a relationship kind of guy, so when you bust Charlie you don't have to feel guilty about your quick exit from the scene. Is that about right?"

Watching the brave attempt to mask the pain and mortification that pooled in her eyes was like being gut shot.

"You're dead wrong, Mary Alice. That couldn't be further from the truth, and you know it."

"Do I? The evidence is pretty damning, Detective Sergeant."

"The *evidence* that you're wrong is right in front of your eyes." He planted his hands on his hips to prove his point. "Besides, if what you say is true, why would I have stopped to tell you who I am, or what I'm doing?"

Her eyes skittered to the front of his jeans, then rose defiantly, hurt still obvious despite her attempt to cover it with anger. "Basic humanity?"

He pushed out a breath. "Fuck this," he muttered, disgusted with his orders, and even more disgusted with himself. Then he turned and walked out.

Screw Watson.

Screw Grayson.

Screw the whole goddamn task force.

Let them get some other poor slob to move in and endure her haunted looks. He couldn't do it. And if that meant being demoted to traffic duty, or even fired…well, it was worth it not to be reminded of what a slimy bastard he'd been to the only truly wonderful woman he'd known since the day his mama died.

Chapter Twenty-Three

When Bridge rolled into the station the next day after his road crew shift was over, Captain Trujillo called him up to his office.

"Got your message last night," the cap said.

Bridge grunted noncommittally. He'd called in late to report his failure to arrange the move-in at Mary Alice's place.

"And Miss Flannery phoned me this morning."

Drilling a hand through his hair, Bridge dropped into a chair, preparing himself for an ass-chewing of epic proportions. "Thought she might."

"You can move in tonight."

His head shot up. "I don't understand. When I left she—"

Captain Trujillo held up a hand. "She still doesn't like it, but I was able to convince her it was her civic duty to cooperate with us. Her father would roll over in his grave if she refused, and she knows it."

"You told her it would be me?" Bridge hardly dared to hope.

The cap tapped a pencil thoughtfully on his desk and

nodded. "You can pick up a key from her any time before seven. She's going to stay with a friend for the duration. You'll have full run of the cottage."

Bridge didn't know whether to be relieved or furious at the captain's news. He wouldn't touch her again—he swore he wouldn't—but if he was going to be in her house, he really wanted her to be there with him. He felt cheated. Like a kid opening a beautifully wrapped present on Christmas only to find an empty box—a sibling's cruel prank.

After checking in with the task force, he headed home, showered, grabbed a toothbrush and change of clothes, then drove over to her place. When she answered his knock, she wouldn't even look at him. Her hair was wound so tightly in its bun her eyes tipped up at the corners. She wordlessly handed him the key at her front door, stalked down the driveway, and drove off, stiff-backed and thin-lipped, without a backward glance.

Okay, then.

So much for her being there with him. Or ever speaking to him again.

God, sometimes he hated being right.

He ground his teeth and went inside, feeling out of place and decidedly out of sorts. After checking out the rooms he hadn't seen last night, he decided to set up his surveillance gear, alarms, listening devices, and his laptop in her spare bedroom, which she used as a home office.

Too bad there wasn't a guest bed in there, too, along with the desk and bookshelves. The only choices for sleeping seemed to be either Mary Alice's bed, or on a short, antique couch which looked like it had been designed by the Marquis de Sade.

Which was only fitting, since this whole scenario would no doubt have suited the Marquis' torturous sensibilities perfectly.

Bridge chose the couch.

And for two long afternoons and even longer nights after knocking off the road crew, he rattled around her bungalow, desperately manufacturing ways to keep himself occupied while watching the singularly boring and inactive Charlie Watson. And trying not to think about Mary Alice Flannery.

He cursed his weakness for the damned woman.

He was going crazy. Sitting in her living room after it got too dark to work or prowl around outside, everywhere he looked he was reminded of her—and of the disdain for him she'd shown by leaving. Closing his eyes didn't help. He was only assaulted by the seductive, lingering scent of her sweet strawberry shampoo.

His first night there he'd discovered the shampoo bottle sitting on the edge of her old-fashioned claw-foot bathtub. He'd done his best to avoid it and the memories it stirred. But on his second night, after doing a late perimeter check of Watson's place, he finally surrendered to the inevitable. He set his motion detector beeper on the bathroom counter and soaked in the tub until the water went ice cold, just squeezing that shampoo bottle and breathing in the scent. Imagining what it would be like to have her there with him in the tub, her hair loosened from its horrible up-do and cascading over his bare skin, her eyes warm and gazing at him with desire, her arms tender and loving.

As they had been the other night.

Get real, Bridger.

After dragging himself out of the tub and suffering through a lengthy self-lecture on the futility of such fantasies, he moved the beeper to an end table in the living room and tormented himself again attempting to catch a couple hours sleep on the overstuffed, undersized torture sofa. He found a quilt and wrapped himself in it, only to find he was again surrounded by the smell of the woman he'd do anything to forget.

The woman who had haunted his every waking thought now for two punishing days and two tormented nights.

He couldn't sleep.

Not without dreaming.

And every time he closed his eyes he would dream of his mother singing in her garden back home. He'd reach out to her, but she would always slip out of his grasp and start to walk away.

"Mama," he'd call, and she would turn to him.

But always, it was Mary Alice's face that looked sadly back at him.

He didn't know how much more of this he could take. Even Charlie Watson seemed to be in on the conspiracy, not going out except to his job, and not receiving any interesting visitors, or even packages that Bridge could check out the labels on.

In short, he was going stark, raving mad.

On the third day of hell, he walked up the street from his truck to Mary Alice's cottage, sighed, and scoped around for Jose and Enrico, the two gardeners who had been tending Mary Alice's yard when he'd knocked off from his final shift on the road crew an hour ago.

He'd nearly forgotten about Watson's guys doing her lawn every week. Since Bridge had mowed it just a few days ago, they'd decided to trim some bushes instead. Upon discovering the two men in the bungalow's yard earlier that afternoon, and desperate even to hear the sound of her name spoken aloud, he'd spent a few minutes discussing the garden with them, exchanging lawn tips, and sharing a chuckle over Watson's obsession with his precious water lilies. They'd been curious about Mary Alice's new live-in boyfriend, and he'd endured a few male barbs about his intentions concerning her.

But apparently Jose and Enrico had finished and were now gone.

Bridge hoisted the duffel bag with fresh clothes he'd brought over from his place for the weekend, grateful he wouldn't have to do a grimy load of road crew laundry every night any more. The task force had picked up chatter that Watson's buy was happening soon, so the captain had insisted Bridge go on surveillance duty full-time. A rookie officer, Jason Deane, was taking over his undercover spot on the construction crew starting on Monday.

Bridge headed into the house, taking the front steps two at a time. But when he inserted the key in the door, it swung open, unlocked. He froze, his cop instincts instantly setting off inner alarms.

Dropping his bag, he quickly grabbed his small back-up gun from his boot holster. Easing himself through the door, he quietly shut it. It was still full daylight, so he could readily see that nothing in the open-concept living-dining room had been disturbed. Sliding along one wall, he peered down the hallway to the bedrooms.

Clear.

He sprinted for the kitchen, pausing before he whipped in, crouched with weapon raised, aiming first left, then right.

Empty.

He sucked down a breath, slipped around into the hall. Breaking a light sweat, he crept along the wall. Checked the spare room. The bathroom.

No one.

Only Mary Alice's bedroom was left.

Door closed.

He listened intently.

There! A soft scrape. Something being dragged along the floor.

He leaned against the door jamb. Took a deep breath.

Collected himself.

If Watson had discovered the motion detectors the FBI techs had installed around his property, he could have put two and two together and deduced the man staying at Mary Alice's might not be her new lover, but a Fed. He'd be out to investigate the possibility and eliminate the opposition, if necessary.

Bridge gripped his weapon, thinking wistfully of the Berretta in his gym bag. Hell, the pea shooter he was holding now wouldn't stop a determined chipmunk. He wasn't even carrying his handcuffs.

Nothing to do about it now.

Stretching out his fingers, he finessed the doorknob until the latch clicked open. His adrenaline surged.

He burst through the door, launching himself at the figure leaning into the closet. "Police! Freeze!"

She screamed.

"*Jee*zus!" he yelled, yanking his weapon away from Mary Alice's neck. He spun away from her and bent over at the waist, gripping his knees, heart thundering. "What the *hell* are you doing here? I could have killed you!"

Chalk white, she stood plastered to the corner of the room, her eyes wild, peeking over her trembling hands as they clamped tight against more screams he could tell wanted to escape.

He holstered the gun in his boot, then straightened. "Are you all right?"

She nodded once, loosening the death grip on her mouth and lowering her hands to grab her arms instead. She was still shaking.

Damn. In a single stride, he'd pulled her into his arms, holding her close, soothing the shakes that wracked her body. "God, honey, I'm so sorry. I wasn't expecting you— I thought you were Watson."

"No. It's not your fault," she whispered hoarsely against his chest. "I'm sorry I'm being such a baby. I just have this thing about guns. My fiancé and my father—"

Guilt washed over him at the reminder. This was exactly why she didn't want to be around cops. And he'd brought it right into her bedroom.

Just as his dad had done to his mom.

Anguish filled him as he remembered once when he was about seven and his dad had been away on a three-day stakeout. After the first night, his mom had taken to her bed and stayed there, just staring at the wall. Bridge had felt so helpless, watching her fold into herself more and more, and lose touch with reality.

He'd tried to tell her Daddy was a good cop and was being extra careful. That he'd be okay. But Mama had just looked at him with her dark, doleful eyes.

"My baby boy," she whispered, beckoning him into her embrace. He'd held her for hours that time, singing their favorite songs to her in a high, shaky voice, desperately feeling like nothing he could do or say would help.

And he'd been right.

He knew now, as an adult, that she had more psychological issues than simply being married to a police officer. That she had been mentally fragile to the extreme and might not have made it even if she'd been married to a poet or a baker. But that was his head talking. And what he always heard was his heart whispering that promise he'd made her as she lay dying.

"Don't do this to another woman, *mijo*. Promise me you'll only marry a strong, independent woman. A woman who won't fall apart if you're—"

Her expression had gone utterly stricken then, and her words had died, along with the little light left in her eyes. He'd called to her, grasping her hand in grief and distress as she'd slipped away from him forever.

Holding Mary Alice now, Bridge steeled himself against the wellspring of emotions bubbling up within him. As much as he wanted her, wanted to try for something real with her, he had no business with a woman like Mary Alice. She had too many bad memories. She'd never be able to make a life with another cop. And he refused to kill her sweet, gentle spirit, watching it wither and die as she waited at home, worrying over another man whose whole world was filled with violence and uncertainty. Another man who one day might not return home because of the profession he'd chosen.

Eventually Mary Alice stopped trembling, and he let her go, but only after wrapping her tenderly in a fuzzy blanket from the bed.

And silently vowed never to hold her again.

That was when he spotted the overnight bag sitting on the floor by the dresser.

"What are you doing back here?" he asked with a frown, crossing his arms and pinning his hands beneath them so he wouldn't reach for her again.

She plunked down on the bed, eyeing him, suddenly defiant despite the shadows of fear still playing in the depths of her eyes. "I live here?"

He was already painfully aware of that, thank you. "I thought you were staying with a friend as long as I'm—" He set his jaw.

She pulled the blanket tighter around her shoulders, lifting her chin. "There's been a change of plans. Nancy's husband just got some disturbing news about his health. I don't want to intrude on their privacy while they deal with it."

He stared at her. "You're moving back in?"

He wasn't sure whether to pump his fist, or run as fast as he could back to the station and resign from the case.

She glanced at his face and scowled. He snapped his jaw shut but it was too late.

"Don't worry, Detective Sergeant, you'll still have the run of the house," she said brusquely. "I'll stay out of your way. You won't even know I'm here."

Yeah, that was real likely.

He turned and walked toward the bedroom door. "No problem. And I really wish you would call me Bridge."

"Of course, you'll have to find somewhere else to sleep, *Detective Sergeant.*"

He stopped dead and jerked a glance at her, then at the bed behind her. "I've been sleeping on the couch."

She blinked. "Oh."

Was that disappointment he saw flit through her eyes?

Who was he kidding? More like abject relief.

He gave in to the bitterness scratching at the edges of his heart. "Don't worry, Miss Flannery. I'm here to do a job and nothing more."

With that he strode out and closed the door firmly behind him.

Now, if he could just convince his loudly protesting heart that was all he wanted.

Chapter Twenty-Four

Mary Alice looked out the kitchen window to the back yard, searching for Bridge. He'd been avoiding her all morning, and that made her feel like crap. Okay, so she was still furious to the max with him for lying to her, and for nearly giving her heart failure when he'd assaulted her and practically shot her head off last night. But as much as she hated to admit it, she'd missed him. Missed him a lot.

How was that even possible?

When Nancy and Ben had gotten the frightening news from Ben's doctor that a large tumor had turned up on his head scan, Mary Alice had known they needed their privacy to deal with such a scary and serious situation. Nancy had assured Mary Alice she was still welcome to stay, but the last thing her best friend needed during such a time was an extra wheel hanging around the house.

So, Mary Alice had decided that despite Bridge's presence, she should move back home.

She hadn't expected his negative reaction, nor his avoidance. She'd actually been worried she'd have to fend him off every time she turned around.

She should have known better. Once he'd gained access to her house, it was obvious she held little interest for him.

Which was a good thing. A *very* good thing.

He was a cop, and she did *not* get involved with cops. No way. No how.

Hell, she didn't want to get involved at *all*. Not anymore. She'd learned her lesson. Just look at what had happened when she'd only contemplated the idea of it.

Even so, his complete rejection was more than a little humiliating. And yes, she was hurt by it.

"Mary Alice?"

She jumped and whirled around, grasping the edge of the kitchen counter. "Bridge, you'll really have to stop scaring me like that."

"Sorry."

She winced inwardly, wondering if he noticed she'd accidentally called him Bridge, not Detective Sergeant. "How anyone can sneak around wearing cowboy boots— What?"

He was looking at her—her hair to be specific—with a peculiar expression on his face.

Embarrassed, she reached up self-consciously and grasped a lock of the unruly mess. She'd really meant to put it up in a neat twist. "Scary isn't it? Be thankful you don't have to look at it every morning."

His hooded gaze dropped to hers.

Damn.

She faltered, heating from the unintended innuendo. "In the mirror, I mean." Spinning back to the sink, she busied herself with the potato salad she was fixing for lunch.

After an endless moment of silence, he said, "I was just thinking how pretty you look today. I like your hair down." Before she could possibly think of an appropriate response, he went on, "Do you have an old coffee can I could use? Or something like that?"

She nodded and opened the cupboard under the sink, where she kept the stuff she saved to use at school. "Down here. Take whatever you like."

They both stooped down at the same time, meeting eye to eye in front of the cupboard.

"Quite a choice," he said, not looking at the cans at all. Then he cleared his throat, picked out a large green can, and strode out the door, leaving her wondering what exactly had just happened.

At lunchtime they sat across from one another at a picnic table under the big magnolia in her back yard, straining to make polite conversation. It wasn't as if she could eat without inviting him to join her. Her mother had brought her up right, even if his hadn't.

"What are you working on today?" she asked politely.

In the last three days, he'd managed to mend the wobbling pickets in her fence, repair the sagging shed door and back porch stairs, and trim several undisciplined trees. And all morning she'd heard mysterious noises coming from inside her ancient garage.

"I found an old rose arbor stashed in the backyard. Thought I might have a go at restoring it." He glanced at her uncertainly.

She sat up. "Really? Do you think it's possible?"

"You like it?" His expression warmed.

"I love it. I just thought it was beyond repair."

His face relaxed. "It's falling apart, all right, but mostly because the nails are rusting out. Wrong kind. Replace them with stainless steel ones, slap on a fresh coat of paint, and it's good as new. The wood itself is in great shape. I think it's teak or something."

Torn, she put down her fork. "You don't have to do all this. I happen to know fixing fences and rose arbors isn't part of a cop's job description."

He took a swig of iced tea, then twirled it in his hand. "Easier to keep watch from outside."

"I do have a hammock."

His lips curved. "Now, how suspicious would that look, your new boyfriend spending the whole day in a hammock without you?" He shook his head. "Dead give-away."

She shook off an instinctive shiver at the word "boyfriend." She couldn't believe she'd gone along with that ruse. Her father's old friend, Captain Trujillo, had suggested it when she called him to say she was moving back in…hoping she could talk him into kicking out Bridge in favor of someone less…disturbing. Instead, Trujillo had seen right through her protestations and turned the tables on the idea. In a moment of shocked witlessness, she'd agreed to let Bridge pose as her boyfriend.

She picked up her fork again and toyed with her salad, thinking of all the days Jack had spent in the hammock without her, back when it had hung in her parents' backyard. "Still. I'm starting to feel like I'm taking advantage of you," she managed.

He raised a brow.

"The situation," she corrected, fumbling with a tomato.

He raised the other.

God.

"Having a man around."

He cocked his head and she slammed her eyes shut.

"To fix things and such."

"No need," he said, finally rescuing her from herself. "I told you, I enjoy doing it. It's been a while since I've been able to putter."

She stole a glance at him from beneath her lashes. How could any mortal man look so good sitting at a picnic table with dead leaves clinging to his shirt and gardening gloves sticking out his back pocket?

She had to remember she wasn't interested in him, mortal or no. Besides, he wasn't attracted to her unless his job depended on it. He'd made that crystal clear by ignoring her for the past three days.

But if she wasn't interested, then why did her heart still flutter every time she looked at him or heard his deep voice?

He lifted a forkful of potato salad to his mouth and, suddenly, she noticed his knuckles were scraped and raw. "You're hurt. What happened?"

"It's nothing." He dismissed her concern with a wave of his hand.

"The nails on that arbor looked awfully rusty. When was your last tetanus booster?"

"Probably last time I got shot."

She blanched, staring at him for an endless moment, her heart stalling in horror. Then she slammed down the lid on her knee-jerk reaction and jumped to her feet. "You should put some antiseptic on it. I'll be right back." She hurried into the house.

Last time I got shot.

The graphic, disturbing reminder of his profession had her stomach lurching. Against her will, visions of, first Jack, then her father, lying in some alley in a pool of blood, flashed through her mind. She grabbed the bathroom sink and took a deep, cleansing breath, pushing the images away. She'd thought she had managed to banish those vivid memories long ago, but Bridge's unexpected statement had caught her by complete surprise and she'd reacted badly. He probably thought she was a complete wuss.

Straightening, she pulled the yellow tube of antiseptic and some cotton balls out of the medicine cabinet, and returned determinedly to the picnic table. "Let me have your hand."

For a few seconds he didn't move. Then, with the look of a

man indulging a woman in a silly but harmless whim, he gave his hand over to her.

Feeling at once terribly self-conscious about touching him, she forced herself to take hold of his fingers. They were long and bronze against her much paler, smaller hand. She could feel his pulse beating in his fingertips. They were warm. So warm she thought hers might melt away under them.

Swallowing heavily, she swabbed his knuckles with a water-soaked cotton ball, then dried them and gently spread on a layer of antiseptic cream. He watched her face the whole time, an inscrutable look on his own, ignoring his hand completely. Red-cheeked, she suddenly realized she'd been stroking his fingers much longer than necessary.

Struggling against the urge to kiss away the hurt, she placed his hand on the table. "All done."

"Thanks." He pulled it back and quickly finished up his lunch without another word.

She really hated this awful tension between them. She was sick of walking a tightrope between suspicion and lust. She wanted their fun, comfortable friendship back. They had been so relaxed and happy together before his confession—when they weren't all over each other—and she missed that.

To be honest, she missed the being all over each other part, too. But she wasn't going there again. Still, talking would be nice.

Maybe if she apologized for doubting his honor. Perhaps then she'd get back the other Bridge—the new friend she'd been growing so fond of.

He started gathering up his lunch dishes.

She quickly ventured, "Captain Trujillo said you argued to keep me out of this case. But the FBI SAC ordered you to use my house, however you had to get my permission."

He looked at her for a moment, then shrugged. Crumpling up his napkin, he tossed it on his empty plate. "It was really the only option."

"I accused you of all those horrible things. I'm sorry." And she really was. On more than one level.

"No big deal," he said. "You had every right to be angry."

"Maybe so, but not to go off on you like that. I know you weren't trying to—" She faltered. "That you wouldn't have—"

With a grim expression he stood and picked up his plate and glass. "Don't make me into something I'm not, Mary Alice. Believe me, if you'd been willing, I would have screwed your brains out in that truck and walked away a very happy man. But I would have walked away."

As if to demonstrate, he turned and walked away from her then, disappearing through the door that led into the kitchen.

And her heart quietly broke in two.

Chapter Twenty-Five

B ridge carefully set his dishes down on the counter—before he could throw them at the wall. He raked both hands through his hair and cursed himself long, hard, and vile. He'd never actually hated himself before. Not until this past week.

Turning on the tap full blast, he stuck his fingers under it and scrubbed at the antiseptic lotion till his raw knuckles sang with the sting of the hot water.

He looked out the window and saw Mary Alice sitting at the picnic table, looking every bit as beaten as during that horrible moment he'd held a gun to her neck. Her head was bowed, her shoulders slumped, and her pretty hands were clasped tightly in her lap. He'd bet good money they were shaking.

God, he was a son of a bitch.

He had to keep away from her.

He wanted her in the worst way. And the best way. But he couldn't commit to spending the rest of his life with her—or anything more than a short time. And she'd want more than that.

But he couldn't ask a woman to stay with him. Not if he really loved her.

He wouldn't risk it. He couldn't. Especially not with this woman, who had already managed to turn his world upside down.

He shook his head. Even to himself, his reasoning sounded hollow. Like a lame excuse, rather than a solemn promise being fulfilled.

Funny, it had never rung false before.

Then he thought of his mother. Her death certificate said it was a stroke, but he knew better. That's not what had killed her. She could have fought the depression, might have won, but she had deliberately chosen not to. Every time Dad had been late coming home, she was convinced he wasn't coming back at all. She'd retreated further and further, gotten more and more remote, until finally even her baby boy hadn't been able to bring her back.

Bridge inhaled a long, deep breath, and released his white-knuckled grip on the edge of the sink. His mother might have been overly fragile, but the fact was, every cop's wife had a hell of a stressful life. Not something any woman should have to endure, let alone a woman with so many reasons to avoid it. He'd be damned if he'd put Mary Alice in that position.

He just couldn't do it.

So he spent the afternoon taking apart the rose arbor, pouring his frustrations into sanding the pieces till they were smooth as silk—smooth as Mary Alice's thighs—to his touch. He caressed the curves of the wood with his thumbs, closed his eyes, and let his mind take him where he wanted to be. Instantly, his body was as hard as the wood beneath his hands.

Groaning, he threw aside the sandpaper and opened a can of white paint. He had to exercise an iron grip on himself to keep from running to her, getting down on his knees, and begging for her forgiveness. But doing so would surely lead him to hug her, touch her, kiss her. And more.

And that would be disaster.

No. He had to put a leash on it. He was a grown man, for godsakes, capable of rising above the temptation of this situation.

Shit.

That damned promise had always been so easy to keep before. What the hell had happened over the past week to make him think of nothing more than how much he wanted to break it?

Chapter Twenty-Six

The next morning, Mary Alice woke to the smell of bacon frying. For a second she thought she was back at Nancy's, but when she opened her eyes the fog cleared from her brain as she recognized her own room.

Well, most of the fog cleared. A slight headache thumped against her temples. She moaned in self-recrimination and eased out of bed. She'd had three glasses of wine with dinner last night—something she never did.

Bridge had grilled burgers, and they'd sat out back under the magnolia again, relaxing over a glass of wine with the meal. Or rather, they'd tried to relax. She'd done her best to present a facade of sangfroid against his cool, distant conversation, but the tension had proven too much for her, and she'd resorted to two extra glasses of wine to get through dinner.

It was embarrassing to have a hangover from three glasses of wine.

And now she had to face the man and his stupid bacon. She gritted her teeth and considered sneaking out a window instead.

Unfortunately, nature wouldn't allow her that option, even if she could bang the sticky window screen open without waking the whole freaking neighborhood. For the first time since she'd bought her quaint old bungalow, she dearly wished she'd chosen a modern house—with a master bath instead of the single bathroom down the hall.

But there was no way around it—she'd have to leave the sanctuary of her own room and brave seeing her houseguest.

Maybe if she was really, really quiet, he wouldn't notice her.

Chapter Twenty-Seven

Naturally, he saw her right away.

After two aspirin, a splash in the sink, a fresh dress, and a bit of make-up, Mary Alice felt much better. Still, when she ran headlong into Bridge as she came out of the bathroom, her legs were suddenly as wobbly as a Catalina tourist stepping off the hydrofoil.

"Breakfast?" he asked.

He looked suspiciously cheerful. And unbelievably attractive wearing nothing but a pair of cut-off PPD sweats and a spatula.

Mary Alice gave herself a firm mental admonishment for her weakness, and avoided looking below his neck. "I'm not really hungry," she said, attempting to hurry past without touching him.

"Nonsense. Breakfast is the most important meal of the day." He parked himself in front of her, blocking her retreat. "I made Denver omelets."

Reluctantly, she allowed herself to be herded toward the dining room. "How's a woman to refuse?" she mumbled.

When she was seated, he placed a plate in front of her with the most delectable-looking omelet she'd ever seen, along with a steaming mug of coffee.

"Smells wonderful," she admitted, her stomach growling appreciatively. She reached for her coffee, but Bridge just continued to stand there, looking suddenly nervous. "What?" she asked warily.

He stared at her for a moment, then seemed to gather himself. "I want to apologize," he said, shocking her speechless. "I've been acting like a complete jerk, and I'm sorry."

Remnants of the pain she'd endured for the past few days zinged through her at his words. She couldn't deny he'd hurt her badly, first with his deception and then by his cold attitude after she'd returned. She licked her lips and grappled for something to say, but before she could formulate a single thought, he went on.

"The truth is, I'm attracted to you. Very attracted. But I also know how you feel about getting involved—with me in particular." His mouth thinned. "Being this close to you...well, I'm just having a little trouble dealing with the whole situation."

Her overloaded brain homed in on one phrase. *I'm attracted to you.*

Surely he— No. He couldn't possibly mean he was interested in her...*interested* interested. Not beyond a superficial physical desire. His pretty speech about the truck had made *that* abundantly clear. It was just sex he was interested in.

The man had a hell of a nerve.

She set her jaw. "And that's supposed to excuse your behavior, I suppose?"

"No." Slowly, he scraped the second omelet from the skillet onto his plate. "It doesn't matter how much I want to—" He stopped abruptly and cleared his throat. "Nothing justifies taking out my frustrations on you."

Her face blazed and she looked away, toying with the

edge of the tablecloth. She figured she knew exactly what he wanted. "Bridge, please don't. I—"

"It's not just sex, you know," he interrupted, shocking her again. Was the man a mind reader?

"Bridge, honestly—"

"I like everything about you. Your generosity, your sense of humor. The way you love those kids you teach, and wear those pretty dresses instead of jeans. Even that man-eating lawnmower of yours that should be illegal makes me like you even more for not wanting to pollute the environment."

He reached for her hand and caressed the tender underside of her wrist, looking as earnest as an altar boy. "Please, Mary Alice. If I promise to be very, very good, can we go back to the way it was before? I miss you. I liked being your friend."

Stunned, she opened her mouth, couldn't think of a thing to say, and shut it again. Her vision suddenly blurred. "I miss you, too, Bridge."

He smiled, and she held her breath as they gazed at each other for a long moment, happiness filling her to the brim.

Then a mischievous grin slid over his lips. "Of course, the sex part ain't bad, either."

Her breath whooshed out and she smacked his arm, blinking back the tears that had inexplicably dampened her eyes. "You are completely incorrigible."

He pulled her into a hug. "Another one of my more endearing traits."

His chest was warm and his arms strong and tender. And she knew if she stayed in them for one second more, she'd forget all about her new resolve to avoid him. So she pulled away. "Sex isn't an option. I'm sorry, but it really isn't."

He held up his hands, walked around to his side of the table and sat down. "I know. I know. You deserve a nice, stable guy with a nice, stable job. Someone who is willing to make all the right commitments. I can't do that, so I'll suffer in silence and not pressure you. I promise."

"I'm glad you understand," she said, and forced herself to take a bite of omelet. It should have been delicious but it tasted like sawdust.

He was right. She *did* deserve a nice, stable man who wasn't afraid of commitment. If she was going to take the awful risk of another relationship, she had to make sure her heart wouldn't be broken because she chose the wrong man.

Unfortunately, she suddenly couldn't imagine herself with any man but Russell Bridger.

Which left her…where?

Fresh out of luck. Because he'd only love her, then walk away. That's what he had said. He would make love to her, then walk away a happy man.

No, it wasn't worth it. Better to be just friends.

She eased a smile onto her face. If it was a bit more subdued than it could have been, well, it *was* honest. She *did* like him as a friend and was glad she could have at least that much of him.

"Mary Alice?"

She jerked her attention up, and realized he was waiting for her to say something. "*Um…?*"

"So, friend, would you like to help me paint the rose arbor this morning?"

"Yes, of course," she answered, sensing her taste buds awaken again to the flavor of cheese and salsa. "I'd love to."

He winked, and she dug into the omelet.

It would be all right. *She* would be all right. She'd just have to be vigilant. Keep her defenses up around him. Lots and lots of defenses. And she could absolutely not let him catch her off guard. Off balance. Because then she might do something crazy.

And if she did something crazy, there would be no stopping herself. Or him. And she'd be lost for certain.

Hopelessly lost, in love with Russell Bridger.

Chapter Twenty-Eight

"*Uh-oh*, Watson has company," Bridge whispered under his breath to Mary Alice, watching a car turn into the neighboring drive.

She was sitting next to him on the back lawn, cross-legged and leaning over a jumble of newly painted wooden arbor parts. The faded T-shirt and old cut-offs she'd changed into carried smears of white paint, as did her thighs where they weren't covered.

He'd been severely distracted by those thighs all morning and nearly forgot what he was saying when he glanced over at her. There was paint across her nose, too.

"What are you going to do?" she asked.

"Do?" *Damn*. He was going to concentrate, that's what he was going to do. He jumped up and asked in a loud voice, "How about some iced tea?" The woman had definitely scrambled his brains.

"*Uh*, sure."

He went as quickly as he could into the house and straight to the spare room, where he peeled off his painting gloves and turned up the listening apparatus on the phone surveillance. The small electronic device planted in the receiver unit in Watson's house was also able to pick up conversations in the room where the phone was kept.

Within five minutes he concluded that the visitors were just boating buddies of Watson's, not connected to the technology thefts at Conrex Data Systems. But he left the recorder on just to be safe. Grabbing his digital camera, he fixed a couple of iced teas and returned to Mary Alice in the backyard.

"Thank you," she said and raised her brows in question as she took a sip.

He shook his head and pulled the gloves out of his back pocket. "Think I'll take some pictures when we get a bit further along with the arbor," he said casually, nodding at the camera.

When Watson's visitors were getting into their car to leave, Bridge snapped several photos of them under the cover of taking shots of Mary Alice next to their painting project.

Of course, he took a few of Mary Alice, too. She looked so cute with her hair straying from the confines of her ponytail, paint smudges everywhere, wearing a glow of happiness a blind man couldn't miss. He was pretty sure he was wearing that same glow. They'd been having a fine time all morning, painting and talking about everything under the warm California sun. Everything but what was really on both their minds.

But that was okay. It was dangerous territory, what was on their minds. And they both knew it.

So he had to be content with catching her staring at his face, his chest, his biceps when he reached for the paint, and knowing she might just share the craving he felt every time he looked at her. Once, he swore she was about to lean over and kiss him. His body had zapped him so badly that, after she'd merely pulled a ladybug out of his hair, he'd had to go into the kitchen for a cold dunking in the sink

Oh, man. He didn't know if he'd make it through the weekend. At least during the week, she'd be at work and out of temptation's way.

His temptation.

"I'll just take the camera inside," he said when Watson's buddies pulled out of the driveway.

In the spare room, he uploaded the photos into the task force cloud storage, and emailed Sam Grayson at the station to have him run them through facial recognition. He added a note to his growing file on Watson's activities, then went back outside to continue his watch from the back lawn.

And more sweet torture being so close to Mary Alice.

After dinner, he volunteered to do the dishes.

They'd both avoided wine that night. He was still on duty, and he guessed she had overindulged the night before and didn't want a repeat.

Just as well. The last thing either of them needed was to relax their inhibitions.

They'd had fun together today, combining work and play so seamlessly the day had flown by before he'd realized it was gone. But the electricity that still swirled and crackled about them was unmistakable, and gaining strength by the second. Mary Alice could deny it from here to next week, but Bridge knew she wanted him just as badly as he wanted her.

Not that he'd do anything about it. He'd made her a promise to keep things platonic, and he meant to keep that one, too.

Just as long as she kept her hands off him.

If she touched him, really touched him, he didn't know if he could be responsible for his actions.

He took his time with the dishes, and when he finally came out to the living room, she had settled down on the sofa with a book.

"What're you reading?"

She glanced up and her face instantly turned bright red. The book disappeared into the folds of the dress she'd changed into after her shower. "Oh, nothing."

Amused, he strolled over. "*Aw*, come on now, you can tell me. I won't give away your secrets." With a finger he flipped over the cover she was trying to hide.

Mistake. *Big* mistake. It depicted a nearly bare-breasted redhead swooning in the arms of one of his mother's Native ancestors. *Ho-boy*. He licked his lips, briefly imagining what he'd look like in long hair and a loincloth.

"Looks, *uh*—"

There was no possible way he could sit in the same room with Mary Alice and that book cover. His imagination was far too inventive.

Her eyes were large and liquid, gazing up at him with a mixture of embarrassment and…something else. Something he shouldn't even think about.

He let the cover flip back. "I need to get some work done. I'll be…"

Letting his words trail off, he did an about-face and strode to the spare room, lecturing himself the whole way.

For the first time, he noticed the bookshelves lining the walls, filled with early childhood education texts—and romance novels. He stared at them for a full minute before forcing himself to sit down in front of the various monitors and his laptop.

He'd be far safer surfing the net than having one of those suggestive covers in his hands, prodding his fantasies even farther into dangerous territory. They'd already gone far enough all on their own.

His email had built up from neglect, so he took a couple of hours to answer it, sent a quick note to his dad, then checked in on a few blogs and forums he kept up with. He ran through the recording from Watson's phone conversation, just to make sure there was nothing on it that he'd missed the first time around. Finally, having run out of distractions, he grabbed the perimeter beeper and headed for the bathroom. He took a shower, intending to kick Mary Alice out of the living room so he could toss and turn on the sofa for a few hours before getting up for his usual nocturnal reconnaissance of Watson's property.

Standing naked in the middle of the bathroom floor, steam from the shower swirling around his legs, he rubbed his hair dry with a towel. Suddenly, the door flew open.

Mary Alice halted halfway through.

He froze.

Her mouth opened to exclaim, but no sound came out. Her eyes fastened on his body.

Kick-starting his momentarily paralyzed brain, he resumed drying his hair. His pulse hammered. Normally he wasn't into exhibitionism, but at her reaction to his nakedness, something primitive took over. An erotic wave licked through his belly. Excitement surged.

"Sorry, I forgot…" Her words faded as his arousal grew. Her grasp on the flaps of her long flannel robe tightened. But her lips parted. "Oh, my," she whispered.

"You should leave, Mary Alice," he warned, his voice low and rough. "Right now."

"Yeah." But she didn't move a muscle. Slowly, she catalogued his body parts.

Every last one of them.

He waited several beats, then said, "This isn't smart."

She swallowed. "No, it's not."

He wondered where he got the fortitude to resist just ripping that robe right off her and tossing her to the floor.

Then it came to him. He wanted—no, *needed*—the

decision to be hers. Completely hers. He cared too much for her to have it otherwise.

A burst of surprise shot through him. *Holy crap*. He *cared* for her. Gut-deep cared. When had that happened? The realization almost scared the physical craving right out of him.

Almost, but not quite.

"Something I can do for you, angel?"

She blinked, tearing her attention from his body. His pulse pounded.

"How about some iced tea?" she asked weakly.

He almost laughed. But this situation was too loaded for humor. He shook his head. "No."

She gazed at him. "What would you like to do?" she finally whispered.

It was pretty damn obvious what he wanted to do. His cock was at full stand, straining toward her.

"You."

The following silence in the small, steamy room was deafening.

She swallowed heavily. Her grip on her robe loosened. As her hands fell away, so did the robe, revealing a long, narrow wedge of bare skin.

His temperature spiked. "Jesus," he choked out. He should chase her off. *Now*.

She took a step toward him.

"Mary Alice…" he began, searching her eyes for a hint of her intent.

She stepped back, knocking into the door. It smacked shut behind her.

Tossing his towel over the rim of the tub, he eyed the gap in her robe. She nervously smoothed her hands down the flannel. But didn't pull it closed.

Step by step, he approached her, until they were practically touching. "This really isn't smart," he repeated.

"I'm tired of being smart," she whispered.

A potent mixture of fear and excitement swirled in her eyes. Her body called to him, an irresistible siren song that left his best intentions scattered.

He slowly, deliberately, opened her robe and pushed it off her shoulders, then let it drop to the floor. Taking one more step, he braced his feet apart. Her naked body grazed his. The hard points of her breasts whispered across his chest as his arousal nestled in the hollow of her abdomen. He could feel the light tickle of her curls between his thighs. Every muscle screamed at him to pick her up and carry her off to bed.

"Sweetheart, are you sure?"

She looked up into his eyes, a little dazed. Hesitantly, she lifted her hands and ran her fingers down his damp chest, stopping at his waist.

His skin burned from her touch, but his mind howled with warning. *They should not be doing this*. It was a huge mistake they'd both regret in the morning.

And yet, he couldn't tear himself away to save his life.

"Please," she whispered.

Her quiet plea snapped his willpower in a thousand pieces. He grasped her hips and pulled her a shade closer. "No assumptions?"

"No assumptions." She looked serious. Like he could trust that she really did know what she was letting herself in for.

The question was, did *he*?

He rolled his hips against her in a sensual rhythm that left no doubt about what he was asking. Her soft breasts pillowed against him. "Just tell me you don't want me and I'll let you go."

She licked her lips and tilted her face up. "I—"

He pulled her tighter against him. If she changed her mind now he'd die. Simply keel over dead.

Her gaze dropped to his mouth and her green eyes grew

dark as a forest in a storm. Her hands slipped an inch further around his waist. "I don't want—"

He knew a moment of pure panic. With steel restraint, he leaned down and drew his tongue along her jaw. "You don't want...?"

From her hip, he let one hand snake around her waist and crawl up her back. She drew in a sharp breath. He painted over her lips with his tongue.

"I don't want you to—"

Her words were lost on a moan as he took her breast in his hand. With a thumb and forefinger he gently rolled the tip. She arched, and her body pressed into his, fitting like a fine weapon in the hand of a man who loved to shoot.

"Baby, tell me."

"I don't want..."

He urged her mouth open under his, plunging deep inside with his tongue.

"I don't want you to stop," she said on a gasp when they came up for air, minutes later.

With a triumphant growl he lifted her off her feet, burning a path of kisses along her throat.

She *would* be his.

He drove his fingers into her silky hair and tugged it out of her ponytail, letting it cascade around her shoulders.

He knew this was all wrong, insane. But he couldn't stop himself.

He wanted her. No, he *needed* her.

Needed to feel her goodness, clasp her sweetness close to his heart. He could deal with the consequences. He would give her as much of himself, of his heart, as he possibly could, for as long as he could. And try like hell not to hurt her. He'd do anything not to hurt her.

"Where's our first prize box?" he asked hoarsely.

She nodded at the drawer under the bathroom counter.

"There."

In two steps he carried her over, and tore the drawer open. With one hand he reached for the box and flipped up the lid. "You choose."

For one horrible second she hesitated, and he really thought she would change her mind. But then she dipped into the box and pulled out a packet, placing it in his hand.

"God, I want you," he murmured, folding her in his embrace. "From the first moment I saw you. I'd use that ridiculous stop sign to hold up traffic, just to flirt with you twice a day. I've wanted you like crazy."

Damned if it wasn't true. He'd never felt this way about any woman before. Ever. He was ready to burst from wanting her. Just *her*. Not some random feminine body, warm and willing.

Only Mary Alice would do.

And that scared the hell out of him.

But he wasn't about to analyze it right now. Or let it stop what was happening.

He kissed her deeply, and he could feel her nervousness in her darting tongue. While he prepared himself for her, he could feel her pulse hammering in her wrists as they circled his neck.

He slid the drawer shut with his thigh, pushed aside his beeper, lifted her bottom onto the marble counter, and stepped between her legs. "Tell me this is really okay. That you want me, too."

"I want you, Bridge." She softly kissed his lips. "I've tried to tell myself I didn't. That I wouldn't do this. But I've known all along, deep inside, what would happen. Some things are just meant to be." Looking down to where their bodies met, she wrapped her legs around his hips. "I want you so much I don't know what to do with myself."

His heart melted, then swelled till it hurt. It would be all right. Somehow, they would make it all right. Together.

For a while, at least.

He wrapped his arms around her, covered her mouth with his, and drank her in. She trembled, and gave herself over to him completely. He could feel her surrender in the way her body turned soft and pliant, molding itself to him, responding to his every wish almost before his body asked.

Hot, primal need roared through him. He would claim her now. Claim her as his.

His alone.

"Hold me tight around my neck," he urged, then hooked his hands under her knees, pulling her legs up and wide apart.

She gasped at the way he exposed her. "Bridge!"

It only inflamed him more. "Don't get shy on me now, baby. Hang on." It was an incredible turn-on to know she trusted him enough to do something that was apparently so out of her experience. The primitive male in him shouted in triumph. A fierce need for absolute possession coursed through his blood. "Guide me in, angel."

Hesitantly, beautifully, she reached down and placed him right where he wanted to be.

So wet.

So hot.

"Oh, yeah." He leaned into her, pushing in to the hilt.

He groaned in ecstasy. *So good.* As he'd known all along. "You feel so damn good."

She threw her head back, her face etched with pleasure. He pulled out once, then thrust in.

Her eyes shot wide open. "What *is* that?"

A grin fought itself through the sweat beading his lip. "Ribbed condom."

She gasped as he pulled out again, and plunged back into her. "My God," she said breathlessly.

He pulled out and thrust in again, loving the way her eyes

fluttered at the unfamiliar sensation of the ribs.

"*Oh*. My. God. That's…" Her words faded on a low moan.

He loved that he was the one making her feel such pleasure for the first time. He wanted to hold her close, so damn close, and never let her feel anything but pleasure again in her life.

If only that was possible.

Pushing away that unsettling thought, he covered her mouth with his and explored her with his tongue as he thrust in and out. She groaned. He plunged harder.

God, she was so damn sweet. Sweet and fine, and everything a woman should be. He wanted to eat her up, devour her, until she was his completely.

Sliding her knees over his arms, he held her body closer, relishing her fingers digging into his shoulders and back. He murmured encouragement in her ear and was rewarded with a nip on the neck. He growled a few more explicit demands.

Her body turned molten in his hands, the heat gloving him ignited to liquid fire.

He plunged into her again and again, faster and faster. He talked her higher and higher, until finally his name tore from her lips. She shuddered in his arms, her body racked with waves of deep tremors.

He kept pounding, wanting her to experience every last sensation, pushing himself to the limit, bringing her quickly back to panting, moaning desire. Feeding his own aching need for her, for this, for her urgent response to his body's possession.

"Stay with me, angel," he commanded when he felt the hot coil between his legs tighten beyond bearing. "*Now*," he demanded, and he felt her body obey, just as he lost control of his own.

He exploded with thick, heated pleasure. A shock of fire streaked through him down to his toes and all the way back up to the roots of his hair. He buried himself deep inside her, as deep as physically possible. So deep, he thought surely he would disappear and never have to leave the blissful, enveloping cradle of her body.

God, how he wanted to stay like this, always. To feel nurtured and cherished, held in the loving arms of a woman who adored him.

This woman who adored him.

After several breathless minutes, their bodies calmed. Carefully, he lowered her legs and wrapped his arms around her. "Incredible," he murmured into her hair. "You are incredible."

"No, you are," she said on a sigh. "I don't think I'll ever walk again."

He chuckled, his ego pleased with her praise. He loved this change in their relationship. It was good to know so unquestionably that she felt the same way he did, that she wanted him as much as he wanted her.

After long minutes of just holding each other, he nuzzled her neck. "Shall I carry you to bed?"

Her arms around his waist tightened for an instant, then loosened and she looked up. Before his eyes, her expression slowly went from warm, sated happiness to careful neutrality.

"Maybe just the bathtub?"

Her words hung heavy in air that was spiced with the scent of their lovemaking. He regarded her closely. *What the hell?* Did she really mean what he thought she meant?

He couldn't believe this was happening—not this soon.

"You giving me the kiss-off, Mary Alice?" he asked quietly. "Seriously?"

Her fingers toyed with the black hairs on his chest, careful not to stray lower. "I, *um…*"

Anger suddenly swept over him. He grasped her arms. "What the fuck? Is this some kind of twisted revenge?"

She bit her bottom lip and looked away. "I thought this was the part where you walk away a happy man. No assumptions, right?" She shrugged. And still wouldn't look at him.

His anger deflated, and he cursed inwardly his own monumental stupidity. *Great strategy, Bridger. Just great.*

"Oh, honey. It doesn't have to be like that. I'd like to be together. I really would. I just don't want you thinking it can be…"

"Permanent?"

He nodded, hating that it had to be this way. Wishing it were possible to try for more. There was nothing on earth he'd rather have than a chance to be with this perfect woman for always.

But there wasn't. It was for her own good.

She exhaled. "Maybe it would be better if we both walked away now and pretended this never happened."

His heart plummeted. "Just because I can't promise you forever?"

A shadow of pain flashed through her eyes, and his heart went out to her. He knew damned well that wasn't the reason, or at least the main reason. She was afraid to get involved with someone like him, a cop who would remind her every day of those she'd loved and lost in the past, and that she could so easily lose everything again.

And he also knew she was right. Had known it from the start. What had just happened didn't change a thing.

"You're a cop, Bridge. You're all wrong for me," she said quietly.

Letting out a long breath, he took her in his arms and sank into the warm solace of her heavenly body. "I know," he whispered, pain searing through his heart. "So, why do you feel so damned right for me?"

Chapter Twenty-Nine

When Bridge stepped out of Mary Alice's embrace and walked through the door, closing it quietly behind him, her anguish was complete. If it hadn't been for the fact that he'd looked just as miserable leaving as she felt letting him go, she would have sunk to the floor and wept.

Damn, damn, *damn*.

She'd gone and done it—exactly what she'd vowed would never happen again. She had given herself, her body—*and her heart*—to the exact man she shouldn't have.

Why did he have to be a cop?

It wasn't fair.

Her skin still tingled where it had touched his. Her breasts were imprinted with the sensation of his rough chest hair scraping over them. The flesh between her thighs echoed with the memory of his cock thrusting hard into her, bringing her to heights she hadn't known existed. And her heart…it swelled with emotions long suppressed. Emotions she didn't want to feel. Not for this man.

She stepped into the shower and turned on the water,

forcing herself to remember why she couldn't take his hand and lead him to her bed, and welcome him into her body again and again.

Even if she got past her own fears, and his refusal to make commitments, she just couldn't live with the constant uncertainty of loving a cop—whether for a hundred years or one year, or even just a week. Bridge's tame undercover assignment watching Watson wouldn't last forever. He'd told her he was with SIS—which she knew was the most dangerous section of PPD outside of SWAT—dealing daily with the most vicious criminals that existed. He could die at any minute, leaving her far worse off than she was now.

As her father had, and her uncle.

And the last man she'd loved.

No, it was better this way. Better to stop this doomed relationship right now, before it got started. They could be friends.

Friends.

Nothing more.

And her aching heart would just have to accept it.

Chapter Thirty

Breakfast the next morning was a conspiracy of denial. Mary Alice acted as though nothing had happened between them the night before. Bridge didn't look too happy about it, but thankfully he went along with the pretense.

He announced he'd wrangled his replacement on the road crew, Officer Deane, into spending his Sunday afternoon off watching Watson for him.

"Let's go to the Pasadena Policemen's Street Fair this afternoon," he said.

Mary Alice stared at him in consternation over her French toast. Was he serious right now? "No. I can't."

The last thing she wanted was to face a park full of Jack's and her father's old buddies and fellow cops.

Especially on Bridge's arm.

"It'll do us both good to get out," he urged.

She shook her head firmly. "No. Not going there."

"Give it a shot. Maybe you'll find you don't hate cops so much, after all, and I'll have a chance with you."

She couldn't help half-smiling at his ironic but hopeful

expression. "I don't—"

"Come on. It'll be fun. Booths crammed with crafty stuff for the cottage." He winked. "Kettle corn and funnel cakes."

He looked so encouraging she actually considered it for two seconds. She glanced down at her plate as her insides slowly twisted into tight knots.

Could she really do it?

He smiled and nodded. "You'll be okay. I promise."

Maybe it was time she faced her demons.

Maybe it was time she tried to put the unhappy past to rest.

And with Bridge's support, she might just be able to get through it.

Chapter Thirty-One

It was a gorgeous, hot day. One of those days when Southern California basked in the glory of its splendid weather. A light wind had blown the smog clear to Amboy, leaving the sparkling San Gabriel Mountains proud and tall as the rugged backdrop to the riot of skyscrapers, fragrant blossoming trees, and the usual colorful inhabitants.

Bridge looked particularly handsome in crisply pressed khakis and a jade-colored polo shirt. He offered Mary Alice his arm when they approached Central Park, where the Policemen's Fair was being held. As she looped hers around it, she bit back a nervous swallow. It was usually so comfortable being with Bridge. He always made her feel so pampered and nurtured. So safe. As though he'd take care of her, no matter what.

If only that were really so. But she knew the feeling was just a cruel illusion. Because there was no guarantee he would even be there tomorrow.

At the entrance, he stepped up to buy their tickets. She took one look at the table and eased behind him. The officer sitting at the cash box, Lieutenant Washington, had worked with her father.

"Bridge, old buddy! Good to see you. I hear the feds've got you pulling twenty-four hour shifts. That sucks."

"Yeah, had to bribe Jason Deane to relieve me this afternoon so I could—"

"Mary Alice, is that you?" The lieutenant peered around Bridge. "I'll be damned. Come here, girl, let me take a look at you."

She fumbled for something to say, and Bridge slipped a supportive arm around her.

"Say, you aren't with this old reprobate, are you?" Washington guffawed, then wagged a finger at Bridge. "You be good to her, you hear? None of your usual shenanigans. This is Seamus Flannery's little girl." He looked back at her, and she could see the memories flash through his eyes. "We still miss him down at the station, Mary Alice. He was a real good man."

"Thanks," she mumbled, wanting to turn around and run for home as fast as she could.

Bridge accepted their tickets, making some comment about taking care of her, then led her into the maze of booths and attractions. She stopped to take a couple of deep breaths.

"You okay?"

She nodded, looking around. "I'd forgotten there would be so many uniforms." They were everywhere in the crowd—hundreds it seemed. Blue, gray, khaki, of every rank and jurisdiction in four counties. "I haven't seen this many since—"

The funerals.

Turning quickly so he wouldn't see the sudden glaze of tears in her eyes, she folded her arms tight across her midriff. "So, which way first?" She raised her chin, determined not to fall apart, and scanned the booths. "Oh, look! The hat lady."

Grateful for something that might genuinely distract her,

she grabbed Bridge's hand and tugged him over to a stall brimming with every type of second-hand hat imaginable.

"I always used to stop by and pick up a few hats for the kids' dress-up corner."

Back before—

"Well, hi, love! Long time no see."

Delighted to see Mrs. Daniels who ran the booth, Mary Alice purged the bad memories from her mind and chatted for several minutes. Off to one side, Bridge entertained them by trying on every hat he could reach—men's and women's. He'd drawn quite a crowd before running out of examples, and everyone was in stitches.

"You are such a ham!" she said with a laugh as they walked away, yanking the brim of his newly purchased Panama hat down over his eyes. "Have you ever considered a career in stand-up?"

"Would it make you like me any better?"

She gave him a wry look. "Bridge, it would be downright dangerous for me to like you any better. That's the whole problem."

"I don't see this as a problem," he said teasingly.

She rolled her eyes.

"We could have a fast and shallow, but deeply satisfying"— he waggled his eyebrows—"relationship. Until you walk out on me for a stable, boring accountant. Everyone's happy. Right?"

"Has anybody ever told you that you have a one-track mind?"

"Frequently. It's one of my more endearing—"

"Traits, right."

He chuckled. "In the end I always get my man. Or in this case, woman. It's why I'm such a good—" He winced.

"Cop?"

"*Oops.*"

"Mary Alice?"

She whirled at a familiar voice, and her heart lodged in her throat. "Mr. and Mrs. Maxwell."

Mrs. Maxwell smiled broadly. "I thought that was you. How are you, my dear?"

In a million years, Mary Alice wouldn't have thought she'd run into Jack's parents here. When his mother gave her a long hug, Mary Alice could barely keep from shaking with emotion. She accepted another hug from Jack's dad. "I'm okay. How are you both?"

"We're doing well. Work on the anti-handgun bill is going great. I think we'll win this next round."

The Maxwells had poured their tremendous grief over their only son's death into efforts to change the gun laws.

Mary Alice still felt horribly guilty every time she saw them. She hadn't kept up their friendship. Seeing them had only reminded her of her loss…and she was sure that was even more true for them.

"I'm so glad," she said, floundering in the guilt. "You are doing such good things out there for society, and all I do is worry about my roses."

Mrs. Maxwell patted her arm. "That's not true, dear, and you know it. Every day at school you teach those kids in your class how to solve their differences using words instead of fists—or guns. That's more important and far more effective than any gun law could possibly be."

Mary Alice bowed her head, then remembered Bridge and introduced him. When they looked slightly taken aback, he rescued her once again.

"Mary Alice is helping me with a case I'm working on."

Mrs. Maxwell quickly recovered, and looked from him to her. "Well, Mary Alice, it was wonderful to see you," she said with a wistful smile. "I'm so glad you are finally getting out. I know Jack would never have wanted you to hide yourself away like you've been doing."

Jack's parents kissed her cheek and said their good-byes.

And suddenly, she knew his mother was right. Jack had been her best friend, her fiancé, but deep down she knew he would have totally disapproved of the lengths she'd gone to keep her heart safe after his death. He'd have taken her Master List and torn it up into little, tiny pieces with a snort of derision. If he were here, he'd be the first one to tell her to get over it already, and get on with her life.

The insight hit her hard.

But she knew it was right.

She just didn't know if she could actually follow the advice.

Chapter Thirty-Two

"Nice couple." Bridge said as they walked away. He watched Mary Alice carefully. So far, she'd been holding up fairly well, but he'd seen clearly that this last encounter had thrown her for a major loop.

"They really are nice. We sort of helped each other through the early days, after…"

Bridge sent her a frown. "Didn't the Department give you someone to talk to?"

She took a breath and shrugged. "Yeah. But I didn't need a shrink. I just needed a hug every once in a while."

He had his doubts about that. But she looked as if she could use a hug right now. He wanted nothing more than to take her in his arms and give her the comfort she needed.

Not a good idea. Touching her would only make him remember how much he wanted her in his bed. Besides, she needed more than simple comfort. She needed far more than he was able to give.

"Come on," she said, squaring her shoulders. "Let's look at some more booths."

They wandered around, and Bridge couldn't believe the number of people who came up to her, saying a few words about how good it was to see her again, or how great a guy Jack or her dad had been. By late afternoon she was looking more than a little shell-shocked. He hoped he hadn't made a huge mistake by bringing her here.

"How about a treat before we go home?" he asked. "Do you like Cactus Cooler floats?"

For the first time since the hat booth, she broke into a broad grin. "Are you kidding me? I love them! Damn, I haven't had one of those in years."

"That settles it, then."

Although they'd never caught on in the big world outside SoCal, the concoction of pineapple-orange soda and sherbet was a local favorite, especially at the fair, where they were sold exclusively in the food booth run by the Sierra Madre Fire Department.

"What kind of sherbet would you like in it?" the firefighter doing the scooping asked her.

"Rainbow. Definitely rainbow."

Bridge grinned. "Oh, you brazen thing, you."

She grinned back. "Only when I'm with you, bad boy."

He caught himself just in time, right before he impulsively slung an arm around her and gave her a big kiss.

It was a constant struggle, not reaching out to her. Not pulling her close. Or kissing the hurt and sadness from her eyes, to put a smile on her pretty face.

They settled at a wobbly table and dug in. A few minutes later, several young police officers piled around a table right behind them and started discussing a recent shooting that had occurred in their district. Mary Alice paled when one described the way the victim had been left in an alley to bleed to death.

"Let's go, okay?" Bridge suggested quickly. "We can stop

at the Fisherman for some shrimp, and I'll barbecue them for dinner."

Wordlessly, she rose and followed him.

When they arrived home, he conferred for several minutes with Officer Deane about the activity at Watson's place. Together, they filled out the log, then he walked Deane out to the front porch.

"How's it going on the road crew?"

"No worries, Sarge," the kid replied. "Kinda fun, actually."

"Good. And thanks for filling in for me today. I appreciate it."

The young man cast a meaningful glance back through the door, where Mary Alice had settled on the sofa. "Tough assignment, eh?"

Bridge gave him a stony look. "Don't even think it, rookie."

"Sure, Sarge, whatever you say."

The kid's face as he jogged down the steps said plainer than words that he found the idea of Russell Bridger staying in the same house with a beautiful woman and one bed, but not touching her, to be patently absurd.

Bridge had to agree.

What was with him, anyway? He still wanted her. Like crazy, he wanted her. And he was fairly certain with very little persuasion he could have her again.

So, what was holding him back?

He jettisoned a frustrated breath. He just hated it when his capricious sense of honor reared its untimely head. It was damned annoying. What was it about this woman that made him want to tuck her under his wing and protect her, rather than tucking her under his body and—

"Bridge?"

Her voice fired him out of his uncharacteristic thoughts. "Yeah, angel?"

"You going to stand out there all night?"

She was leaning against the doorjamb, looking so pretty and fragile and inviting. He wanted to scoop her up and kiss her until she forgot all about cops and shootings and her dad and fiancé's deaths, and the fact that she'd ever known any other man but Bridge.

Damn, but he had it bad for her.

He ground his teeth. "Think I'll move your car into the cut-out so you can get to work tomorrow morning."

She nodded and went to get the keys. He could feel her eyes on him the whole time he walked to the car and back. Afterward, they went to the backyard where he stoked up the grill and uncorked a bottle of wine for her. Too bad he was still on duty and couldn't down half that bottle himself. He could really use a drink.

Relaxing in a lounge chair with an iced tea, Bridge toasted her and the private paradise he found himself sitting in. "Man, I could get used to this."

In the other chaise, she smiled. "*Uh-oh*, the big bad bachelor shows signs of cracking."

He closed his eyes and basked in the cozy warmth of twilight. A pair of mourning doves called out from the roof of the house, their melancholy song wafting about the yard.

"What the hell," he agreed. "Gorgeous evening, a beautiful woman, good food. A man'd have to be insane not to appreciate it."

"But only for the short term."

He lifted a shoulder. He didn't dare open his mouth. He might say something he'd regret. Like, *hell no. For an entire lifetime*.

"What makes a man like you so opposed to marriage and kids?" she asked.

God. He *so* did not want to go there. "Why does it bother you so much?" he returned.

The doves took wing and circled the yard once before heading off up the canyon, flying so close their bodies practically touched.

When she didn't answer, he rolled his head on the chaise and looked at her. She had showered and changed into another one of those cute, silky dresses she favored. This one hung loose around her body, reaching to her calves. It flowed over the side of the chaise lounge, dangling onto the grass beside it. She'd left her hair wild and free like he loved it, and still-damp wisps curled about her head like a halo.

She looked just like an angel.

His angel.

What would she do if he just swung off his chaise and onto her? The backyard was so private, no one would see them. Even Watson's view was obstructed by the many trees along his property line. Bridge could—

"Who was she?"

Mary Alice's question yanked him out of his fantasy. He blinked and shifted, immediately uncomfortably. "Who?"

"The woman who hurt you so badly."

He pressed his lips together. "Who says there was a woman?"

"I do."

A spear of guilt stabbed through him and he forgot all about his libido. He'd unwittingly dragged Mary Alice through hell today at the street fair, making her face her painful past in ways he hadn't imagined. He figured a little turn-about was probably fair play.

He sighed. "My mother."

As they grilled the shrimp kabobs and ate, he told her about his mom and how kind and gentle she'd been. How much she'd loved his father. How hard it was on the two of them when his dad was gone for days at a time on some risky undercover assignment or another.

They moved to the living room for coffee, and he talked through his frustration over how powerless he'd been to help her depression.

"I felt she wanted to be there for me, but she just didn't have the strength to fight the black moments. Dad was gone more and more, and she just kind of gave up."

Mary Alice gave him a sympathetic look. "That must have been awful for you."

"She needed help—should have been seeing a therapist. Or something." He battled back from the unbearable pain that swallowed him every time he remembered how little he'd done to help her. "I should have said something to Dad. Done something."

Her expression turned incredulous. "But you were just a little boy. How could you possibly have known?"

"I knew. When she had the stroke…" He soughed out a long breath. "I was holding her when she died. She'd refused to go to the hospital, telling me it was just a migraine. If only I'd—"

"Oh, Bridge, you can't possibly blame yourself for what happened!"

He slashed a hand through his hair, his whole body wrung out from spilling his guts. "Maybe, maybe not. What's important is, I can't put some other woman through that same torture." *Or another kid.* "No woman should need therapy to deal with her husband's job." He glanced up from his chair. "You, of all people, should understand that."

Mary Alice sat on the sofa, looking suddenly owlish. "Yes, I guess I do understand." She twisted her hands in her lap, studying them as if they could give her insight into the predicament they found themselves in. "My God, even if we wanted to, we really wouldn't stand a chance together, would we?"

He wanted to tell her, hell yes, they would! That, for her,

he'd be willing to risk everything and gamble on a different outcome. If she'd been any other woman with any other past, who'd had any other father, uncle, and fiancé, Bridge might have said the words.

But he knew, of all the women he could choose to fall in love with, this was the one woman who wouldn't ever take a chance on him.

And it was killing him. He knew he'd never find another woman who had Mary Alice's combination of fun-loving wholesomeness, goodness, and natural sensuality. She appealed to every part of him—the man, the lonely soul searching for a real friend, the father in him struggling to get out. She was perfect in every way. If he let her go, he knew he'd never get another chance at this kind of happiness.

But he also knew if he pressured her, and she stayed with him, she'd be miserable. He would be sentencing her to a life filled with anxiety and fear. And if they had kids… *Shit*.

He chuffed out a breath. He just couldn't do it. To her. To either of them.

"Tell me about Jack and your father," he murmured. "Then tell me if you really want us to have a chance."

She swallowed, and after a long moment, slowly shook her head. "You're right. I can't."

He swiped a hand along his jaw, still beating himself up mentally. "It must have been tough on you this afternoon, all those people talking about your dad and Jack, and the funerals. I'm so sorry. I didn't realize what I'd be putting you through."

"Not your fault. I honestly thought I could take it." She gave a strangled little laugh. "It's been three years. I should be able to take it."

"Says who? You lost two of the most important people in your life, one right after another. Hell, your whole family, if you count your mother and future in-laws, who were doing their own grieving and no doubt didn't have time to deal with yours."

She closed her eyes, and he assumed she was once again lost in awful memories. Her bottom lip trembled. "I needed to be strong for her. Her brother had died the same way when I was little, so she totally lost it for a while." Mary Alice caught her lip between her teeth. "There were things to be settled, arrangements to be made. Bills to be paid. Someone had to do it all."

He nodded. "So, you were the strong one."

She lifted a shoulder. "It wasn't so bad."

He scooted up to the edge of his chair, wanting desperately to reach for her, to give her the comfort she'd needed back then. Still needed.

"The guys from the station helped a lot," she said. "After the funeral, someone would call every day to give me news on the case, and later the trial. Ask if I needed anything."

"You didn't go to the trial?"

"No," she said quietly. "I went the first day, but had to leave. I couldn't take listening to how—" Her face crumbled, and she covered it with her hands.

Fuck this.

In an instant he was next to her on the sofa, gathering her in his arms. "It's okay, angel. Let it all out. I'm here with you now."

He held her and rocked her and listened to her story as it poured out between the tears. About the horrible phone call about her fiancé, and all the blood in the alley when she'd hysterically insisted that the idiot patrolman sent to bring her to the station stop at the crime scene on the way downtown. About the senseless motives of the arrogant young perps. And then having it happen all over again, only a few short weeks later, to her dad.

The wrenching experience of seeing the two men

she'd loved lowered into the earth in flag-draped coffins, accompanied by bagpipes and gun salutes, just a month apart.

Eventually, the words stopped flowing and her sobs softened to hiccoughs. He kissed her hair over and over, stroking her back.

"Seeing them all again today, everything just came rushing back at me," she whispered.

"I could see that. I'm so sorry." He handed her a pile of tissues from the box he'd fetched from the kitchen. "Feeling better?"

She lifted her head from his tear-soaked shoulder, dabbed her eyes, and gave him a tremulous smile. "Yes. A little. No, a lot. Thanks."

"Anytime." He pulled another tissue and held it to her nose. "Blow."

"You're spoiling me rotten," she said after taking the tissue.

"About time someone did." He turned and lifted her onto his lap, circling her with his arms.

She sighed and nestled into his chest. "You know the worst thing that happened at the fair today?"

"What's that?" With his fingers, he combed back the curls that had fallen over the side of her face.

"When I saw Jack's parents," she said softly. "Mrs. Maxwell took one look at me with you, and, well— When she said what she did about getting out more, she was giving us her blessing. I've never felt so guilty in all my life."

For a moment he couldn't speak, for surprise. He cleared his throat. "I'm sure she never expected you to remain true to her son's memory for the rest of your life, regardless of how much you loved him."

Mary Alice sighed heavily. "That's the whole problem. When she said that, suddenly I realized I *hadn't* loved Jack. Not as much as I should have."

Bridge froze. "You don't mean that. It's been three years and—"

"No." She shook her head with certainty. "Oh, I loved him, of course. A lot. We'd grown up together and everyone always assumed we'd get married, us included. He really was my very best friend, always. But when I watched you talking to his mom today, all I could think of was how different I feel when I'm with you. How happy I am. How good you make me feel. How much I wanted you last night. It's an amazing feeling that takes over my whole body. My whole world."

Jesus. "Mary Alice—"

She put her fingers to his lips. "I tried to remember just one time when I'd felt the same passion and desire with Jack, and I couldn't. I just never did." She looked into his eyes, her expression open and honest.

Bridge's heart stood still in his chest. "What are you saying, angel?"

"I guess maybe I'm saying…I really wish there could be a chance for us, after all."

Chapter Thirty-Three

As far as shocks went, the one reflected in Bridge's face registered somewhere between eight and nine on the Richter scale. Judging by his stunned reaction, Mary Alice figured her heart would be found in the morning, buried somewhere beneath the rubble of their teetering relationship.

But before he could utter a single word one way or another, the beeper alarm for the motion detectors at Watson's place went off.

"Saved by the bell," she mumbled, eyeing it sardonically.

"Don't count on it." Bridge gave her a firm kiss, slid her off his lap, and ran for the spare room to check his laptop and fetch his night-vision gear. "It's the perimeter alarm. I'll be right back," he called over his shoulder.

Just that quickly, he disappeared out the back door and was gone. Leaving her with a creeping unease about what he'd run into at Watson's, and feeling slightly foolish and extremely vulnerable.

What insanity had possessed her to say something like that? That she wanted a chance with him?

It must have been the catharsis of having finally let out all those festering emotions about the deaths of Jack and her father, and the difficult truth of her feelings about Jack. She felt wrung out, but strangely lightened. As if maybe—just maybe—she really could, finally, get on with her life.

A *full* life.

Without Master Plans or itemized lists of goals.

That heady feeling must have been what prompted her reckless declaration.

Next he would want to know what *kind* of chance she wanted with him.

And for how long…

Damn. How would she answer that? How could she possibly tell him she'd do anything he wanted, be anything and everything he desired, if only he'd quit his beloved job?

He'd probably laugh out loud.

Where the hell was he, anyway? How long would he be out there in the dark?

After fifteen minutes of agonizing, she decided his reconnaissance was going to be a long one. Depending on who Watson's visitor was, Bridge could be out watching for a few minutes or several hours. He'd told her that sometimes it wasn't even a person, but a deer or coyote or some other animal that set off the alarm, but he still had to make certain what had tripped it.

But the longer he was gone, the more anxious she became.

She glanced at the clock and squeezed her eyes shut. Maybe this was a sign. She would put on her PJs and go to bed. If she was asleep she couldn't worry about him. And when she saw him in the morning…

With any luck he'd have forgotten all about the dumb things she'd said.

Chapter Thirty-Four

The next morning Mary Alice woke early. She'd been dreaming again. About Bridge, of course.

She lay for a moment on her side without opening her eyes, smiling to herself and luxuriating in that warm, sensual fog halfway between awake and asleep. Her body still hummed where he had touched her in her dreams, and the smell of him was so real she'd swear he had just left her bed. Her blood pumped thickly through her veins, and she hummed out a sigh, wanting to hang onto the dream for as long as she could.

She licked her lips and moved her head so the warm breeze from the window flowed lightly over her exposed neck.

Funny, she didn't remember opening a window last night.

She rolled a little in order to let it cool the heat burning in her breasts from his dream touch. Something large and solid blocked her movement, and a hand closed around her—.

Her eyes flew open.

Holy crap.

He was in bed with her! Pressed up against her back with one leg hooked possessively over hers, an arm coiled around her waist, and a hand kneading her breast through her nightgown.

She sucked in a breath and tried to move away.

A low growl rumbled through his chest and he pulled her back, snuggling into her, then sighed contentedly. His breathing continued rhythmically in her ear.

He was still asleep.

Thank God.

She took a quick sensory survey and decided he must be on the outside of the disheveled quilt, and apparently still fully dressed. She could feel the hard metal of jeans button against her bottom, and when she looked down she could see the long sleeve of his flannel shirt above the hand that clasped her.

Swallowing, she watched in fascination as his hand continued to caress her, then tried to find its way beneath her nightgown. She knew she should stop him when his fingers worked one, two, three buttons loose.

Then again, what could happen? The man was on the other side of the blanket, fully clothed, and thankfully asleep.

"God, you feel good to wake up to," he whispered in her ear.

She bit her lip. Okay. Two out of three?

He slid his hand over her, and she was lost down a spinning vortex of hot sensation. She moaned in pleasure, murmuring his name. The hand on her waist moved down to her hip and pressed it backward into the long, hard evidence of his intent.

"You feel pretty good, yourself," she whispered back, unable to help herself.

He inched away and turned her on her back, then canted halfway over her. His mouth came down hard on hers, and the musky tang of sleep quickly melted into the sweet taste of desire.

She felt him lower the blanket and spread open her

bodice, baring her pebbled breasts to his touch. The pads of his fingers skimmed over the tips and they spiraled into taut points of achy longing. When he grasped one and rolled it, she arched up into him, gasping, her body shocked by ribbons of fiery pleasure.

He broke the kiss and nipped her bottom lip with his teeth. "Good morning, yourself."

She looked up at him, barely able to focus because of the waves of sensation he had created within her. She hooked her arms around his neck, drowning in the sight of his dark, angular face above hers. His sensual eyes were hooded. The dusky shadows of sunrise danced across the black stubble of his morning beard. She gave a purr of feminine appreciation. "You look good enough to eat."

A slow smile spread across his face. "You'll get your chance, believe me." He kissed her again. "But not this morning. I have to get up in fifteen minutes to go to the station. That's not enough time for what I've got in mind. Not even close."

She nearly groaned in disappointment, then realized with a start just how close she'd come to disaster. My God. This was *not* the way to keep her heart or her sanity intact.

She attempted to move away.

He made a noise of protest, holding her fast and burying his face in her hair. He must have sensed her mental withdrawal. "Don't go yet. You're safe. Please."

Safe? She'd be out of her mind to believe that.

But he felt so good, the last thing she wanted was to leave the warmth of his body. And he'd promised she would be safe—for the moment, anyway—and as nuts as it was, she believed him.

So, she yielded to her weakness and murmured her assent. "Fifteen minutes?"

"*Mm-hmm.*"

"If you're sure I'm safe."

"Count on me."

After a few moments she gave in to it completely, and whispered, "Bridge?"

"Yeah, angel."

"How long do you suppose it would take you to count to a hundred?"

Chapter Thirty-Five

Bridge leaned back at his desk in frustrated — but blissful — contentment. He hadn't felt so thoroughly kissed in decades. He grinned as he applied his newly acquired Chapstick, feeling like a horny teenager. He'd forgotten just how torturously aroused one could get sucking face. Well, and one or two other places.

He'd been an hour late for the task force meeting, but it had been worth the tirade. Special Agent Grayson would get over it, eventually.

Gulping down a cup of coffee, Bridge tried to wipe the silly grin off his face and get back to work. He was supposed to be writing reports, conclusions, and recommendations on the Watson case. Not mooning like some lovesick puppy.

But he had to admit it, lovesick he was.

He wasn't sure how he felt about this development, but it was high time he stopped kidding himself. He was falling head over heels in love with the delectable Mary Alice Cathryn Flannery.

The question was, what was he going to do about it?

Captain Trujillo breezed by the desk, calling out, "How's it going, Bridge?"

"Great!"

Trujillo stopped on a dime and did a one-eighty, raising a wary brow. "Really, now."

"Couldn't be better." As the cap's other brow shot up, Bridge scrawled his signature on the bottom of a report and slapped the jacket shut. "Can you see that Grayson gets this before he blows a gasket? I've got a couple of things to do before my shift on Watson starts."

"*Uh*, sure."

"Thanks, Cap." He rose, grabbed his new Panama brim, and eased it onto his head. It felt a little strange, and he probably looked like a damn pimp, but he figured he owed it at least a week before deciding if he could trade in his old baseball cap. Old habits died hard, and he wanted to start out slowly, one old habit at a time.

He came to with a jerk when he realized Trujillo was still standing in front of his desk, a suspicious look on his face.

"So… What have you been up to that's put you in such a good mood? Dare I ask?"

Bridge shot the cap a lopsided grin and stuffed the file into his hand. "Math," he said, tipped his hat, and strolled out the door into the bright June sunshine.

Chapter Thirty-Six

"Bull," Nancy whispered succinctly in Mary Alice's ear. "If that's an allergy on your face, I'm Mother Theresa."

Mary Alice forbade herself to blush, instead gluing her attention on the student reports they were discussing at the teacher's meeting at school that morning. "*Shh!*" She giggled.

"Yes, shellfish can be very unpredictable," Lucinda, their director, agreed in response to the excuse she'd stuttered regarding her stubble-burned cheeks. "Now, Mary Alice, tell us what progress you've been making with Ivy."

Mary Alice nodded and tried to concentrate on her favorite student instead of her new favorite morning pastime. "Ivy's social interaction with most of the other children is good and has been steadily increasing. But she still has difficulty dealing with the parents who are working in the group."

"Has she started talking at all yet?"

Mary Alice shook her head sadly. "There are times I feel she really wants to break through, but I just haven't found the key yet."

"Well, keep working at it. But we may have to resign ourselves to starting over after summer vacation. Are there any more students to discuss? No? Then—"

The office door opened and a large shadow fell across the transom. Mary Alice's heart leapt as she looked up and saw Bridge standing there, a cardboard box balanced on his lean hip.

"May I help you?" Lucinda asked him, obviously puzzled at his appearance.

Mary Alice felt an elbow poke her in the ribs.

Bridge glanced around at the five teachers seated on the window seats lining the office walls, and his eyes homed right in on her.

"I'm here to see Mary Alice, ma'am." He tipped his Panama hat like a gentleman, but his polite manner in no way disguised his wickedly roguish smile. "I've brought some things for her class."

He might as well have said, "I've come to carry her off and ravish her," her reaction his words produced in her pulse and her temperature couldn't have been any stronger.

Again, the jab of an elbow registered subliminally.

"How nice," said Lucinda, beaming like a mother hen. "Mary Alice, can you take the box from him?"

"Oh, no, ma'am, I wouldn't dream of letting her carry this heavy thing," he assured Lucinda, then turned to Mary Alice. "Maybe you could show me where to put it?" He lifted a devilish brow.

"Y-yes, of course," she stammered, continuing to stare up at him until she realized she was supposed to be moving. She jumped to her feet, spilling the papers in her lap all over the floor.

Next to her, Nancy let out a snicker.

Stacy, the kindergarten aide, hadn't taken her eyes off Bridge since he'd arrived. "Aren't you going to introduce us,

Mary Alice?"

Ignoring Stacy, she started walking to the door but nearly tripped over the heap of papers on the floor.

Nancy stifled another chuckle. "I'll get 'em, hon. You go on ahead."

"Thanks," Mary Alice said absently, then smiled at Bridge as she led him off.

"Who *was* that hunk?" she heard Stacy quietly persist. Through the closing door, Nancy's innocent voice drifted back as she and Bridge walked through the Pre-K room. "Russell Bridger. He's in paint removal, I believe."

Bridge gave Mary Alice an incredulous look.

"Don't ask."

Grinning, he stroked a finger over her cheek. "New blusher? Nice shade."

"*Mm-hmm*. It's called barbarosa. You brute."

His grin didn't even flicker. "Next time I'll shave first."

"Don't you dare." She slanted him a glance, aching to kiss him right there in the middle of the Pre-K. She'd forgotten what a virile specimen of manhood he was. After all, it had been two whole hours since he'd held her tight against his hard body and kissed her into a quivering pool of gelatinous mush.

"Wanton," he admonished in a gravelly voice, giving her a quick goose on the bottom as they went through the door to her own Toddler Group.

Immediately, they were surrounded by a dozen three-year-olds.

"Who's dat?"

"What's he got?"

Little Marina's stage-whispered "Is dat youwr boyfwiend?" got a smile from Bridge.

"Yes, but it's a secret," he whispered back, loud enough so all could hear. He winked, including Mary Alice in its reach.

"Don't tell anyone."

"Ow-kay," Marina assured, then ran over to her mother, who was working in the group that day, and shouted, "Mommy! That's Miss Mawy Alice's boyfwiend!"

Mary Alice tried to ignore the heat that crept up to her ears, but relished the warmth that rushed to her heart at hearing him claim her as his own. Even to a three-year-old. It was crazy. They would never work. Not in a million years. But, there it was. She wanted to be his.

Only his.

She watched Bridge squat down and set the cardboard box on the floor and open it. "I brought you guys some good stuff."

"Wow! Hats!"

"Vests! Yay!"

"Oh, Bridge. You went back to the hat booth," she exclaimed.

He shot her a self-satisfied grin. "Yep. Didn't even notice, did you? Picked them up from Mrs. Daniels this morning."

The kids tumbled the box and scrambled for the treasures, donning the hats and scattering to the corners of the room and out through the double doors to the yard, followed by the parent aides. Little Jarrod hung back and eyed the box covetously from behind an easel a few yards away, and Ivy, of course, watched from the safety of Mary Alice's skirt.

Bridge gave Jarrod a wink and sat down amidst the wreckage of the spilled box contents and stirred around with a hand among the leftover hats. Flipping off his Panama hat, he pulled out a corduroy tennis visor with an aardvark perched on the bill, and placed it on his head. Jarrod grinned shyly in amusement.

Warmed and smiling all over, Mary Alice slowly backed away to the outside doors, letting Bridge work his magic. Surprised, she realized that Ivy had stayed behind, transfixed by the big man playing so incongruously on the floor.

Pursing his lips, Bridge discarded the aardvark and plucked up a baseball cap fitted with twin cool cups on either side of the crown. Two attached flexible tubing straws flapped in the air beside them. Mary Alice could barely suppress her laughter at his ridiculous appearance when he set it on his head. Jarrod giggled and took a few cautious steps toward him.

Mary Alice's heart swelled when Ivy stuck a finger in her mouth and actually smiled. But her heart nearly froze in her chest when Bridge turned to the little girl and winked at her, too, beckoning her closer. He had no way of knowing about Ivy. Mary Alice had to restrain herself from running to intervene. *Let it play*, she told herself, somehow trusting that Bridge would know the right thing to do.

Hadn't he always known with Mary Alice, herself?

Just then, one of the parents called to her from outside to come settle a dispute over the swings. Casting a nervous glance at the drama unfolding on the classroom floor, Mary Alice reluctantly turned to the yard and went out to help the frustrated kids to use their words and inventiveness to solve the swing problem.

A couple of minutes later, deep into that situation, she smiled to see Jarrod streak by on his way to the sandbox wearing the aardvark visor. When she was through at the swing set, she'd have to remember to go inside and dig Ivy out from her usual bed of pillows under the loft.

It took everyone a little longer than she'd expected to come to an acceptable swing solution, and when she went back into the classroom, she didn't see either Bridge or Ivy. Frowning, she glanced around. The inside-the-room-parent and a few kids were busy in one corner with the puppet theater, and another couple of children were looking at Lizzie the Iguana with magnifying glasses. A gentle plucking of guitar strings caught her attention from under the loft.

Cautiously, Mary Alice peeked around a bookshelf blocking her view. She couldn't believe her eyes. Ivy stood next to Bridge, his Panama hat nearly swallowing her head at a winsome angle. Ivy passed her fingers across the neck of the guitar, while her other little hand clutched Bridge's forefinger. He was stooped over, and now he let himself ease down onto the floor beside the little girl, careful not to break the tenuous bond.

"You like the guitar?" he quietly asked her.

To Mary Alice's surprise, Ivy looked over at him and nodded.

Bridge nodded back. "Me, too. Does someone play for you?"

She could see Ivy's throat contract as she shook her head and looked sadly back at the guitar.

Bridge sighed. "Me, neither. My mom used to play for me."

Ivy's head jerked up and her eyes grew round.

"Yours, too?" he asked.

The little girl blinked, her eyes growing shiny, and Mary Alice placed a trembling hand to her own lips.

Gently, Bridge picked up the guitar with his free hand and placed it on his lap. "My mom's voice was so sweet and soothing. Whenever I'd get scared, she'd take down the guitar and we'd sing until I felt better." He looked at Ivy from where he sat. "How about yours?"

She drew a tiny finger across the strings, a look of heartbreak on her face, then nodded solemnly.

"What was your favorite song?" he asked in a whisper.

Mary Alice thought her heart would shatter. A tear broke loose from her pooled eyes, and in the moment when Ivy whispered back to him, "Puff," she knew she would never love any other man but this one, as long as she lived.

He began to strum on the old, out-of-tune guitar, and soon his deep voice blended with Ivy's high thin one, singing about magic dragons and children's fantasies. By the end of the song other kids had gathered around them, joining in a joyful chorus.

Mary Alice wiped her eyes and punched the record button on a kid-proof digital recorder that was sitting on a shelf next to her. Then she waded into the circle, giving Bridge a tender kiss right on the lips, and scooped Ivy onto her lap and sat next to him singing songs until the parents came, her heart brimming with love.

Chapter Thirty-Seven

Bridge pulled into the driveway of his father's house in El Monte, leaned back in the seat, and contemplated his mother's roses in the front yard.

He was scared shitless.

Something had happened to him back there at that nursery school with Mary Alice, and it had him running like a marked man. It couldn't possibly have been *him* having those thoughts as he sat surrounded by kids, his pretty woman by his side, feeling more content and at home since…well, since forever.

He'd actually been thinking about picket fences and planting roses. Imagining what it would be like to have his own kids. Fantasizing sharing his life and growing old with Mary Alice.

Fuck.

It was one thing for a man to admit he was in love. *That,* Bridge could contend with—given some strict lifestyle management techniques. But it was completely different to start having mushy dreams about something that just plain wasn't possible. Kids? Seriously?

He hopped out of the truck and wandered over to the roses.

No, it really *wasn't* possible.

Was it?

He closed his eyes and breathed deeply of the spicy, dusky scent of the blossoms, his mind conjuring up a picture of his mom in her gardening dress, kneeling among them.

"What should I do, Mama?" he murmured under his breath. "I'm terrified."

He could almost hear his mother's voice whispering among the fluttering leaves. *Does she make you happy, darling?*

"Oh, yeah," he whispered. "More than I ever thought possible."

Can you make her happy?

He ran a hand over his temple and sighed. "I wish I knew, Mama. I really wish I knew."

The squeak of a screen door brought him back to reality.

"That you, son? Come on in and have some lunch."

Bridge looked up and saw his dad standing at the front door of the house, motioning for him to come inside.

"Hi, Dad." He stuck his hands in his pockets and headed in, shaking off the uncertainty lingering in his heart. "What's new?"

While he listened to his father's latest deep sea fishing adventure, complete with swordfish and, as usual, some curvy fifty-five year old, Bridge considered his options.

He could go back to Mary Alice's place, pack his bag, and bail. Probably the wisest choice, but the coward's way out. Russell Bridger was a lot of things, but a coward wasn't one of them.

Or, he could keep his distance, ignore his feelings, and hope they would go away.

Yeah, right.

Or, he could go ahead and tumble her again, keeping his emotions locked up tight, then force himself to leave when things got too heavy to handle. The most tempting choice, but the chances of a clean getaway were slim at best. And Trujillo would have his job. Besides, Bridge's irritating sense of honor probably wouldn't let him do it, anyway.

Which left only one other option that he could see. He'd have to face up to his feelings, confess, and throw himself on her mercy.

And hope like hell she told him to drop dead. Because he didn't know what he'd do if she'd been serious this morning, and actually wanted to try having a relationship with him.

A real relationship.

What if the same thing started happening with her as with his mom? What if he couldn't stand watching it and had to leave her? It would kill her if that happened.

Hell, it would kill *him*.

Maybe it would be better to go back to option two, after all. He let out a deep sigh.

"What's eating at you, boy? You haven't answered the last three questions I've asked you."

"*Hmm?* Sorry, Dad. A, *uh*…a rough case has got me second-guessing myself."

"Tell me about it. Maybe I can help."

Bridge got up to pour himself another cup of coffee. "Why didn't you ever get married again after Mama died?"

His dad's jaw stopped in mid-bite. "What kind of case are you working, anyhow?"

Bridge chuckled humorlessly. "Not the case. Just wondered. It's been over twenty-five years, and it isn't like you haven't had ample opportunity."

"You know me, footloose and fancy free. Suits me."

"Even after you retired?"

His dad looked offended. "What's retirement got to do with it? I'm as fit as ever."

"No, I just thought… You know, your job affecting Mom the way it did, I figured maybe that's why you'd shied away from remarrying. Didn't want to risk it happening again…?"

His dad squirmed a little, and gave him a long, searching look. "I didn't always make the best choices, son, but I loved your mother very much."

Bridge bowed his head over his coffee and jetted out a breath. "I know, Dad. It wasn't your fault she couldn't take the stress of being a cop's wife."

"Russ, the stress was—" His dad stopped, shook his head, and said, "You thinking about getting married?"

"Yeah. *No!*" Bridge looked up, aghast at his slip. "No way. Just getting in a little deeper with someone than I'm comfortable with."

"You're worried because you're a cop? Because of what happened with your mother?"

Bridge nodded glumly. "Mary Alice reminds me a little of Mama." He swiped a hand over his face. "Remember three years ago, those two cops were shot in Pasadena a few weeks apart? That was her dad and fiancé."

"*Ouch*. Bad combination. And you in SIS, too—as dangerous as it gets. Maybe you ought to leave it alone."

"Yeah, maybe."

"Never pegged you for the marrying type, anyway. Like father, like son, you know. Are you really willing to give up your freedom for one woman?"

"I don't know, Dad. If you'd asked me two weeks ago, I'd have said no. Now, I'm not so sure." He looked at the clock and went over to put his plate and cup in the dishwasher. "Gotta get back to work. Mind if I cut some roses?"

"Take all you want. They're wasted on me." His dad gave him a slap on the back. "Well, worse comes to worst you can always take that promotion Trujillo's been preaching at you."

Et tu, Dad?

It was a damn conspiracy to get him behind a desk.

Bridge grabbed a pair of rose shears from the drawer and a vase from the cupboard. "What, and give up all the bullets and excitement? Things aren't *that* serious with her."

Were they…?

As he cut a big bouquet for Mary Alice, Bridge thought about what to do. He was a man of action, and once he'd made up his mind about something, he did it. But this time he wanted to get it right. If he was going to throw himself on Mary Alice's mercy, he'd better make damned sure he could live with her decision.

What he needed was a plan.

A good plan.

And subtlety was optional.

Chapter Thirty-Eight

"**Y**ou've been keeping secrets from me, Mary Alice."

Charlie Watson's voice sailed over the low picket fence dividing the side of her front lawn from his driveway.

Mary Alice jerked her head up in alarm from the Stanwell Perpetual she had decided to dead-head after getting home from work that afternoon. "What?"

"I'm crushed," Charlie said, his tone teasing. "You have a new boyfriend."

She let out a silent sigh of relief. Honestly, she wasn't cut out for this cloak and dagger stuff, even if her own father *had* been a cop. Knowing Bridge thought her neighbor was a ruthless criminal had her jumpy as a cat crossing a freeway every time she saw him now.

She shook herself, remembering that she was supposed to be Bridge's girlfriend. "Yes, I do have a new boyfriend," she confirmed brightly.

"From the road crew, isn't he?"

"*Uh-huh.*" She smiled over at Charlie. "But they moved him to another site this week," she added, thinking he might be wondering why Bridge had suddenly disappeared from the crew out front.

He locked the door to his red Porsche and ambled over to the fence, grinning. "Picking up a man right off the street. My, my. I would never have believed it of you, Mary Alice."

"Me, neither." She grinned back. "He sure is cute, though. And all those muscles." She fanned her face with a hand. "Wow."

Charlie snorted. "I'll take your word for it." Catlike, he jumped over the low pickets, landing close to her. "I guess he's handy for yard work, if nothing else."

She glanced around at the recently neatly trimmed trees and bushes, the freshly painted fence, and her beautifully restored rose arbor. "He has a second floor apartment and misses gardening. For which I am very grateful," she said with a low laugh, trying to cover her blossoming unease. Why all the interest in Bridge? Or was it just her over-active imagination?

"Anyway, it's good someone's here to watch out for you. There were a couple of strange characters hanging around the neighborhood last week. I had to call the police."

"You're kidding." She looked out toward the street, at the construction guys just starting to pack up, and hoped he hadn't also noticed that Bridge had left the crew and moved in with her the day after those "strange characters" had disappeared.

"I'll be glad when this damned road construction is over and done with, that's for sure," he muttered.

"Tell me about it," she said with a sigh. "I have to dust twice a day even to find the furniture."

"Hell, I need to take the boat out next week and can't get it out of the damned driveway." Charlie snapped off a delicate pink blossom from one of her rose bushes and stared down the street. His eyes narrowed.

Mary Alice followed his gaze. Bridge's truck was pulling in behind her car in the cut-out.

"Speak of the devil," Charlie muttered.

At the sight of Bridge walking swiftly toward them, a lump lodged in her throat and her concentration took a nosedive. "*Hmm?*"

Her emotions had gone completely out of control today. First in bed this morning, and then during the incredible hour at school. Bridge's lethal combination of sensuality and sensitivity had swept her away completely.

There was no denying, she was hopelessly in love with the man.

But hopeless was the operative word. She had to stop weaving fanciful, impossible dreams of endless love and a happy future with Russell Bridger. He was a cop. And he didn't believe in lifetime commitments. She had to remember that.

She needed to be strong and resist the temptation to let herself be swayed by his gentle, loving ways. By his incredibly arousing body. By his protectiveness, and his understanding. She had to force herself to think of the long-term pain she'd be saving herself, not of the short-term heartache she would suffer when he walked away from her after this assignment was over. She could deal with that.

At least, she tried to tell herself so. Over and over. But her heart just wouldn't listen.

And neither would her body. She couldn't take her eyes off Bridge's imposing figure as he approached.

The man was gorgeous. Tall and lean, dark and angular, thighs rippling under snug jeans. Today, his bright orange construction vest covered a white T-shirt that stretched tantalizingly over his broad shoulders and well-defined biceps. He still hadn't shaved, she noticed, her mouth going dry as the Mojave Desert in August.

Cool, Mary Alice, be very cool, she admonished herself as he came up to her and Charlie.

"Hi, baby," he said simply, and swept her into his arms, his mouth covering hers in a breathtaking hello kiss. "I missed you."

Heat sizzled everywhere he touched. He held her intimately against his body, apparently unwilling to surrender her even as his head rose and he took inventory of her neighbor. "Hi. I'm Russ Bridger." He didn't have to add, "*And this woman is mine.*" The look he cut Charlie said that plainer than words.

Mary Alice wondered suddenly if this was Bridge-the-cop playing his undercover roll to the max, or if it was Bridge-the-man staking out his territory in the face of a potential rival. She couldn't deny the thrill that ran through her at being the object of his claims and desires, and felt her body yield to his.

Charlie stuck out his hand. "Hi. Charlie Watson. I live next door." He tipped his head toward his house.

Bridge kept his left arm firmly around her while he extended his right. "Nice place you have," he said noncommittally.

"I came to invite you guys to a little party I'm having Saturday night. Mary Alice always comes over. I hope you'll be able to make it too, Russ."

She wriggled around in his grip so she faced Charlie, her mind clicking back to the reason for Bridge's being there. What a break for him to have been asked into Charlie's home.

But before she could accept, he said, "I don't know. Mary Alice and I have been enjoying staying in evenings lately."

Ears burning, she reached back and jabbed him with her elbow, gratified when he let out an *oof*. "Don't be silly. Of course we'd love to come, Charlie. It's very nice of you to invite us *both*."

With a satisfied smirk, Charlie looked from her to Bridge. "Good. I'll expect you about nine o'clock, as usual. See you 'round, Russ." He flipped the flower in his hand onto the ground and leapt back over the fence.

Bridge tightened his grip around the front of her body, and something hard dug into her shoulder blade. He murmured, "Count on it, Watson."

As soon as Charlie was out of earshot, he muttered, "Asshole."

She slipped around in Bridge's arms and peered up at him. "What's gotten into you?"

He braced his legs apart and snuggled his face into her neck. "You." His hands found her bottom and lifted her into him as he kissed the sensitive junction between her neck and shoulder. "I didn't like the way he was making time with my woman."

His woman? *Mmm*, she did love the sound of that.

She smiled into his hair, then reluctantly took a step backward. "He wasn't. And I'm not your woman, Bridge."

He ran a thumb down the side of her face. "Then why do you wear my mark on your cheeks?" He darted a glance over the fence. "And why else would he be staring down the front of your dress?"

"I like how you kiss," she said absently, frowning down at her neckline. No, he had to be kidding. Looking up, she caught him grinning and mocked a scowl. She decided to change her tack. "You almost threw away a perfectly good opportunity to get inside his house without a warrant. Good job, Dirty Harry."

"Hey, watch it." He smacked her bottom.

"*Ow!*" She skipped away from him. Laughing, she backed up the walkway to the door, holding her hands behind her protectively.

"I'll show you Dirty Harry, and you won't be laughing then," he called after her with a cartoon-villain chuckle. "Put on some coffee, woman. I have to get something from the truck."

She made a face at him. She should let him make his own damn coffee. But she went in and did as he asked, anyway. Where were her feminist streak and fine Irish temper when she needed them?

Undoubtedly keeping her good sense company, wherever *that* had gotten off to.

The front door closed just as she pressed the brew button on the coffee maker. Behind her, she heard Bridge walk into the kitchen, his boots hardly making a sound.

She smiled. She was getting better at knowing when he was sneaking up on her. "You know, you really—" She turned and exclaimed, spotting the huge bouquet of roses he held out to her. Her heart skipped a beat, and she immediately forgot whatever scolding she'd been about to give him. "Oh, Bridge! They're beautiful!"

"The old varieties aren't very good for cutting, so my mom kept a few teas, too. Thought you might like these."

A few perfect white buds were mixed in with a large bunch of fragrant, mauve-colored blossoms. He'd even cut ferns to give the bouquet a nice frame. She inhaled the delicious, spicy fragrance, and hummed, "*Mmm*. They're wonderful. Thank you."

Accepting the vase from him, she took it to the living room where they could both enjoy the flowers. She knelt by the low coffee table and fussed a little with the arrangement.

"Speaking of roses, I got a letter today from the Historical Rose Society, confirming the board's appointment here Friday." Her fingers found a curly strand of ribbon among the flowers. "What's this?"

Then she looked up, saw him, and let out a big gasp.

Chapter Thirty-Nine

B ridge watched Mary Alice's horrified reaction to the sight of his weapon in its shoulder holster and the badge hanging from his T-shirt pocket. He'd put them on when he fetched the flowers.

Her face paled, her eyes widening in shock, and her hand flew to her mouth. "What are you doing with those?" she squeaked.

He went to the coffee table and knelt down in front of her, bringing them eye-to-eye. Gently, he removed her hands from her cheeks and held them in his. "I'm a cop, honey."

Her gaze faltered badly, then dropped to the Beretta hanging at his side. "But why wear them now? You're supposed to be undercover, aren't you?"

"SAC Grayson just called to let me know his informant is sure something's cooking with Watson and he'll make a move any time. I have to be ready."

"So soon?" Lines of fear were suddenly etched around her pretty green eyes. "Will you be in danger?"

He gave her a reassuring smile. "No more than usual.

Don't worry. I'm very good at what I do. Ask anyone."

"So was my father." She sank back on her heels, and her eyes squeezed shut. "Sorry. I have no right."

"You have every right," Bridge said softly, his heart going out to her. "I've been officially upgraded to "boyfwiend," remember?"

She opened her eyes, joy lighting them again. "Oh, Bridge, you were wonderful at school today. I'm so glad I had the recorder set up. I'll treasure that tape of you singing forever, and so will the kids."

He smiled, remembering how comfortable it had been. How contented he'd felt strumming the guitar for a bunch of toddlers. "I had a good time. I didn't realize kids could be so much fun."

He looked down at her and she looked up at him, and he'd put good money on that they were both thinking exactly the same thing. "Mary Alice—"

"Bridge—"

They both laughed, and suddenly he felt shy for the first time since he was five. "You go first," he said, squeezing her hand.

"I just wanted to tell you how special what you did today was to the kids, especially Ivy. You simply have no idea…"

She took a deep breath and looked back at his shield, a sad expression capturing her lovely face. Slowly, she reached out to touch the badge. Her hand shook slightly as she ran her fingers around the edge, then over the pattern of city hall, the letters spelling Pasadena, and his number.

"You are a cop," she whispered, as if reminding herself.

She lifted her hand and touched his chin, then traced his jaw with the same trembling fingers that had tested the cold metal on his chest. After a moment, she moved on to his lips, his cheekbones, his ears.

"A cop who doesn't believe in marriage," she said.

He wanted to cry out in protest. Yes, he *did* believe in marriage. *He did.* Just not for himself.

But he didn't speak, for fear of breaking the hypnotic spell of her seeking fingers. His face felt alive with nerve-endings, tingling and tickling where she touched him, the cells of his skin crying out with loss when her fingers moved on.

He closed his eyes and let her explore his eyebrows and lashes, his eyelids. He felt her brush back a lock of hair that had fallen over his forehead, then bury her fingers among its mates. He let his head fall back, loving the sensual way she stroked his head, rubbing small circles with her fingers at his temples, across his forehead, behind his ears.

She trailed them along his neck, across his shoulders, and down his arms until her hand met his gun in its holster. Slowly, she drew the weapon out of the leather.

He snapped his head up and opened his eyes. "Baby…"

She held it delicately in her hands, resting it palms-up across her lap. "Such a small thing to be capable of so much destruction."

He could see the struggle within her—a reluctant fascination clashing with the urge to throw it as far as she could. She was trying to come to some kind of terms with it, he figured, and resisted yanking the weapon from her hands. He watched her, knowing instinctively that his own future was being decided at that very moment.

"It's part of you, isn't it?" She looked into his eyes. "As much as your hands or face. Or your blood."

Moment of truth. "Yes. It's part of me. Of what I am. It always will be."

"Love you, love your gun."

His gaze locked with hers. "Do you, Mary Alice? Do you love me?"

He thought he saw the answer in the deep green of her eyes as she looked at him. Or maybe it was only wishful thinking. Either way, he had to know for sure.

Carefully, he lifted his weapon from her and reholstered it, then took her hands and kissed them. "I want to hear you say it."

Her lips parted and her eyes went liquid and fearful.

A loud, strident beep suddenly screeched from his pocket, where he kept the alarm beeper.

"Fucking-*A*," he spat out in supreme frustration. "This guy's got bad timing down to a fine art." He snatched up the beeper and glared at it, furious over the untimely interruption. "It's the front door. Watson's going out. Damn it to all hell. Gotta go."

No choice. As much as it killed him to leave, he was on duty and had to do it. He kissed her fast and firm, then ran for the back bedroom to grab a jacket, his Kevlar, and his go-bag.

When he came out she was screwing the lid on a thermos of coffee, studying it fiercely. "You haven't eaten. Take some pears." He plucked up a few of the fruits from the basket on the counter and put them in his bag, along with the thermos she gave him. "Thanks," he said, tipping her chin up to face him.

"Please, be careful," she whispered.

She looked so scared, he caught her around her waist and held her close. "I will." Next door a car started, and he knew he had to hurry. "Will you be okay?"

"Bridge, I—"

"I'm going to be fine, sweetheart. I give you my word on that."

"Oh, Bridge," she said brokenly. "I don't know if I can do this."

He swallowed the words that threatened to come out, then kissed her one last time, and strode quickly out the front door—before he made her promises he could never keep.

Chapter Forty

Bridge called Officer Deane for backup on his cell phone and arranged to meet him at the parking lot of the upscale liquor store where Watson made his first stop.

"We'll take your car," Bridge said when he arrived.

He locked up his vehicle and slid into Deane's Honda, just in case Watson recognized the truck.

Watson spent an hour at the store, finally coming out with several boxes full of bottles, which he loaded into the back of his Porsche. An hour and a half later, after following him all over the city, they pulled up to the third grocery store Watson had visited, this one a small Russian deli.

Jesus. The man took his parties seriously. Bridge could hardly wait for Saturday. His stomach was already growling.

Good. Maybe his hunger would distract him from the fantasies that had been playing in his brain ever since he'd asked Mary Alice if she loved him. What would she have said if they hadn't been interrupted? God, he wanted to rush home and find out.

He dragged the last pear out of his bag and demolished it in four bites, tossing the stem next to the empty thermos.

"Watson's going to have to start strapping bags on the ski rack at the rate he's going," he muttered.

Deane passed him one of the two sodas he'd just purchased while checking out Watson inside the deli. "This'll be the last one, guaranteed."

"How can you be so sure?"

"He's buying caviar. On ice."

Bridge shot him a grin. "Hot damn, we'll make a detective out of you yet, Deane." He pulled out his cell phone. "I better call Mary Alice and see if anyone's dropped off my truck." He'd arranged for a uniform to pick it up earlier.

The Deane kid had the audacity to snicker.

"And what's that supposed to mean?"

"Aw, hell, Sarge. It don't take a detective to spot that Magnum you're packing just thinking about her."

Bridge clamped his jaw in the face of irrefutable physical evidence. "Sometimes a man can be too good at his job, rookie." He hit the speed dial for Mary Alice's number. "It's me."

"Bridge! Are you all right?"

"Everything's fine. I should be back soon. Listen, is the truck back in the cut-out yet?"

"Yeah. Someone from the station dropped it off a while ago."

"Good. Watson'll never know I was gone."

"Should I heat up some dinner? Are you hungry?"

"Ravenous."

Deane snickered again, and Bridge realized he'd lowered his voice to a suggestive drawl. He cut the kid a warning look, but smiled to himself. *What the hell.* May as well bite the bullet and admit to the world how he felt. Obviously he was a total bust at hiding it. "See you soon."

"Thanks for calling. I feel so much better knowing you're okay."

"I'm glad. And angel?"

"Yes?"

"Looking forward to finishing our conversation."

Chapter Forty-One

Mary Alice heard the dial tone in her ear and mentally scraped herself off the ceiling. *Oh, lord.* Was he really going to make her answer his terrifying question?

What would she say?

Did she love him?

Of course she did. Madly. But should she actually say the words out loud? *Hell,* no.

Everything had been just fine…as long as she thought all the feelings were one-sided—*her* side—and that all he was interested in was a short, sweet, physical affair. Emphasis on short. And physical.

Sure, she'd be hurt when he left, but ending it was for the best, all around.

However, she feared his insistence on her answering his question could only mean one thing—that he also wanted to take a chance on being together.

And maybe…just maybe…that he loved her, too.

Love changed everything.

Didn't it?

No doubt, he would expect her to accept his job along with him. But she knew she couldn't deal rationally with his life as a cop. She was already so frightened that he would be taken from her any minute. She couldn't go on if he were hurt.

And what about his vow never to put another woman through what his mother had gone through? Was he willing to break that promise?

Which begged the next question…

What kind of relationship did he have in mind?

He didn't want to get married, and she didn't want just an affair. How could they possibly hope to make anything between them work? She had to be a fool even to consider getting more involved with him.

Yet, the thought of losing him caused a pain in her heart so great it threatened to completely undo her resolve.

What she needed was some advice, and fast. Before he got home.

She dialed Nancy's number in a blind panic.

"Oh, Nan, what have I gotten myself into?" she moaned after telling her all the gory details.

"Sounds like you've gotten yourself into the best thing that could possibly have happened to you, girl. Don't fight it. Grab your chance at happiness and enjoy it while you can."

There was a poignantly sad edge to her friend's voice. Mary Alice pried her mind off her own problems long enough to ask about Nancy's. "How's Ben? Have you gotten his new test results?"

"Yes, today. Oh, Mac, I'm so worried. The doctor says his tumor is growing, but it might not be operable. We have to meet with her tomorrow to go over options."

Mary Alice was horrified. "Oh my God, Nancy, I'm so sorry. Here I am, prattling on about my silly troubles, and you're facing that." She couldn't believe she'd been so selfish not to have noticed her best friend's distress. And Ben! Good lord, he had to be okay! He just had to.

"Stop," Nancy said. "I'm really glad you called. It'll give me something nice to think about. Seriously, hon, listen to me. Don't let Bridge get away from you because of something that happened in the past, or something that might or might not happen in the future. Be strong and live for today. Today might be all you ever get. If this is the real thing between you two, don't miss the opportunity for love, however short that time may be."

Chapter Forty-Two

When Bridge walked through the door, dropped his go-bag, and held out his arms to her, Mary Alice forgot all about her anxiety and the problems left to be solved, and ran straight into his embrace.

Nancy was right. It was time Mary Alice accepted that hiding from life was not being tough. It was being a coward. She loved Bridge and had to take this chance with him, even if it meant making adjustments, and accepting the risk of being hurt.

His lips met hers and she surrendered, giving herself into his care, surrounding herself with his strength. With her kisses she told him she desperately wanted to be his.

She had stars in her eyes when he finally let her up to catch her breath, maybe because their kiss had put her into orbit. "We're both completely crazy, you know that, right?"

"Yep." He let out a deep growl, giving her another hug. "I am, anyway. About you." When he looked like he wanted to say more, she quickly led him into the kitchen. She wasn't ready to face that part quite yet.

He kissed her hair as she fixed him a plate. "Smells great."

"It's lasagna."

"*Mmm*, that smells good, too."

She smiled, and suddenly wished that after her shower she'd put on something a little more sexy than flannel PJs and her Snoopy slippers.

She watched as he peeled off his jacket and settled at her table, all legs and shoulders and dark bedroom eyes. She was swamped by desire. Even the sight of his gun and badge boldly displayed on his chest couldn't deter her longing for him.

Lord, she wanted him. She'd probably regret it in the morning, but tonight she wanted to revel in this new feeling of being totally out of control. Tomorrow was soon enough to figure out where to take it from here.

Tomorrow was soon enough to deal with this new reality that neither of them had thought they could live with.

Chapter Forty-Three

After dinner, Mary Alice settled next to Bridge on the sofa in the living room.

He put an arm around her and fingered the collar of her PJs. "That was delicious. Now, what's for dessert?"

Leaning back on his arm, she smiled coyly. "I've got some chocolate chip cookies."

He ran a forefinger down her sleeve. "I had my heart set on something a little hotter."

"Coffee?"

"Sweeter." He unbuttoned the top button of her top and nuzzled her neck.

When she put her hand on his chest his gun nudged her. She touched it tentatively. "You're still on duty, Detective Sergeant."

"Only until the lights go out at Watson's place." Lifting his head, he checked his watch, then glanced down at her hand. "Until then, you, *uh*, wanna play with my weapon, little girl?"

She squelched a giggle. "Is it loaded?"

He grinned. "Hell, yeah. Full barrel."

"In that case, better not. Wouldn't want it to go off accidentally."

"It does like a light touch." His eyelids went to half mast, his thick lashes casting long shadows on his cheekbones. He tipped her chin up and kissed her long and slow.

A warm, delectable lethargy seeped into her limbs as she nestled there in the crook of his arm, his lips roaming over hers. All the reservations she'd had about letting down her guard and allowing herself to be swept into this frightening, wonderful experiment seemed suddenly trivial. How could this possibly be wrong? It felt so right. She sought his mouth and pulled him close, losing herself in his taste.

After a long time, Bridge gave a groan and pulled away, dropping his head onto the back of the couch. "Baby, we've got to stop or I won't make it till lights-out."

She snuggled up against him, basking in the earthy male smell of him. But a niggling doubt kept prodding at the back of her mind. He hadn't pressed her about her feelings for him…but maybe only because they'd been too busy kissing to actually converse. She was terrified to bring it up, but she was even more terrified to leave things up in the air.

She gathered her courage, and asked, "Bridge, should we talk about what we're doing here?"

"Probably. But I'm afraid if we do, we'll talk ourselves right out of it." Taking a deep breath he looked down at her. "Honey—"

Before he could get any further, she said, "We both know everything's against it working between us."

"No." He shook his head. "Not everything." Flashing her a sly look, he reached across the coffee table and slid over the vase of roses she'd put there earlier. He pulled out the ribbon that dangled down from among the flowers. "I wonder what's tied at the end?"

She glanced at it uncertainly.

"Go on."

When she gave it a tug, a small box appeared. She sucked in a breath. "What's this?"

"Open it and see."

Her hands shook as she held it, contemplating the possibilities. She didn't know whether to be relieved or disappointed that the box was the wrong shape to be a ring.

Impatient, he pulled off the ribbon for her, and she tore the paper from around the box.

Inside, two shiny gold apples winked back at her, dangling brilliantly from a pair of gold earrings. "Oh, Bridge. They're lovely. But I couldn't possibly accept these, they're—"

"Sure, you can." Pushing her hair back from around her ears, he carefully removed the porcelain ladybugs she was wearing and slipped one gold wire through the hole in her earlobe. "Just a couple of apples for the teacher, that's all."

The corners of her lips turned up. "You wouldn't be angling for teacher's pet, would you?"

He nibbled on her other earlobe then slid its earring home. "No. I'm angling to pet the teacher," he whispered, pulling her close.

A small, needy sound escaped her throat.

He dragged his wet tongue around the shell of her ear. "Want to know why I chose these little apples?" He caught her earlobe between his teeth, apple and all, and sucked.

She felt the erotic pull clear to her center. "Why?" she managed.

He played his tongue over the heavy ball of the earring. "Because they remind me of the tips of your breasts when I get you excited. Hard, round, smooth." He rubbed his thumb over her nipple and streaks of electricity shot through her body. "Like they are now."

She moaned his name, melting into his arms, her own arms winding around his neck. "Every time I wear them I'll think of you touching me."

And she would, too. For the rest of her life she'd have this reminder of Bridge and how he made her feel, inside and out.

He plowed his fingers through her loose hair, holding her face in his hands. He kissed her then. A long, demanding kiss that swamped her with its urgency.

"I want to touch your breasts," he murmured hotly, "and everywhere else."

Her body shivered against his. "Yes," she whispered.

"I won't walk away, I promise you. I was so wrong before. I want you, angel. I want to be with you."

She held him tight. "I want you, too, Bridge. More than anything."

"Tonight," he coaxed, crashing through her fears and reservations. "Tonight, when Watson's lights go out and I'm back from my night check. I want to come to your bed and find you naked and willing, waiting for me to touch you all over. Waiting for me to make love to you."

A wall of desire nearly knocked the breath from her lungs.

Nancy's words echoed through her mind. *Today might be all you ever get. If this is the real thing, don't miss the opportunity…*

Mary Alice closed her eyes and surrendered. Yielded to the unstoppable emotions flooding her heart. She wanted more than anything to confirm them in the most fundamental of ways.

"Come to me tonight, Bridge," she whispered tremulously.

Regardless of the cost to her heart.

Chapter Forty-Four

When Bridge's half-nude body appeared in her bedroom door, tall and shadowed and completely filling the darkened space, Mary Alice had to swallow twice to push her heart from her throat back down to where it belonged.

He stopped in the doorway, backlit by the hall light like a Hollywood movie hero. His freshly washed hair glistened, the grooves left by his comb alternating silver and black. A bundle was tucked casually under his arm and he held a pair of boots in one hand. A fresh hint of soap along with a dark note of musky spice wafted through the dim, silent room to tease her nostrils.

He looked like a man who'd come prepared and was planning to stay awhile.

She sat up on the bed and hugged the thin summer quilt to her chest. Her nakedness under it felt strange—exciting. In her whole life, she'd never done anything quite this premeditatedly daring. Their first time, she and Bridge had come together so quickly she hadn't had a spare moment to consider what was happening. And with Jack, sex had always been more of a pleasant, comfortable pastime than this overpowering physical need she felt for the man who now gazed heatedly at her from the doorway.

"Still time to change your mind," he said in a low voice that dared her to try.

She could see the ridge of his powerful arousal pushing at his jeans, and in her final second of rational thought she wondered how he found the strength to stand there unmoving and wait for her reply.

Fearing her vocal chords were as paralyzed as the rest of her, she shook her head. She had no intention of changing her mind.

Slowly, she drew the quilt from her body, letting her actions speak for her.

He stood a moment longer, watching the quilt's descent, his gaze stroking over her bare skin as ardently as she hoped his hands would soon be doing. He dropped his boots with a dull thud, closed the door, and approached the bed. The shadow of his Adam's apple slid down his throat and back up before he tore his eyes from her and searched for a place to put the bundle.

Unrolling the flannel shirt holding it together, he took out the few things that had been wrapped inside, then opened the drawer of her nightstand and slung the shirt over it, sliding his cell phone into the breast pocket, ready to grab at a moment's notice. As she held her breath, he carefully placed the other items on top of the nightstand. In a sliver of moonlight slanting through the bedroom window, the dark objects took shape. She recognized his alarm beeper, his badge, his gun in its shoulder holster, and finally the box of condoms from the bathroom.

It was an explosive combination.

Her heartbeat thundered in sudden consternation.

Oh, Lord, what was she doing?

She was about to have sex with a big, dark, dangerous male who stared death in the face every day. A cop, whose uncertain job could snatch him away from her at any moment on a whim of fate.

A man who made her tremble just looking at him.

She clutched the edge of the quilt and inched backward, staring first at him, then at the dreaded grouping on the nightstand.

Several seconds went by as her thoughts whirled. He moved to the side of the bed and peered intently at her. Even in the dimness of the room she could see concern on his face, mixed with the hard edge of desire.

Concern.

She licked her lips, regaining control. She deliberately calmed herself.

This wasn't some cold, jaded stranger she was accepting into her bed. It was Russell Bridger, the man she loved. The man she loved so much she was willing to overlook the small detail of his having the one profession she'd thought she could never accept in a mate.

And no, they weren't about to have sex.

They were about to make beautiful love.

Chapter Forty-Five

Mary Alice took a deep breath and met Bridge's gaze.

His pulse almost stopped dead. He could practically hear the gears turning in her mind, the last-minute argument she was having with herself about whether or not to take this chance on him.

What would she decide?

He hated the apprehension he saw in her expression. Especially a moment ago when she'd caught sight of his purposeful arrangement on the nightstand—set dressing for the reality of his life. But he'd had to do it. He needed to be absolutely certain this was what she wanted. That she could take him as he really was, and not as she wished him to be. He may have started this relationship under false pretenses, but he wouldn't continue it that way. That wouldn't be fair to either of them.

Nervously holding his own explosive feelings under tight rein, he observed the emotions vying for dominance in her eyes.

He hoped like hell that love would wind up the winner.

Or at least hope. Hope for a future with him.

When she looked up, he tamped down on an almost desperate need to influence her decision in his favor. As casually as he could manage, he asked, "How'd I come out?"

A small smile relaxed the tension in her expression. She released her white-knuckled grip on the quilt and stretched out her hand to him. "On top."

His lips curved in relief. "My favorite position."

He took her hand and let her pull him down next to her on the bed. With a sigh, he gathered the ragged tatters of his nerves and held her close. Only for a moment. Having Mary Alice naked in his arms threatened to push everything from his mind—except gloving himself in her velvet heat.

But he had one more little test to perform before he could risk what was about to happen between them…along with their unspoken commitment to one another. He forced himself to ignore the satin feel of her body against his, and eased out of the warmth of her arms. If she could get through this last test, they might actually have a chance at making this unlikely relationship work.

Her eyes searched his questioningly.

Providing *he* didn't crack.

Chapter Forty-Six

Mary Alice leaned forward, her blood pounding, her body hungering for Bridge's touch.

He met her halfway and their lips brushed. But before she could even taste him, he pulled back. He grasped her hands, firmly lacing his fingers through hers.

"I want you," he whispered, and her breath backed up in her lungs. The startling realization of her precarious position—on the brink of taking huge risks, both sexually and emotionally—and the even more startling realization that she actually savored that position, nearly scared her to death. It was not Miss Hiding-From-Life there in bed with this modern-day gunslinger complete with boots and six-shooter.

It was finally her true self who sat shivering hot and cold, waiting for him to make his move.

Wanting him to do it now.

As if reading her mind, he did.

Still holding her hands captive, he nudged her down onto her back until her head sank into the pillow. He kissed her, deep and seductive. She reveled in the moist pressure of his mouth on hers, the quick teasing nips from his teeth and short parries of his tongue.

Mmm. This was what she wanted. *Exactly* what she wanted.

His lips moved down her body, leaving erotic trails of wet kisses on her skin. He paused just above her breasts and blew lightly over them, sending her nipples into tight spirals of delicious sensation. Her body arched toward him, wanting contact, wanting him to take her breasts into his mouth and suckle her until she cried out with the sweet agony of her need.

He sat up, and instead she cried out from her loss.

"*Shhh,*" he whispered.

He didn't release her hands, or let her move. His eyes blazed out from his shadowed face, the angles of his cheekbones sharply defined in the moonlight.

"Do you want me?" His expression was intense, almost savage.

Her heartbeat kicked up another notch. "More than anything."

"Good."

He raised her hands and positioned her arms in a curve around her head. Then he gently gathered and spread her hair over the pillow.

She tried to bring her hand up to touch him, but he quickly pushed it back down. "No. Don't move."

She shivered again, vividly aware of her body being put on display for him, her breasts round and thrust upward because of the position of her arms. She felt a blush rip down her chest, heating her skin until her flesh felt on fire.

She had never felt so acutely sexual in her life.

His slow, hot-blooded inspection embarrassed her, but at the same time it aroused her beyond words.

Studying her reaction, he drew his fingertips softly down

the sensitive insides of her arms, from the crossed wrists above her head to her underarms. Then he circled her breasts with his barely-there touch.

"Relax. Let yourself go," he urged.

His fingertips circled her again.

She moaned softly. "I'll try."

How could she relax when all her deepest, darkest fantasies were on the verge of coming true?

His nails scraped gently over her again. She hitched in a sharp breath, her skin quivering from his silky touch.

Ever so slowly, he bent over her and placed his tongue on one quickened nipple. He lapped at it, then blew a sharp stream of air over it. Ribbons of exquisite sensation streaked through her. She moaned louder, and tried to reach for him.

Again, he replaced her arms. "Don't move. I know it's difficult for you—letting go. But I need you to trust me."

She licked her lips, a prick of uneasy excitement stabbing at her. Why didn't he want her to move?

"Do you trust me, angel?"

"I—"

She forgot his question as his hands traveled down to her waist, then lower, to her hips. His thumbs caressed the crease where her legs joined her torso, drenching her body with a deep yearning. Every one of her muscles melted in the deluge. She'd had no idea her body could feel like this—so languid, so vulnerable to a man's will, so physically needy.

His hands continued their journey down her thighs, pushing them apart, and she was helpless to deny him access to the most intimate part of herself. Not that she would. She wanted him more than anything she'd ever wanted.

"*Do* you trust me? Completely?"

She did. Of course she did, or she wouldn't be here now, naked, exposed, and willingly putting herself in his power. "Yes."

But the mere fact that he'd asked caused a ripple of apprehension to purl through her.

He ran his hands along her inner thighs, spreading them even farther apart. "Enough to put your body totally in my control?"

Desire slammed into her, an irrational craving for the man—and for the danger she instinctively knew he posed to her and her safe little world. Because of his job…but also because of his powerful sensuality. This side of sex was new to her. Not edgy, exactly, but a far cry from the safe, routine lovemaking she'd enjoyed with Jack. Instinctively, she knew sex with Bridge would never be routine.

"Yes. I trust you."

With her words, her body surrendered to him completely. Her limbs yielded to his commands as he proceeded to arrange her on the bed in a sultry pose, arms up, breasts out, legs spread with one knee up and one bent on the bed. The look on his face sent goose bumps clear down to the tips of her toes. He looked like a predator laying out a feast he intended to savor down to the last crumb.

Oh, Lord. Now that she had given permission, how would he choose to devour his feast?

She closed her eyes and let herself enjoy what was happening to her body. His fingers smoothed over her skin, her breasts, down her legs and ankles, dipping into her navel and her mouth, setting off sparks and igniting fires wherever he touched. She felt the last vestiges of her willpower slip away, leaving her entirely open and vulnerable to him.

A heady, erotic thrill shot through her. For the first time in memory she didn't have to be the strong one. The one in charge, making the decisions. She didn't have to do anything at all. She could just lie back and let it happen.

And God, it felt so damn good. On every possible level.

Chapter Forty-Seven

Bridge smiled in satisfaction. Mary Alice's slumberous gaze and her heartfelt declaration were redolent with invitation.

"I know," he said with a smile, feeling a powerful tug of control deep inside him.

He intended to take full advantage of that invitation—now that he'd learned what he'd needed to—that she trusted him completely.

He swept his gaze down the length of her beckoning body. "You are so incredibly beautiful. I want to see you. All of you."

A lamp stood on the chest of drawers on the other side of the room. He slid off the bed, strode over, and switched it on. He turned back to her, drinking in the sight of his woman.

His woman.

The scent of her body, all lush and eager for him, filled his senses. The golden earrings he'd given her were dangling from her ears. A kind of primitive possessiveness seized him as he looked at her, as if he had somehow bound her irrevocably to him with those thin gold wires.

He only wished it were that easy.

She hadn't moved from the position he'd put her in, but she shifted her muscles now as he gazed at her, her body undulating suggestively. His already hard arousal jumped with impatience.

Soon, he promised himself. Soon he would slake his tremendous need to be inside her. But first, he must thank her properly for her trust.

He fingered the top button of his jeans. She caught the movement and surprised him with a little moue of disappointment.

He hiked a brow. "On or off?"

The tip of her tongue peeked out from between her lips and flicked over her bottom lip. Her cheeks flushed rosy and when she raised her eyes to his, they glittered with a heat he hadn't ever seen in them before.

"On," she said. "But unbuttoned."

He nearly fell over. Clearly, her choice was not due to modesty. He grinned, absurdly pleased with this new, adventurous side of her. He decided to test how far it went. "Shall I get the orange vest?"

Her eyes dipped to his chest for a moment before the corners of her mouth lifted. "Maybe next time."

Ooh, baby. He was going to thoroughly enjoy discovering the secret fantasies of the formerly prim and proper Mary Alice Flannery. He sent up a silent *thank you* that he was the man she'd built those fantasies around, and made a solemn promise to her—and to himself—to uncover every last one of them.

Even if it took a lifetime.

He climbed back on the bed and knelt between her legs. One by one he unfastened the metal buttons of his jeans, then spread the fly. He'd dressed commando, so his sex sprang free, hard and thick and ready.

"Grab the bars on the headboard, angel," he ordered huskily. "You're going to need to hang on."

Chapter Forty-Eight

Mary Alice felt her eyes go wide at Bridge's command. But she didn't stop to ponder what she'd gotten herself into. She just obeyed.

The brass columns were chilly in her hands, but smooth to the touch and a perfect fit. She closed her eyes and imagined it was Bridge she was holding instead of cold metal. Excitement twisted through her.

He dropped down, and her body sighed in pleasure when he lowered himself onto her. The rough texture of denim against her bare thighs and his hot arousal jutting into her belly made her squirm with anticipation. Coarse chest hair scraped against her breasts, sending sharp jolts of desire to her center.

She arched under him, wanting to get closer, wanting to feel his body covering hers, all the way down.

He kissed her deeply, passionately, and she moaned into his mouth.

"Please." She needed to be even closer, as close as was possible between a man and a woman. She needed him inside her.

She wrapped her legs around his hips and felt the uneven seams of his back pockets bite into her bare calves. Her fingers grasping the brass headboard, she kissed him back until she couldn't breathe.

She was his, and she loved the heady feeling. Loved belonging to him, loved what he did to her, loved the joy he'd brought into her life.

Loved him.

He left her gasping as he eased down her body, tasting each and every inch with his lips and tongue and nose and cheeks. His touch was sublime. By the time he reached her feet she was a quaking mass of molten need.

"Bridge, please," she pleaded, crazy with wanting him.

"Not yet. There are one or two places left."

Then he spread wide her shaking legs and started working his way up the tender inner flesh. There was no doubt in her mind where he was heading.

When he reached the brink of her intimate triangle, he paused and looked up at her. "You okay with this?" His hot breath tickled the ultra-sensitive area, making her wriggle in his grasp.

"I—" How could she tell him she'd never done this before?

"Surely, you've…?" His voice registered the incredulity she saw reflected in his face when she shook her head. "Oh, honey," he said on a groan. "Hang on tight. I think you'll like this."

He burrowed into her with his mouth, kissing her and using his fingers to open her fully to his caresses. She slammed her eyes tight and squeezed the brass in her hands.

His tongue painted over her flesh. Jolts of pure electric craving stabbed through her, straight to her clit, which he circled with his clever tongue, over and over. She felt herself slip away, draining into the hot, wet ecstasy of his loving.

It felt incredible. Better than incredible.

She moaned his name, panting with each lick and stroke. Her body writhed under him, his fingers digging into her waist, her thighs, her back, as he held her.

God, he felt so good.

The hot knot of pleasure wound tighter and tighter in her center, threatening to splinter her into a million brilliant pieces. The back of her knees started to tremble, the weakness working up her inner thighs, where all the sensations met in a blinding shock as she felt his teeth close over her clit. Her body exploded.

"Bridge!" she cried out, her hands releasing the bed to find him. Her thighs clamped around his head, and she rode his tongue as it wrung every last bit of pleasure from her body.

"Oh my God," she groaned when she finally floated back to earth. She'd had many, many orgasms before, but that had topped every single one.

"Feel good?" he asked, the cocky grin on his face telling her he knew exactly how amazing it had felt.

Lying limp on the bed, barely able to move, she slid her hand over his hair. "I had no idea."

He scooted up, the weight of his body settling enticingly on top of her. She managed to put her arms around his neck.

"I'm glad. Call me a chauvinist, but it turns me on that I'm the only man you've done that with."

She hummed out a long sigh. "I imagine there must be other things, too…"

He kissed her, a sultry smile gracing his beautiful mouth. "Oh, yeah. And I won't rest till we try every one of them."

She smiled. "I can't wait." Suddenly, she was struck with her own urge to explore. She rolled him off her and onto his back, and straddled his thighs.

"Hey!" he protested. But not really. His eyes shone with

anticipation.

"In fact, I think we should start right now."

"In that case, take me." Bridge lay back like a good captive and stretched his arms out in mock capitulation. The muscles in his neck and shoulders bunched and he lifted his arms over his head, positioning them as he had hers. "I'm at your mercy."

She studied the magnificent body under her. Midnight black hair and brows accentuated his eyes and clean-shaven cheekbones. His broad, sturdy chest dwarfed her bed, and for a second she shivered at having such a powerful man in such an intimate position. She swallowed. Although she was on top now, that could change with a mere flick of his wrist.

He studied her closely as he waited for her to move, his gaze daring her to be bold.

Although he had just given her the most incredible release of her life, her body heated and tightened under his intense scrutiny, craving his possession again.

She moved her fingers over his chest, down his ribs. And felt a small, round, pitted scar. She halted, moving back to investigate. "What's this?"

His half-lidded eyes watched her, full of pure, feral hunger. "Old football injury. Can't you find anything more interesting to touch?"

A smile bowed her lips.

She smoothed her hands over his flat belly, tangling her fingers in the dark arrow of hair, letting them be drawn toward the awesome length of his arousal. The fly of his jeans was still spread wide where his cock lay erect.

At the last minute, she veered off and grasped the waistband. With his impatient help, she pulled off his jeans and tossed them aside.

She figured turn-about was fair play. So she crawled between his legs and spread his thighs.

"My turn."

Then she bent to taste him. And she moaned in pleasure.

Bringing the wild beast to heel with her hands and lips and tongue, she soon had him growling and moaning in sensual torment. She savored every moment. His body was hard and firm and tough and masculine. She loved the way the hair crinkled crisply over his iron-hard legs, pooling around the straining length of his manhood.

Moments later she heard his strangled groan, and suddenly found herself on her back under him, his hands gripping hers above her head.

"Feel good?" she ventured, a smile teasing her lips as she licked them and peered up at him. Still tasting him.

"You," he ground out between his teeth, "are a hell of a quick study, teacher lady," he concluded on a sharp exhale.

She could tell he was pleased at the revelation.

He reached a hand over to the nightstand and grabbed the box. "Choose."

This time she riffled through the packets and extracted the one she wanted. Ultra Thin. "I only want to feel you tonight," she whispered.

A muscle jumped in his jaw. In three swift movements, he was up on his knees, readied, and down again.

She stretched out luxuriously under him, every inch covered by his hot, impassioned body. His mouth clamped over hers and they melded together in a long, fevered kiss.

He tasted of heat and forbidden things.

He tasted of desire and love, and everything she'd ever wanted.

"Spread your legs for me, angel. I want to come home."

She hooked one knee over his butt and the other over his thigh, and wrapped her arms around his back. He slid all the way into her, long and thick, and she trembled at how very right he felt there.

"You're mine," he whispered hoarsely, holding her close.

"This makes you mine."

"I'm yours for as long as you want me," she affirmed.

She kissed him, letting her tongue and body tell him without words that she was his and would never belong to another man as long as she lived.

He began to move over her, thrusting in and out, building a steady rhythm. Their lips parted and met again, parted and roamed, panting in half-open bliss, hotly whispering words of love. Their bodies slickened, slipping against each other in a moist, satiny heat.

He pumped faster. Plunged harder.

She dug her nails into his back and hung on, burrowing down under him, pressing her cheek against the wildly beating vein in his muscle-corded neck. With each staccato breath she took, she could taste the sweet-musky scent of their coupling, mingled with the salt of his sweat-dampened shoulder.

He drove deeper into her.

Every racking plunge brought his body tighter against her, closer over her, deeper into her, until she was sure their bodies had melded together and become one, burning with hunger. Their voices joined in aching cries of need, of love, seeking the sweet torture of release.

When it came, she ignited in a firestorm of pleasure. She called out his name and he answered with a last powerful, stiff thrust, a harsh cry tearing from his throat.

He collapsed onto her, and she gathered him in her arms, holding him tight. She never wanted to let him go. Never, ever.

She may have to, one day soon. But whatever happened, she would never regret this moment. She knew she was meant to be his. It was absolutely certain that, no matter what the future brought, in her heart she would always belong to Russell Bridger.

Chapter Forty-Nine

B ridge awoke the next morning with Mary Alice's warm body snugged against his, their limbs tangled, her hair draped across the pillow they shared, the sweet scent of strawberries and love filling the air around them.

He sighed contentedly and pulled her close. Last night had been amazing. He had to be the luckiest man on earth to have landed in this position with this generous, passionate woman. Sure, there were still things to work out between them, but this morning he figured life was just about perfect.

Right up until the cell phone rang and Captain Trujillo ordered him downtown to take part in a raid.

Damn.

"Aw, hell, Cap. I just came off a really hard double shift. I didn't get an hour's sleep last night. Give me a break."

Bridge winked at Mary Alice, who had awakened when he reached over her for the phone. Now she lay under him, laughing and trying to stifle the little moans his fingers were causing her to make. He glanced at the clock. Six-oh-five a.m. *Double damn.* He'd been counting on sleeping as long as the perimeter beeper let him.

"Sorry, Bridge. We got a hot tip and we're moving on the Bienvenido Street thing. I knew you wouldn't want to miss it." The cap's voice left little doubt that he had better not want to miss it, if he liked his career.

Bridge blew out a breath and stilled his fingers. He'd been working on that case for sixteen months and it was going down in less than an hour. The captain was right. He'd kick himself if he wasn't part of it. "When do we roll?"

"Seven. Be here and suited up."

"Got it."

Bridge tapped off the cell phone and reinserted it in the pocket of the shirt hanging over the drawer. "Bad news, sweetheart. I have to get to work."

The laughter in her face faded. "So early?"

"Yeah. Big case going down." He gave her a kiss filled with regret. "I'm really sorry."

A thousand questions and emotions shadowed her eyes, but she only said, "It's okay. I understand."

"Of all the damned mornings," he muttered, and pulled her close for a hug.

"Guess I better get used to it, if we…" Her words trailed off.

There wasn't a lot he could say to that, so he kissed her again, then rose to get ready.

He ground his jaw in frustration. *Fucking hell*. This was not remotely what he'd had in mind for the morning after with Mary Alice. He'd expected to have a few more hours before reality intruded—love play and leisure time to cement the relationship they'd truly begun last night. The timing on this bust was just plain rotten.

Last night, he'd shown her graphically how much she could trust him, and that she could rely on him when she put that trust to the test. That good things could, and did, happen when she let go and lost control of what was happening, putting her fate in another's hands—in *his* hands. He only hoped she would make the connection between bed and his job. He'd wanted to explore the concept a bit more before trying it out in a potentially explosive situation.

Like this one.

He grabbed a quick shower, and when he came out to the kitchen, she had made him a thermos of coffee and a sandwich.

"For the road," she said in a thready voice as she put them into his hands. "You need to eat."

He took them gratefully, and said without thinking, "Thanks. You're a lifesaver."

For a second she looked stricken, and he instantly regretted using a word containing any hint of mortality. She tried hard to hide her fear, but it was there, plain as day, making her pretty face ashen.

God, he hated leaving her like this.

"Trust me," he said as he kissed her goodbye at the door. "I'll be fine. I promise."

She nodded. But she didn't believe him. That was also on her face, plain as day.

Damn.

Nothing like trial by goddamn fire.

Chapter Fifty

It wasn't that she didn't trust Bridge, Mary Alice thought miserably at school that afternoon. It was all those criminals and weirdoes out there she didn't trust.

She'd made it through the morning okay. No reason to panic yet, right? But as the hours went by and she still didn't hear from Bridge, she'd gotten more and more worried.

She was valiantly fighting it—the growing anxiety gnawing at her stomach. All day she'd wanted to call or text him to make sure he was okay. As she always had with her dad. But she forbade herself from doing it.

Her calling hadn't helped her dad, or Jack. And she would rather bite off her tongue than ask Bridge to text her every five minutes like some wayward teenager checking in with an overprotective mother.

This was just another day on the job for him. And like she'd said, if she was going to be a part of his life, she'd better get used to it.

But damn, she really, *really* hated this.

Losing the battle, she gave in and wrapped her fingers

around her forehead and squeezed tight.

He would be all right.

He *was* all right.

He had to be. He'd promised, hadn't he?

"Mac, what's wrong?" Nancy slid into a pint-sized chair across from Mary Alice at the craft table she was attempting to set up for tomorrow. "You look like my reflection."

Mary Alice came out from behind her hands and smiled weakly at the attempt at humor from her friend. Nancy had been a total wreck ever since Ben was diagnosed with his brain tumor last week. Mary Alice must really look terrible if even Nancy had noticed.

"That bad, *eh*?" she murmured.

"You tell me," Nancy said. "Things okay with your new man?"

"No. Yes. No." Mary Alice fought to keep her eyes from filling. "Oh, Nan, I don't know whether I'm coming or going."

"Come on," Nancy said, standing. "Let's go get a drink and you can tell your old buddy all about it. Frankly, I could use a stiff one, myself."

It was only three-thirty, but extreme measures seemed justified under the circumstances. And besides, she might just have a nervous breakdown waiting by herself until either Bridge walked back through her door or—

Not going there.

They went to the Fisherman—the place where she and Bridge had bought fresh shrimp to barbecue just a few short days ago. They sat at a quiet table for two, and after listening to Nancy pour out all her terror and feelings of uncertainty about Ben's condition, Mary Alice finally allowed all her own fears spill out into Nancy's sympathetic ear. How she was slowly starting to lose it, how she was petrified Bridge would be hurt or killed, scared to death for him when he'd simply been called in to do his job.

"Strange that we're going through such similar anguish," Nancy said bleakly. "Even though our men have such different jobs."

"It's not fair," Mary Alice said vehemently. "Ben is an accountant, for crying out loud. You shouldn't have to go through this kind of thing."

Nancy slowly shook her head. "It is what it is. At least you have a choice."

Mary Alice nodded miserably. "I do. And I don't think I can take it, Nan," she said with a moan. "I think I'm in love with Bridge. No, I *am* in love with him. But I'm terrified I'll drive myself nuts worrying about him. And make him hate me for it. Last night, everything seemed so perfect. I was ready to face anything to keep him. Now, I'm not so sure I can actually deal with the reality of it."

Nancy gazed at her sympathetically. "I wish I could give you a magic formula to make things easier. But sometimes all you can do is let go and roll with the punches."

Mary Alice watched Nancy refill her wine glass from the carafe they'd ordered, thinking about the major, heartbreaking punches her friend was being forced to roll with these days. "I haven't had much practice rolling," Mary Alice murmured. "Things always seem to knock me down completely. How do you do it?"

Nancy smiled weakly. "If you really love him, you'll find a way to face this. You can do it. You have it in you, Mary Alice. Just reach deep."

"I'll try. But I don't know if I can, Nan," she whispered. "I just don't know."

Chapter Fifty-One

It was after five o'clock when Mary Alice drove the few blocks up the Canyon to the cottage—well past the time Bridge would normally be working his first surveillance shift. Her heart sank. The road crew was gone, and the cut-out was empty of vehicles. She parked and walked dejectedly up the front porch steps, fishing for her key. When she inserted it, the door swung open on its own.

Bridge!

She ran inside and threw her canvas tote bag on the sofa. The kid's digital recorder with Bridge's singing on it spilled out onto the cushion. She'd brought it home from school, thinking that listening to his voice might help calm her nerves.

"Bridge?" she called, peeking into the kitchen. It was empty.

She cocked her head, listening. *There.* She heard the sound of him typing on his laptop in the spare room. Her whole body sagged in relief that he was home and presumably in one piece. She rushed in, only to skid to a crashing halt behind a stranger sitting at the desk.

She screamed.

In one motion, the stranger jumped and turned, slamming the laptop shut and frantically reaching under his arm for a gun that wasn't there.

"Officer Deane! Jesus, Mary, and Joseph, you scared the daylights out of me."

Wild-eyed and bracing an arm on the desk, Jason Deane looked like he might expire on the spot. "Sorry, Miss Flannery. I was, *um*, absorbed in what I was doing and didn't hear you come in. You sort of took me by surprise." He gave a shaky laugh and rubbed his palm on his chest. "Yikes."

"Where's Bridge?"

"Bridge?" The young man grew even paler, if that was possible, and pulled at the collar of his T-shirt. "He, *uh*, well, *um*… That is, we don't rightly know…exactly. I'm here to take his shift." Deane coughed nervously. "Until he turns up."

Every emotion she was feeling must have branded itself on her face, because he looked alarmed and immediately added, "Which he will. I'm sure he'll turn up soon. *Very* soon."

Mary Alice groped her way back to the living room, followed by Deane. She wished she hadn't had that second glass of wine with Nancy. Then again, maybe it was a good thing. Lord knew how she would have reacted if she'd been stone cold sober. Probably would have done something supremely idiotic, like falling into a dead faint.

We don't rightly know?

She drew in a steadying breath. "Officer Deane, I don't know if you are aware of Detective Sergeant Bridger's and my…relationship?"

She paused and he nodded, his ears turning red. His eyes shifted away as he seated himself across from her.

"Please tell me what's going on. How can the Pasadena Police Department *lose* one of its officers?"

She picked up the digital recorder from the sofa and

fiddled nervously with it. Deane studied the device in her hands for a moment, obviously torn about telling her what might still be unreleased information.

Finally, he said, "The raid at Bienvenido Street was only partially successful. The team seized a shit—I mean, a huge stash of cocaine and meth, a bunch of lab equipment, and made a few arrests. But the main guy they were after escaped." Deane glanced away, avoiding her probing gaze.

"And?"

He drilled a hand through his short-cropped hair. "The suspect got in a car and hightailed it. Last they saw Bridge, he'd commandeered an undercover vehicle and taken off after him."

"He—" *Oh, Lord.* Her head spun at the news. "When was this?"

Deane shifted uncomfortably. "Sometime this morning."

She stared at him in increasing horror. Her worst nightmare was coming true. Her lover was going to be killed in a fiery car crash chasing some stupid drug dealer across the whole state of California. "But what about his cell phone?" she asked, grasping desperately at straws. "I know he had it with him this morning."

"They found it on the sidewalk. Must have dropped out of his pocket while he was running. Listen, Miss Flannery. I know you're worried, but really, he'll be okay. Bridge is a pro."

"I know he is, I just—"

Just what?

She didn't want to go into the whole story about her father, her uncle, and Jack all being killed in the line of duty. About how she was on the verge of a nervous breakdown because of her terror that the same thing would happen to Bridge.

"I'm just not used to all this…danger," she said lamely. Her attempt at a smile failed miserably.

Deane waved his hand dismissively. "Aw, heck, this is nothing. Bridge has been in lots worse scrapes. Did he ever tell you about the time he single-handedly surrounded those gang-bangers up on Orange Grove?"

"No. He never did." She dropped her head onto the sofa back, morbid curiosity overtaking her common sense. Deane was only trying to make her feel better, but somehow she knew hearing this was not going to help. She was pretty sure his story wasn't going to involve subduing villains with rainbows and pixie dust.

Deane's mouth split into a big grin. "What a mind!" he said, warming to his subject. "Bridge had the dispatcher patch him through from his cell phone to the two-way radio in his truck. Then he rigged his belt to keep the trigger on the truck's megaphone pushed down while he sneaked around to the back of the convenience store the perps were trying to heist." Deane sounded like he was recapping the latest issue of his favorite superhero comic. "When he was in position, he started shouting out commands from the cell phone through the megaphone in the truck parked out front of the store, and they all started blasting, backing up one by one into the rear storage room—where he was waiting for them."

"Oh, God," Mary Alice whispered. This really *wasn't* helping.

Oblivious, Deane gestured in a vivid illustration of his narrative, a worshipful look on his face. "Bridge just whacked their weapons away and tossed the sleaze-balls into the walk-in freezer. That last bullet just grazed his ribs, really. By the time reinforcements arrived, he'd subdued all five bad guys."

So much for old football injuries. The scar on his side had been from a bullet wound. She should have known. Or maybe she *had* known, but hadn't wanted to.

A *bullet* wound.

She squeezed her eyes shut against a flood of emotions.

By the time Deane had regaled her with several more stories of Bridge's heroics, she was beyond feeling anything. She was numb with sheer panic. Russell Bridger was nothing less than a loose cannon ready to explode at any second, showing total disregard for correct police procedure, and for his own safety.

Wow. Not only was he a cop, he was the worst kind of cop—one who had no concern for his own life. Wild and reckless.

Selfish.

How had she ever thought for a single second she could deal with this? With him?

A feeble whimper rose in her throat and she got to her feet midway through Deane's tale of a double-timing snitch.

"Excuse me," she said softly, barely noticing the astonishment in the young cop's face as she walked out, gathering her hair up into a tight twist. "I have to take a bath now."

Mechanically, she set aside the recorder she'd forgotten she was still holding and filled the tub to brimming with a warm, soothing bubble bath.

Her heart weighed heavy with the decision she had to make.

Not that there was really any choice. She knew which way it had to go.

But that didn't make it any easier.

Chapter Fifty-Two

The next morning Mary Alice's panic had evened out to a sharp, throbbing ache in her chest.

Bridge still hadn't come back, but he had managed to get a message through. Late last night he'd exchanged cars at breakneck speed in a gas station along the freeway heading east, thrusting the keys of the undercover car with an empty tank into the hands of the stunned owners of a tanked-up Jeep, along with his card carrying a message scribbled on the back directing them to call the PPD.

Deane related all this over breakfast with a guarded look on his face, as if he feared the news might push her over some invisible edge she was balanced on.

He wasn't far wrong.

Mary Alice was proud of how calmly she took it. Somewhere during the endlessly long, sleepless night she'd realized that, once again, she had to be the strong one. She could not let this defeat her.

Somehow she would go on living...even without Russell Bridger in her life.

For the rest of the day, blessedly, she would be required to think about something else. Tomorrow the whole board of directors of the Pasadena Historical Rose Society would be at the cottage to meet her, to inspect and document the two roses that were up for inclusion in their registry. So, today after school she had to clean and bake, and make sure the garden was ship-shape for the inspection.

She sighed and drained her coffee, forcing herself to pick up her canvas tote and go to work as usual. For the first time in years, she didn't look forward to seeing the shining, smiling faces of the children. Even the prospect of hearing Ivy's few, precious words shyly spoken didn't shake her out of her indigo mood. Thank goodness it was nearly the weekend. Then she could hibernate without having to face a soul except Deane, who'd gotten pretty good about keeping out of her way.

Unless Bridge showed up.

What would she do when he did?

If he did.

After a stunt like he'd pulled, he couldn't possibly think they had a future together. Not in a million years. Not knowing how much she worried about him. Surely, he'd totally understand why she had to put a stop to this madness right now—before they got in any deeper.

Deane had more news of Bridge when he got to her house after his shift on the road crew that evening. The Bienvenido Street suspect had taken to the desert, apparently heading for an established hide-out. Bridge had lost him in the web of little-used dirt tracks outside of Amboy, and had used a borrowed cell phone to call Trujillo and to arrange for the local sheriff's office to join the hunt and help track the man. They hoped to end up with a storehouse full of product, and enough evidence to bury the perp behind bars.

Once again, Mary Alice stared at the ceiling all night.

Was Bridge lying dead somewhere out in the desert at

this very moment, a bullet in his back and buzzards feasting on his dead body?

She was more convinced than ever that her decision to end their relationship was the right one. Although outwardly calm, she hadn't slept, and had hardly eaten since he'd been gone. Her body couldn't take much more of this kind of punishment. It would be better by far never to know the kind of danger he was putting himself into.

Even if it meant that she would never again know the loving freedom of his arms.

Chapter Fifty-Three

D espite Mary Alice's preoccupation, Friday's meeting with the Rose Society's board went well. Mrs. Underwood, Mrs. Wyeth, and the delightful Miss Beadle gushed over her, and exclaimed their genuine dismay at Bridge's absence.

"Oh, whatever shall we do?" Mrs. Underwood cried. "We had counted on him to take pictures of the proceedings." She glanced in consternation at the small point-and-shoot camera dangling from her hand. "I'm quite sure I would cut off everyone's head if I tried to take them."

Mary Alice chuckled, waving a hand over the fence at Jose and Enrico, who were driving up Charlie Watson's driveway in their dilapidated gardening truck. *Damn*. She'd forgotten all about the lawn. It didn't get mowed since Bridge hadn't been around to do it. Thank goodness the ladies hadn't seemed to notice.

She deliberately returned her attention to the situation at hand. "I'd be happy to take the photos, Mrs. Underwood,"

"But Mary Alice, you should be in the pictures," countered Miss Beadle. "And what a shame your young man won't be in any of them," she added with a mischievous wink.

"Yes," Mary Alice said wistfully. "What a shame."

Miss Beadle looked at her with a hint of concern, but just then Mrs. Underwood said, "Very well," and thrust the camera into Mary Alice's hands.

The meeting was brought to order. Most everything would be done outdoors that day, so she led everyone over to the newly refurbished rose arbor, and the formal proceedings started. Introductions and announcements were made, and Mary Alice took a series of photos featuring the whole group as well as individuals during the subsequent tour of the garden.

"Everything is so lovely," Mrs. Wyeth said, beaming at her over a budding Clotilde Soupert bush. "Where did you get that beautiful old arbor? It wasn't here last time, was it?"

"No, it wasn't. Bridge restored it for me last weekend." She looked at it and could barely keep the tears from filling her eyes. "I'll be sure to tell him you like it."

Miss Beadle gave a huff. "My dear, come and show me the climber you've started over here by the fence," she admonished, leading her away from the group. "And tell me whatever is wrong. No, no, don't pretend with me," she scolded when Mary Alice started to protest. "I can tell. It's something about your fiancé, isn't it? You're worried about him, aren't you?"

"Yes." Unable to deny it, Mary Alice lined up and shot a photo of the kindly old woman as she steadied her voice to speak. "You see, he's a— That is, he's been on a very dangerous work assignment the past few days. I haven't heard from him."

"Oh, dear. That is worrisome. But he struck me as being a very competent fellow. I'm sure he's fine."

Just then, Jose the gardener appeared at the fence. "*Señorita* Flannery, we should do your lawn today?"

"Oh, hi, Jose. We'll be a few more minutes in the garden,

but if you're still here when we go into the house, I'd really appreciate it."

"*Si*, sure thing." He smiled and melted back onto Watson's property.

"Your neighbor has some beautiful water lilies," Miss Beadle commented, peering over at Charlie's pond where Enrico was up to his calves in the murky water pulling out dead pads.

"*Mmm-hm*. We have sort of a rivalry going over our favorite flowers," Mary Alice said with a wan smile. "Naturally, my roses are winning. Well, shall we call the committee inside for some refreshments?"

"Oh, yes! Let's do."

Mary Alice showed everyone into the house, placing the camera on the mantle on her way to the kitchen. She should be elated the selection process was over and her two-year dream of having Mrs. Trent's roses included in the registry was finally coming true.

One more thing on her Master Plan for a Perfect Life was nearly completed. Now she could move on to the next item on the list, which was to find a nice choir to join—to help fill the long evenings. And then start researching that dog.

But the whole Master List thing suddenly didn't seem nearly as important as it had for the past three years. It felt hollow. Empty.

And she knew exactly why.

Because Bridge wouldn't be there to share her life...so things would never be perfect, no matter how many items she crossed off that damn list.

Chapter Fifty-Four

The desert sun rose on Bridge's third day away from Mary Alice, and he gratefully soaked in its warming rays. He pulled his thin police jacket closer to his body and shivered. Most people thought the desert was always hot. Obviously, they hadn't spent the night lying on a rocky promontory with their teeth chattering so loud they were terrified the scumbag hiding out in the ancient prospector's hut down the arroyo would hear and come out shooting.

Damn good thing he and the rest of the local police would be moving in any minute now.

He thought about Mary Alice, and wondered how she was taking this whole situation. When he'd walked out the door that morning three days ago, he'd never expected to be gone this long, nor to be involved in one of the weirdest episodes in his entire career. She was probably worried.

He cringed mentally. *Worried, hell*. She was probably going to kill him. He hoped she was, anyway. Anger would be far preferable to the debilitating stress and anxiety he remembered his mother going through.

But he knew Mary Alice was stronger than that. He'd seen himself how strong she could be. He just had to pray she wouldn't crack on him. Not before he could get back and help her through it.

With any luck he'd be home in time for the party at Watson's tonight.

With any luck she was still speaking to him. And still wanted him.

The sheriff gave a signal, and the deputies that had surrounded the shack started moving in. Bridge drew his weapon and took aim.

He wanted a life with Mary Alice so badly it hurt. He'd do anything to make sure they had one.

He didn't want to have to choose between the job he loved and the woman he'd come to realize he loved even more. But he'd do it in a heartbeat.

And there wasn't a question in his mind which one he'd choose.

Chapter Fifty-Five

Mary Alice stared into the bathroom mirror and sighed in disgust. No amount of make-up was going to hide the ravages the past three days had wrought on her face. Drawn and tired, fine lines surrounded her mouth and dark circles sagged under her eyes. She looked ten years older. The very last thing she wanted to be doing right now was going to a party.

She couldn't believe she'd let herself be talked into this. Lord knew what she would tell Charlie when she showed up at his door with Special Agent Sam Grayson in tow instead of Bridge. But it had to be good, so her neighbor wouldn't suspect anything. At first she'd objected to Grayson coming with her—after all, she'd never even had a boyfriend before, and suddenly she was surrounded by men. Charlie was going to wonder. But Captain Trujillo had convinced her it was critical to the operation, so she'd relented.

Sighing, she gave one last tug on her miniskirt, which she'd paired with a silk camisole for the party. Maybe if she got him to look at her legs he wouldn't notice the fatigue in her face.

Or the guilt, at bringing an FBI agent into his home. She still wasn't quite convinced he could be a traitor selling government secrets to China.

The party was already in full swing when she and Sam finally got there at ten o'clock. Mary Alice had hoped to slip in unnoticed, but Charlie spotted her immediately and hurried over, giving her a floor-lifting hug.

"Darling! I'm so glad you made it. I've been watching for you and— Well, well. What have we here? Where's Russ?" He eyed Grayson up and down, brows lifted.

"Out of town. This is Sam. He's…an old college friend." She tried to ignore Charlie's assessing gaze.

"I see. Well," he swept a hand toward the crowds of people gathered around the built-in bar next to the pool, "make yourself at home, Sam. I'm going to get Mary Alice a drink."

With a shrug, Mary Alice allowed herself to be led away from the FBI agent. So far, so good. It was her job to keep Charlie occupied while Sam did what he called a plain-sight search of the house.

"You're looking very sexy this evening," Charlie whispered in her ear, startling her out of her thoughts.

"Thank you," she mumbled, scooting quickly around the corner of the bar and nabbing an empty stool. Surely, that hadn't been his hand on her bottom?

"I must say, you've changed in the last few weeks. I don't know what Russ did to cause it, but I'm hoping I'll be eternally grateful. Is he out of the picture, then?"

She realized she'd made a big mistake by sitting when she felt his hand settle warmly on her knee. She tried to swing away from it but only succeeded in pressing her other thigh up against his trousers. "*Um*, no. He's not out of the picture, just out of town."

Charlie's hand crept up an inch. "And what about the other one? The young guy that took his place?" Another inch.

"On the road crew. The one I saw sneaking out of your house at an ungodly hour this morning." He leered.

She swallowed and folded her hands across her lap to prevent his from traveling any farther up her thigh. "Jason? Oh, *um*, he, *uh*, had a fight with his girlfriend. Bridge said he could sleep on the couch while he was gone."

"How very generous. And how long will Mr. Bridger be gone?"

She looked around nervously. "I was actually expecting him back by now. He was looking forward to the party." She spied several couples dancing poolside and grabbed his hand before he could do any more mischief. "Anyway. Would you like to dance?"

To her surprise, Sam Grayson was also on the dance floor, with a cute Asian brunette wrapped around him. Mary Alice sent a glower his way. What was he doing? He should be busy breaking into wall safes or something.

After two dances, Sam still hadn't budged from the brunette, and Mary Alice was getting royally tired of fending off Charlie, so she pleaded nature and slipped into the house. Worried he'd follow, she ducked through the first door she came upon. It opened onto the landing of a set of wooden stairs leading down to the bottom floor of the house, where the garage was located.

"Oh, great. Just where I needed to end up. The creepy garage." She jumped when the lights snapped on automatically, then rolled her eyes at her own skittishness. She took a few steps down the stairs and surveyed her surroundings.

It was a huge, super-high-ceilinged, three-car garage, pristine white, adorned with a blue and white marine power cruiser resting on a trailer in the far bay, and a perfectly polished candy-apple-red Porsche convertible parked just below her. Not a grease spot in sight.

Okay, maybe not so creepy.

She descended the stairs and looked around.

"No weekend mechanic, our Mr. Watson," she murmured, running her finger along the hood of the shiny red car. She strolled over to the other side and gazed up at the boat, admiring the spotless white hull and gleaming chrome of the railings.

"I can't imagine what Charlie wants with a boat," she murmured to nobody in particular. He'd never taken it out that she'd seen. Though hadn't he mentioned he intended to next week? "*Hmm*. I wonder…"

She walked around the trailer, looking for a way to get up to the deck. "Not a chance," she muttered, glancing down at her mini-skirt, hose and high heels. She turned and rested her hand consideringly on the Porsche. "But maybe…"

She doubted she'd find anything incriminating in the car, but what the hell, she could at least take a quick look through the glove compartment. Grayson sure as heck wouldn't be getting around to it. "You never know, right?"

The top was down, so she leaned over the passenger door and fiddled with the glove compartment lock. It sprang open.

Bingo. She rooted through the contents—maps, a packet of tissues, a flashlight. No microfilm, thumb drives, or secret spy documents. Not even a gun or silencer. Well, what did she expect? The man was hardly likely to—

"Busted, Flannery," a gravelly voice said behind her at the same time a large hand clamped over her mouth.

She gasped, struggling to right herself, but a powerful arm across her back kept her hanging in her undignified pose, draped over the Porsche's door.

"I'd tell you to assume the position but I kinda like the one you're in."

"Bridge!" His hand left her mouth and helped her up just as the overhead lights automatically clicked off. "Oh, Bridge, you're back. Thank God."

She whirled and threw her arms around him. Never mind that she had to tell him she never wanted to see him again. He was here now—*alive!*—and that was all that mattered.

She breathed deeply of his wonderful, masculine scent and met his eager lips with her own. He crushed her to his chest, pouring his wet, delicious kisses like honey into her mouth. Her knees went weak and her breasts tightened with craving for his touch.

"Angel, angel, I missed you so much. I thought about you every second I was gone." He kissed her cheeks, her ears, her eyes, her lips.

"I thought I'd go mad. I was so worried—"

"*Shhh.* I'm here now, baby." His hand slipped under her camisole and cupped her breast, his fingers tugging aside the lacy wisp that encased it. "You feel so damned good," he whispered into her mouth.

Her moan turned to a gasp when he gently thumbed the aching tip. Slipping a thin strap over her shoulder, he bent his head and feasted on her soft flesh, and she thought she'd die of bliss.

She melted in his arms, trying desperately to remember what she had to tell him. "Bridge, we have to talk."

"Later. Right now I need to feel your heat around me." His hands slid under her bottom and lifted, carrying her to the front of the car. From the windows in the garage doors, moonlight pooled like a spotlight on the shiny hood where he deposited her.

"But someone might—"

"When I saw you, I locked the door to the house. Just try not to scream too loud." A roguish grin flashed in the dim light.

He tipped her onto her back, and she felt herself being stripped of shoes and panties. "Russell Bridger, you can't be serious," she whispered, scandalized.

Warm silk whispered by her ear and after a moment she heard the rustle of foil.

"What's the matter? Never made love on the hood of a car before?"

"Certainly n—" Her eyes widened in shock, as vivid as the memories of her fantasy dreams. The dreams that had started this whole crazy attraction with Bridge. "That is—"

Scrunching her skirt up to her waist, he parted her legs and loomed over her, his eyes glittering in the moonlight. "Yes?" he teased. The long, hard column of his arousal rubbed between her thighs. "So, I'm not the first?"

She swallowed, her body quickening to the fantasy. "I had dreams. About you." The slippery, erotic motion of his slow, slick massage sent tremors tumbling through her. "The night after that first day I saw you on the road crew holding that silly stop sign, I dreamed of you…"

A low rumble came from his chest and his voice roughened. "Tell me what I did in your fantasies, so I can make them come true."

He flicked open her bra, and her breasts spilled free for his caresses. She arched under his hands. He could light her on fire with a mere word, but his searing touch made her forget even her own name.

"Tell me," he coaxed.

She closed her eyes and took a deep breath. "You made me stop my car with that stupid stop sign. You had no shirt on."

He grabbed his T-shirt and ripped it off, flinging it on top of her pantyhose. "What did I do?"

"You leaned through the window. You were a little sweaty and smelled so good, like a real man. I hadn't been close to a man in so long…" She moaned longingly. "Then you kissed me."

"Like this?" He tugged her up and wound a hand in her

hair, urging her head back. His lips covered hers and his tongue slipped into her mouth, taking her breath away completely.

When they came up for air, she moaned. "*Mmm*, just like that. I wanted you to kiss me all over, everywhere. You opened the car door and pulled me out."

He kissed a trail down her throat. "And?"

"Then you stripped off all of my clothes."

He gave an appreciative grunt, and slipped her camisole up over her head. "There, in front of everyone?" It and her bra joined the growing pile of clothes next to her. "My, I am a naughty boy."

"No," she laughed, then drew in a sharp breath when his mouth closed over one nipple, his fingers over the other. "It was dark by then, and we were all alone. You lifted me onto the hood of my car." His suckling grew more ardent. She let out a ragged whimper, leaning back on her hands, offering herself up for his enjoyment. And her own. "The air was chilly on my naked body, but the metal of the car hood was warm. Your hands were so warm, too. Touching me all over, caressing me, stroking me."

She let him press her down onto the Porsche and lay back as he acted out her words, his mouth and tongue working over her in sensual torture. She moaned, writhing under his hands.

"You were so hot," she said, panting breathlessly. "I could see you—big and hard. I never knew a man could be so huge."

"This big?" he urged hoarsely as he covered her, fitting the hot length of his cock to the apex of her parted thighs.

She cried out when he thrust home, but he captured the sound in his mouth and fed it back to her as his own, and thrust again. She wrapped her legs around his lean waist and shivered in ecstasy, sandwiched between the slick, shiny wax of the hood and the iron hard muscle of his torso. He moved over her, driving in and out, slowly at first, then faster and faster, making them both gasp for air.

He felt so good, so right, she nearly wept.

How could she ever give him up?

He rode her like there would be no tomorrow, and she kissed him like this would be the very last time they would ever make love. And as the heat and ecstasy overtook them and they both shot over the edge of oblivion in each other's arms, she cried out again.

Because she knew this *would* be the very last time.

Chapter Fifty-Six

"**O**h, woman."

Bridger let out a half-groan, half-chuckle and handed her the packet of tissues he'd confiscated from the glove compartment. "Just look at what you've done to me. Standing in somebody else's garage, making love with my pants around my ankles like some oversexed teenager."

For a man who hadn't gotten any sleep in nearly four days he felt pretty damned good.

He looked down at Mary Alice and wished like hell he had a camera. Her creamy white skin glowed pearlescent in the puddle of moonbeams lapping at her neck and breasts, highlighted perfectly by the dark backdrop of the cherry-red car hood that matched her kiss-stung lips. Pale ringlets of hair surrounded her shadowed face, sparkling in the dim light spilling in from the garage window.

He sighed, blessing the day he was born to see such a beautiful sight. The words just slipped out. "I'm crazy in love with you, Mary Alice Flannery, and I'm going to spend the rest of the night proving it."

"Oh, Bridge," she whispered, sounding so sorrowful a whip of foreboding prickled at his scalp.

She reached up and delicately touched his chest with the tips of her fingers. He caught them and brought them to his lips, kissing the soft pads one by one. He saw the glimmer of a tear slide down her cheek, and his heart lodged in his throat.

He pulled her up and wrapped his arms around her, cradling her in his embrace. "Angel? What's wrong?"

Her body was still warm from their lovemaking, and he squeezed his eyes shut and breathed deeply, wanting to memorize the feel and smell of her. He figured he knew what was coming, and he wanted to roar in protest.

"You are everything I've ever wanted," she murmured into his neck, and he could feel her hot tears trickle onto his shoulder.

Already, he could feel her pulling away from him emotionally. "But?"

"But the past few days have been hell, wondering if you were lying hurt somewhere. Or worse. Bridge, I just can't do this."

"Oh, no. No, baby—" His heart stalled as the finality of her tone and her statement hit him.

Never to hold her again. Never to walk with her, laugh with her.

Impossible.

He had to talk her out of this terrible idea. He couldn't stand it if she really meant what she was saying. "You can't intend to just walk away from me? From everything we have, everything we've come to mean to each other?"

For several moments she was silent while he rocked her back and forth in his arms, praying for some kind of miracle. Praying she'd change her mind. When she finally spoke, he could barely hear her.

"We should never have started. I knew this would happen. We both did. If I don't leave now, I'll end up driving you away with my worrying."

"But you don't have to worry. Trust me, Mary Alice. You trusted me when we made love the other night. You can trust me about this, too." He held her away from his chest and grasped her arms, looking at her intently. "I won't take any chances on the job, not anymore. I swear. I told you, I'm very good at what I do."

Gazing at him, she smiled bleakly. "I know you're a good cop, Bridge. The problem's not with you. It's with me. I just don't make a good cop's girlfriend."

"I'll quit, then," he blurted out recklessly, meaning every word. If that's what it took to keep her, he was more than willing to do it.

"No!" She shook her head and tightened her arms around him. "I know how much your job means to you. I would never forgive myself if you gave it up for me. And you wouldn't forgive me, either. Maybe not right away, but eventually you would resent it—and me."

"My captain has been trying to give me a promotion. To lieutenant, and a desk job. It'll be better when I'm—"

"No, Bridge. I have to be strong in this. For both our sakes. Have you forgotten about your mother? Your promise to her?"

He let out a measured breath, stroking Mary Alice's hair. How could he explain how fundamentally different she was from his mother? As he'd gotten to know Mary Alice, he'd become more and more convinced she had plenty enough inner courage to deal with her fears—and his—and come out the victor.

He just had to convince Mary Alice of that.

"If you're going to be strong, angel, be strong *with* me, not against me. We can do this if we work together. I know we can. Don't you even want to try?"

She sniffed, and he felt her breath sough raggedly over his neck.

"I'm sorry," she whispered tearfully. "I can't take the chance. I just can't."

Chapter Fifty-Seven

So be it.

Bridger whipped through three of the five stages of grief he'd learned about in Psych 101, and was now firmly mired in the fourth.

Anger.

But this was no damn stage. He'd be angry for the rest of his life. He didn't need any know-it-all psychologist telling him he'd eventually accept reality. *He* knew he wouldn't. Not. Ever.

He wasn't sure what he wanted most—to get Mary Alice back, or to strangle her for her reluctance to give their relationship a real chance. Either way, for his own peace of mind he had to gain some distance and put himself back on an even keel.

Standing under a storm cloud with a deadly glower carved into his face, he watched her dress, then stomped out of the garage after her. He did a spinning double-take when he spied Sam Grayson hustling some curvy brunette at the buffet table, but figured the feeb must have gotten Mary Alice to let him tag along to the party when Bridge hadn't shown up yet.

Good. That got him off the hook so he could collect his gear from her place and head back to his own apartment for a well-deserved week's worth of sleep. Jason Deane had been assigned to take over for Bridge for a few days while he recuperated from his three-day Bienvenido adventure. He planned to make that a permanent switch.

Ignoring Sam Grayson's surprised look, he strode out Watson's door and into the night.

Screw it all.

Chapter Fifty-Eight

Monday morning Bridge was still angry, but he was channeling it better now that he was somewhat rested. At the station, he stalked into Trujillo's office.

"Take me off the Watson task force," Bridge demanded. When the cap looked at him askance, he added, "Please."

Trujillo steepled his hands on the desk in front of him. "If I do, will you take that promotion to lieutenant?"

Bridger dragged a hand down his haggard face. He'd already decided to accept the promotion. He'd made up his mind a week ago, the first time he and Mary Alice had made love. Subconsciously, he'd known from the beginning where things with her were headed, even if his conscious mind hadn't.

So, why was he suddenly hesitating now?

Because I'll probably end up with the boring job and won't get the girl, anyway.

"Yeah. I'll take it," he heard himself say.

Trujillo pursed his lips. "Damn, you must want off this case pretty bad. What the hell happened?" His eyes narrowed. "Or do I want to know?"

"Not a thing, Cap. I'm just going nuts rattling around in that dinky old cottage with nothing to do all day but walk the perimeter and watch the grass grow. Watson's being super careful. Whatever's going down, I doubt it's happening at his own house. Besides, Deane needs the experience in surveillance. I don't."

The captain studied him for a minute, but apparently decided he looked miserable enough and spared him a cross-examination. "Fine. But I still expect you to back up Officer Deane."

Bridge grunted, then mumbled, "Thanks," and beat it out of Trujillo's office before he could get pinned with any more questions.

At the elevator he was promptly accosted by Grayson. "I want you off the Watson task force, Bridger."

He snorted. "Too late. I already quit."

"You know the rules about conduct unbecoming—" Grayson halted and looked over in astonishment. "Wait. What?"

"I just took myself off the task force. You'll get my final report by end of day." Bridge threw himself into his desk chair and leaned it as far back as it went, stacking his hands behind his head. "And speaking of conduct unbecoming, how'd it go with that brunette I saw you with Saturday night?"

Grayson sputtered. "I'll have you know she's the prime suspect for Watson's go-between with the Chinese. She speaks four languages, including Mandarin and Arabic, and has no VMI."

"Her *means of income* seemed pretty *visible* to me the other night." Bridge gave the red-faced Grayson a snicker. "I hear Deane got photos of all the party-goers as they left. Any other leads?"

The other man straightened his tie. For once the knot wasn't perfectly square, and Bridge wondered idly if the pressure was finally getting to him. "Yeah," Grayson said. "We got a couple good leads we're following up. Chatter says a big money exchange is happening sometime this week. We're counting on it to wrap up the case for us."

"Good. Then you won't miss me."

"Ya think?" Grayson perched on a corner of his desk. "But someone else will. Listen, Bridger, Jason Deane told me what's been going on. It didn't take an FBI special agent to see how upset Miss Flannery was after you left the party Saturday night. Deane's done fine replacing you, and I thought if I took you off the case permanently, things might be easier..." He shrugged.

Bridge's jaw dropped in disbelief. Damn. The man was actually trying to make his life *easier*?

"Being in law enforcement is hard enough," Grayson said, "let alone trying to have a normal relationship, too. Believe me, I've failed often enough to know." He sighed, looking so forlorn Bridger suddenly felt sorry for the man. Hell, he couldn't possibly *like* this guy?

"Thanks, Sam," he said quietly. "I appreciate the thought."

"No problem." Grayson slapped him on the back and turned to go. "By the way, friends call me Gray."

Well. Wonders never ceased. Bridge smiled. "All right, Gray it is."

"Anyway, hope everything works out for you."

"Yeah. Me, too."

Chapter Fifty-Nine

Mary Alice walked somberly through the hospital parking lot and got into her car. She dropped her forehead onto the steering wheel and closed her eyes. Her throat ached with the need to cry, but there were no tears left in her. In the six days since Charlie's party, it seemed as if she'd done nothing but weep.

First over Bridge, now for Nancy and Ben.

Despondent, Mary Alice started her car and pointed it toward home. It was late afternoon, almost quitting time on the road crew. Officer Deane would be at her place soon and he would not be expecting her back today, so she wanted to be in plain sight when he arrived — one gun aimed at her neck was plenty for a lifetime.

She had been staying at Nancy's place again to help her cope since Ben was admitted to the hospital two days earlier after blacking out several times. They were doing more tests to see if surgery on the tumor would even be possible, given its sensitive position in his brain. But today, Nancy had sent her home.

Mary Alice sighed deeply, thinking about Ben. They were bringing in a specialist from another hospital, but while the doctors were arguing, Ben's health was deteriorating fast. The prognosis was bleak.

Mary Alice had tried to comfort Nancy, helping her through the days, minute by minute, as her friend had done for her three years ago. But getting Nancy to eat or sleep was next to impossible.

Not that Mary Alice had much use for those activities herself.

She missed Bridge with a physical longing that was all-consuming. Even in her darkest moments with Nancy, she still couldn't forget him. Like Ben's tumor, she feared her sorrow was untreatable, and she was destined to slowly waste away until there was nothing left of her but a shadow.

Like Ben.

Ben, the *accountant*.

Ben, who had the safe, comfortable, benign life of a man whose most dangerous activity was making a bad stock trade, or walking across Baldwin Avenue to get a sandwich at the deli for lunch.

Gazing up at the purple mountains towering over her small hometown, Mary Alice finally accepted the certain knowledge that had crept into her heart as softly and quietly as the clouds that drifted over the distant peaks.

A cop couldn't be taken from this world any faster or more surely than Nancy's Ben was being taken from her at this very moment.

Nice, gentle, safe Ben.

Chapter Sixty

The construction had finally moved past Mary Alice and Watson's houses while she'd been at Nancy's, so she turned into her driveway and parked. She inhaled a long breath and looked around. She frowned when she spotted a stranger holding the stop sign out on the crew. She couldn't see Officer Deane anywhere.

Well, maybe they'd given him the day off. The poor kid had been pulling double and sometimes twenty-four hour shifts since Bridge had gone chasing off last week.

On the other hand, according to Deane, the task force had been convinced Watson would be exchanging the stolen data drives for cash payment by today, so maybe it had already happened and she'd find a note that Deane had moved out.

That would suit her fine. She didn't feel like having company.

Unless it was Bridge.

But Bridge wouldn't ever be coming back. He hadn't phoned her since the party. Or even texted. *Nothing*. She would do anything to hear his voice right now, but the best she could hope for was listening to the recording of him and the kids singing that she hadn't been able to bring herself to return to school.

Walking onto the porch, she noticed the front door was slightly ajar. Her heart leapt with hope.

"Bridge?" She flung open the door and ran inside. "Bridge, is it you?"

There was someone in the living room. Gasping in surprise, she slammed to a stop, right in front of the large man who greeted her.

"Hello, Mary Alice," he said, reaching out to grasp her arms.

She clutched her canvas tote bag to her chest in sudden fear. "Charlie!"

Heaven help her, he must have found out about the surveillance.

"What are you doing in my house?" she demanded. "How did you get in?" She tried to back away from her neighbor, but he held her arms firmly in his painful grip.

"I thought we were friends, Mary Alice."

"Of course we're friends. I don't know what you mean," she said, playing for time. Bridge had said the man was a dangerous criminal, a traitor to his own country. But this was Charlie, her *neighbor*. He wouldn't hurt her.

Would he?

He sighed wearily, and pulled her by the arm over to the sofa where he pushed her down to sit. "I'm very disappointed in you. I had hoped"—he shrugged—"well, that perhaps we would become even better friends. And then I find out you are spying on me."

She sat forward, her heart beating an anxious tattoo. "No! It wasn't me. They didn't give me a choice, Charlie. Please, what are you going to do?"

Casting around nervously for a clue to his intentions,

her gaze skittered onto the photos from the Historical Rose Society meeting last Friday that she had printed out to give to Miss Beadle. They were now strewn across the coffee table instead of sitting neatly on the mantle as she'd left them.

He tipped his head and mimicked hitting on a new idea. "Perhaps we can become better friends, after all. How would you like to go on a little trip with me?"

Tentacles of alarm crawled up her arms. She rubbed her hands up and down the rising goose flesh. "A trip? I don't think so. I've got work, and—"

"I'm afraid you leave me no alternative, Mary Alice. These photos…" His voice trailed off as he pushed a finger through the scattered stack. "Clever. Very clever."

She frowned, staring at the pictures of Mrs. Underwood, Mrs. Wyeth, Miss Beadle, and the other board members posing in her garden. "I don't understand. What have they got to do with anything?"

He narrowed his eyes suspiciously at her. "Don't play dumb with me, sweet cakes. I know you and that bastard cop have it all figured out. But I'm afraid your plans to arrest me won't work."

She shook her head, truly at a loss. "I don't know what you mean. Officer Deane doesn't confide in me."

"I wasn't talking about him," Charlie snapped.

She bit down on her bottom lip, getting more frightened by the second. "He will be here any minute, you know—Officer Deane. He won't let you take me anywhere."

Watson smirked. "Pack a bag, Mary Alice. We leave in five minutes. Deane, you take care of the laptop?"

Mary Alice gasped as she turned. The young cop strolled out of the hall, nodding. "Officer Deane! What—?" She broke off, unable to credit what seemed to be happening.

"I'm sorry, Miss Flannery." Jason Deane stopped by the coffee table, shifting his feet, and glanced at her uncomfortably.

"The money… I couldn't make this much money working for ten years on the force."

Her head spun. Deane? A dirty cop? "I can't believe you'd do this."

"Believe it, sweet cakes." Charlie rose as Deane scooped up the photos. "Now, go pack your make-up and a bikini. Where we're going, you won't be needing anything else."

Chapter Sixty-One

Bridger stood among his mother's roses, his hands jammed in his pockets, contemplating his future.

He was already over thirty, and what did he have to show for it? He glanced over to where his dad was fiddling with a sprinkler head on the lawn. By his age, his dad had made detective, had owned this house for ten years, had his wife die, and was raising an unruly kid all on his own.

By comparison, Bridger's own exploits—on and off the job—seemed selfish, trite, and hollow.

The past week had shown him just how empty his life really was. He missed her terribly—Mary Alice, his red-haired angel. She'd gotten under his skin as he'd thought no woman ever could. He wanted her. He *needed* her. Thoughts of her filled his every waking moment, leaving a black craving in his soul. Like a bad habit he couldn't shake.

But she was no bad habit. She'd been good for him. So very good. And he knew the last thing he wanted was to shake her.

Well, maybe some sense *into* her…

Like a fool, he had let her walk out of his miserable life.

Oh, yeah, Mr. Tough Guy. He'd figured he could do just swell without her. He'd done fine before, and could again. Hell, there were lots of redheads whose skin was silky and body willing.

But he hadn't counted on missing Mary Alice in every way imaginable, and some he never would have thought. From the way she brushed her teeth in the morning to the sound of her silly Snoopy slippers clicking on the floor as she cooked him dinner.

He loved her more than life itself, and he'd just let her walk away.

What a prime idiot.

She hadn't come crawling back, either—hadn't even phoned him. It looked as if she had every intention of staying away from him permanently, just as she'd said she would. Because of his damned job.

The hell of it was, Bridge couldn't blame her. Hadn't he vowed never to get seriously involved because of his job? Tipping back his head, he gazed up at the sky and groaned. Okay, so he'd made the top of the certified list and had told the captain he'd take the jump to lieutenant. But would that make life so much safer that Mary Alice would give him another chance?

Did it even give him the right to ask?

"Looks like you've got the weight of the universe on your shoulders, son."

He looked over at his dad, who stood beside him, vise grips and a broken sprinkler in his hand.

"I'm up for lieutenant," he said.

"Hey, congratulations! Finally came to your senses, *eh*?"

A smile tugged at Bridge's mouth. The old man had nagged him almost as much as the cap had. "Yeah, I guess. Couldn't turn down the big bucks."

His dad grinned, then grew serious. "What's the problem, then?"

Bridge scanned the horizon. "No problem." The quick upward movement of his dad's bushy eyebrows caught his eye.

Much too casually, his dad said, "So. How's it going with that young woman you're seeing? When do I get to meet her?"

Bridger chuffed out a breath. "She left me."

His dad nearly choked in surprise. "Well, that's a switch. Tough break, son."

"Yeah."

"You want her back?"

"Yeah." Bridge shot a hand through his hair. "Hell, I don't know. I shouldn't."

"Why not?"

"I've got no right."

His dad cocked his head, crossing his arms in front of his chest. "On account of what?" Concern limned his voice. It was the old good-cop routine.

What the hell, Bridge could spill with the best of them. "Mary Alice doesn't want to end up like Mama. Worrying herself to death waiting for me to eat a bullet, or worse."

The old man's face blanched.

Bridge sighed. "I understand. I've always said I didn't want a woman waiting at home for me, going slowly catatonic." Let alone a kid who had to deal with it all.

"Listen, Russell. About your mom." His dad took a deep breath and let it out through his nose, staring vacantly at a cat that trotted along the top of the fence. "I, *uh*…. There's something you should know about what happened to your mother."

Bridge's cop instincts perked up when his dad swiped a hand over his face and looked around—at anywhere but at him. Bridge waited silently, his pulse notching upward. What the hell?

"I loved her, you know that," his dad said.

Bridge nodded. "Of course."

"There were some things you were just too young to understand. And, somehow, over the years, well… I've just never found the right time to talk about it."

It was Bridge's turn to fold his arms over his chest. He peered at his father, waiting for the boom to fall.

"It's true, she worried when I went out. And when I was gone for days on end. But it wasn't because she was afraid I'd be gunned down."

Bridge scowled in confusion. "What are you saying, Dad?"

"I—"

His dad let out a groan and turned away, as if unable to bear meeting his eyes. "I cheated on her. Every time I did, I swore it wouldn't happen again. Then, I'd walk out the door and it would. She wouldn't leave me, because of you, but she couldn't handle it. When she got sick, she must have figured it didn't matter if she got better. She just let the depression take over. And I've had to live with myself ever since." He looked down. "It hasn't been easy."

Bridge watched, stunned, as his dad took several steps into the rose garden, away from him, and swallowed.

"You're telling me…?"

When his father turned back, his eyes were wet with tears of regret. "I'm telling you it was my own damn selfishness that wore her down, not my job. Me being a cop had nothing to do with it."

Chapter Sixty-Two

An hour later, Bridge was storming down the sidewalk a block from the station, still trying to walk off the betrayal roiling in his stomach. He stopped in mid-stride in front of an old-fashioned plate glass storefront. Involuntarily, his eyes were drawn to a display of gold bands against a blue velvet background.

Oh, God.

His heart hurt so much he unconsciously reached up and rubbed it.

All these years *his own father* had lied to him.

Lied to him.

Lies that had caused Bridge to push away love and relationships because he was too afraid of what might happen should any woman get too close.

He didn't want to think about the untold regrets that might have been in store for him if his father hadn't found the courage to confess his lies. And he knew the reason he'd done it, too.

Mary Alice.

As long as Bridge had been happy, his father had kept

up the pretense, the deception. But when he saw that his only son was miserable, and all because of his deception, he'd owned up to what he'd done—regardless of the consequences to their father-son relationship. Bridge knew eventually he'd have to find the strength to forgive his dad. But he'd deal with those feelings later.

Right now, he had to fight his way through the morass of emotions clutching at his guts, and figure out what to do about Mary Alice.

Not that there was any question in his mind.

He refocused his gaze on the gold rings displayed in the window before him. Deep down, he'd known all along what he wanted. This new information just eliminated any reservations he'd about trying.

He'd get down on his knees and beg if he had to. Then it would be up to Mary Alice whether she could accept the risks.

Before he had a chance to change his mind, he strode to his car and drove to her house. He was in luck, her car was parked in the driveway.

"Mary Alice!" he shouted as he burst through the un-locked door. "Where are you?"

The house echoed with silence.

Odd.

Uneasiness crawled up his spine. He would've heard if the Watson case had been solved, so Officer Deane should be here, at the very least. "Deane?" he called hesitantly, his inner alarms screaming.

Instinctively, he drew his weapon.

The answering quiet coiled about his nerves like a venomous serpent. The skin pricked at the back of his neck.

Throwing caution to the wind, he pounded through the house, pitching open doors and calling Mary Alice's name.

He found nothing and nobody.

Ice slowly filled his veins and he made a calmer search,

checking every possible place of concealment. There were no signs of a struggle, but Mary Alice's dresser drawers had been left open, their contents disheveled and hanging over the sides. The closet door was gaping wide. In his time with her he couldn't accuse her of being a neat freak, but she would never have left her room this messy.

He hurriedly checked the FBI equipment in the spare room. It had all been shut down or disassembled. His laptop sat on the desk, its lid closed.

Pursing his lips, he fingered the black plastic. He flipped up the lid and turned on the computer, frowned, and quickly punched a few keys. The hard drive had been wiped clean. There wasn't a byte of data or software left on it.

He scowled. Thinking furiously, he walked back to the living room and carefully scanned it for any clue as to what had gone down. The question kept screaming inside his brain, over and over.

Where is Mary Alice? Where the hell is she?

He would not panic. He would not.

He'd be calm and professional about this, methodically eliminating the possibilities one by one, so he wouldn't look like a fool or an hysterical paranoid when he called Grayson.

Like hell.

He *was* a fool and a hysterical paranoid, and he couldn't afford to waste a second.

He whipped out his cell phone.

Suddenly, his frantic gaze snagged on a photo that sat half-concealed under the vase of roses in the middle of the coffee table. Reaching for it, he examined the printed photo. Miss Beadle of the Historical Rose Society beamed back at him. He pushed out a frustrated sigh and was about to toss it back onto the table when his eye snagged on something in the picture's background.

Oh, shit.

Oh, *holy fucking shit.*

Chapter Sixty-Three

Mary Alice swallowed down another bout of nausea. She was locked up in the cabin of Watson's boat. It was rocking, and she could hear the sound of waves sloshing against the hull. But it wasn't seasickness causing her stomach to roil.

It was blind fear.

How had he managed to haul the boat from Pasadena to the marina and launch it without the police noticing? Surely, someone—

But of course, with Officer Deane in his pocket and assigned to watch him, no one would ever find out.

She looked frantically around the boat's small salon, hoping to find something that would help her out of this mess. A phone, a baseball bat, hell, at this point she'd even welcome a gun. *Anything* that would allow her to escape the clutches of her neighbor and Jason Deane in one piece.

Charlie had promised he'd let her go when they reached Mexico, that he only wanted a little insurance for the trip. But she didn't believe him. Not for a nanosecond. And even if he did eventually let her go, his eyes told her he had other plans in mind for her before he did.

She'd just as soon skip the whole unpleasant ordeal.

The cabin was depressingly bare. The boat's long stint in Watson's garage must have rendered things such as spear guns or even forks and knives unnecessary. She fought a rising panic.

She still couldn't believe what was happening. Deane had always seemed so straight and narrow. Even Bridge had trusted him.

Bridge.

Tears sprang to her eyes. Where was he now? Did he know she'd been spirited off to parts unknown, against her will?

No. How could he? He'd gotten himself taken off the task force, and he had no other reason to call her.

She'd made sure of that.

A tear slipped over her lashes and trailed down her cheek. *Why, oh, why had she pushed him away?*

She had made a terrible mistake. On so many levels.

It didn't matter if Bridge was a cop, or an accountant, or a test pilot, or a zoo keeper. She loved him and would worry about him regardless of what job he had. He could be an ice cream man and she'd worry about him getting frostbite.

It was too ironic that it was now her *own* life in danger—and specifically because she'd refused to be involved with a cop.

She drew a hand across her wet cheeks and bit her lower lip. Without Bridge, her life was empty. She knew that now. Denying their love had nothing to do with being strong, and everything to do with hiding from pain and uncertainty. Ben's fatal prognosis had shown her there was no point in hiding. Death could find you anytime, anywhere.

Just look at her present situation. Wasn't she the poster

child for safe and secure—a nursery school teacher with a carefully constructed Master Plan For A Perfect Life? Just look at that awesome plan now. It didn't mean shit, when push came to shove.

Hugging her canvas tote to her chest, she rose on wobbly legs and scrutinized the cabin. She had to get out of there. There must be a way.

She had to get off the boat, because she needed to find Bridge and beg him to forgive her and come back.

After what she'd done, he probably wouldn't want to see her, let alone hear her apology. But somehow she had to make him listen. Show him she'd changed. Sure, she'd still worry when he was out on the streets chasing bad guys. But she felt certain she could handle it now—sure she would no longer feel the irrational, uncontrollable terror for his safety she'd experienced last week while he was gone. She trusted he could handle whatever was thrown at him.

And so could she.

But if she didn't escape this damn boat, she'd never get the chance to plead her case.

So, by God, she was going to escape.

The boat's floor rolled gently under her feet as she rechecked the portholes, the drawers and cabinets, the tiny bathroom, the extra blankets on the bunk. There was a closet with a padlock that wouldn't budge, but other than that, there was no hint of anything useful, and no way out other than the hatch door up to the deck, which was bolted shut from the outside.

New tears of frustration clouded her vision, and she dug into the bottom of her tote for a tissue. As she blew her nose, her disheartened gaze landed on the contents of her canvas bag. Miraculously, they'd let her keep it. Maybe there was something in it she could use.

She picked up the make-up kit she'd hastily packed on

Charlie's orders, and after a thorough inspection she discarded it, followed by everything else in the tote.

Nothing she could use to escape.

Damn!

Sniffing, she finally pulled out the recorder with Bridge singing that she'd forgotten to take out at school today. Well, at least she could die hearing his voice.

She pushed the power button. As she did, something tugged at her memory. She set aside her wadded up tissue and grasped the recorder with both hands, fingering the volume knob thoughtfully.

What was it Bridge had done to capture those hoods at the convenience store up on Orange Grove?

Chapter Sixty-Four

S am Grayson glanced incredulously at the photo Bridge thrust under his nose. "A little old lady? *That's* who you think is in cahoots with Watson?"

Bridge fought back his mounting frustration and sense of urgency. "No, damn it! In the background. Look at what Watson's gardener is doing."

Gray took the photo and stuck it under the desk lamp. In it, Enrico was standing knee-deep in Watson's lily pond, furtively pulling something out of the water. Something that looked suspiciously *unlike* plant matter. In fact, it looked like it could be a small storage drive in a Ziplock bag.

"Well, I'll be damned." Gray looked up. "This must be how Watson's been passing on the data. While he fiddles with the lilies in the morning he slips the bag into the water. Then the gardener fishes it out on Friday and passes it along. No wonder we never saw the exchanges with the Chinese. We've been watching the wrong people. You say you found the photo at Miss Flannery's?"

Bridge nodded. "She's gone, and so is Deane. The FBI equipment is ruined and the hard drive with all the logs on my laptop has been erased. I checked Watson's place before I left, and the house is locked up tight as a drum. His boat is gone, too. The son of a bitch has taken her, Gray. I just know it." His skin crawled at the very thought.

"Seems you may be right."

Bridge slammed his fist on the desktop. "If he so much as *breathes* on her, I swear I'll—"

"Calm down. Deane's with them. Nothing will happen to her as long as he's alive."

"How do you know he's with them?"

"Well, let's see." Gray pulled out his cell phone, punched up a text message, and turned it so Bridge could read it. "Here we are." Deane's text was short and to the point.

EXCHANGE SLIP 17. MARINA DEL REY. HEADING MEXICO. MAC HOSTAGE.

Bridge felt his blood boil. "Fuck! He's really got her." He pulled his Kevlar and PPD windbreaker out of his bottom drawer. "Let's go."

Gray ran after him, grabbing his own vest and slipping it on as he went. "She'll be okay."

"I can't believe Deane managed to get captured, too. Come to think of it, how did he get a message through?" Bridge asked, gunning the engine of his truck and slapping a cherry flasher onto the roof through the window.

Grayson snapped on his seat belt. "He's my informant, working from the inside. We put him in Watson's way a while back and he fell for it. Thinks Deane's young and greedy, and has used him to keep tabs on our investigation."

Bridge's hair rose on his arms. "My God. Double-agenting the Chinese? The kid's barely out of diapers! He could be killed." The tires squealed as he peeled the truck out into traffic. "Hell, *she* could be killed."

Chapter Sixty-Five

Mary Alice knew she'd only have one chance to get it right.

Two tough-looking men had boarded the boat a few minutes earlier, accompanied by the cute brunette Sam Grayson had been dancing with at the party. Their eyes watched in silent curiosity as Charlie led Mary Alice up from the cabin and onto the deck. The men looked her up and down, male interest vying with outright suspicion in their expressions. She shuddered and turned her back on them.

The sun disappeared over the horizon of choppy sea in a molten ball of red. The wind had kicked up, whipping the marina flags and rocking the boat. Mary Alice clutched her tote bag close to her heart, shivering in her thin summer dress.

Deane strolled up and draped his jacket over her shoulders, but she shucked it off immediately. "No thanks. I'd rather freeze to death."

For a split second Deane looked taken aback, but then he shrugged and plucked the jacket off the deck, casually tossing it onto the bench lining the aft railing. "Suit yourself."

Watson watched the exchange with narrowed eyes. "Get below, Deane." He motioned at Mary Alice and snarled to one of the strangers, "Keep an eye on her while we finish up." To her he said, "This'll take five minutes, and then we're shoving off."

He disappeared behind Deane into the cabin, along with the brunette and the second man. Mary Alice noted the stranger was carrying a large satchel. Must be the final pay-off, she thought, squeezing her eyes shut. Which meant…

I know too much.

With a leaden sinking in her stomach, she realized there was no way she was going to get out of this situation alive. Not unless she made her escape. And the odds were not likely to get any better than right now to execute her plan. They were still at the dock, and she had just one guard. The man they'd left with her was armed and muscular, but she was counting on surprise to give her an advantage.

Her only advantage.

Sucking down a long, steadying breath, she shot a sidelong glance at the man, then looked around, pretending to decide where to sit. Deane's jacket lay conveniently on the bench at the back of the boat. Rubbing her arms, she walked over to it as casually as she could, then bent to set her tote down. With a huff and her chin held high, she grabbed the jacket and slipped it on.

Her heart pounded in her throat.

Blocking the guard's view with her body, she held her breath, reached inside the tote, and punched the 'play' button on the recorder.

Sweet Lord in heaven, please let this work.

One thousand one, one thousand two, one thousand three—

She turned to the guard and smiled weakly, then slowly ambled along the railing until she got to where the deck narrowed and ran alongside the cabin toward the front of the boat.

One thousand seven, one thousand eight—

"That's far enough," the man barked, waving her away from the passage. He took a couple of steps toward the center of the deck.

"Sorry," she mumbled, running her hand nervously along the cabin wall as she deliberately turned and made her way to stand with her back to the hatch door. Her knees shook so badly she was afraid he'd hear the bones knocking together.

One thousand fifteen.

Now!

Please start now!

On cue, her own voice, lowered an octave in a poor attempt at disguise, boomed out of the tape recorder. "*FBI! Get your hands in the air! Do it now!*"

She and the man whirled in the same instant, he to the sound of the unidentified voice, and she to quickly slide the hatch door's bolt home. She ignored the panicked look that flashed over Deane's face through the small portal window next to the hatch as she turned back to the man on the deck.

"*I'm not saying it again! We've got you surrounded!*"

The guard yanked his gun from under his coat and searched behind the boat in confusion.

Before he knew what hit him, Mary Alice took a long running leap, gave the man a huge shove, and tumbled him over the back railing into the harbor. As he surfaced, sputtering and cursing in the murky water, she grabbed her bag, shook out her aching shoulder, and dashed up the gangway toward the dock.

Chapter Sixty-Six

"**M**ary Alice!"

Bridge could hardly believe what he'd just witnessed as he, Grayson, and the SWAT team they'd summoned on the way had prepared to launch their attack on Watson's boat. Before they could even move, his pretty angel had single-handedly captured the bad guys—and using one damned cool maneuver.

What the hell was she thinking?

He thundered down the marina dock with the others, catching her up by the waist and swinging her in the air. "Thank God, oh, thank *God* you're safe."

She threw her arms around his neck and dissolved into tears. "Bridge! Is it really you? How did you find me?" She sobbed into his chest, clinging to him as though she'd never let him go.

Grayson and the team streaked past and poured onto the boat, taking charge of the situation and fishing the flailing guard out of the harbor.

"What the hell possessed you to pull a stunt like that?"

Bridge lambasted Mary Alice as he poured kisses over her face. "They could have killed you! I would never have forgiven myself if anything had happened to you."

"I had to get out of there. If I didn't—"

"Honey, you should have let Deane handle it. That's his job—"

"Deane's dirty. He sold out to Watson."

He groaned. Of course she would think that. "Baby, he was undercover. A plant."

"Well, damn." She leaned her forehead against his shoulder, wiping her eyes. "I never thought of that possibility. I was just so scared."

"Don't *ever* put yourself in danger like that again. You've got to promise me. I couldn't stand to lose you. Mary Alice, I—" He blinked at the expression on her face as she looked up at him. "What?"

She just smiled through her tears.

Suddenly it hit him. "This is what it does to you, isn't it? When I'm out on the streets?"

She gave a wry nod, and hiccoughed. "How does it feel?"

"Lousy. No wonder you don't want anything to do with me." *Fucking hell.* He groaned, tipping his head back. "And suddenly, he gets it."

"Bridge, I—"

May as well get it all over with. He raised his hand like a stop sign. "No, before you tell me to go straight to hell, let me just say a couple of things."

"I wouldn't tell you to go to hell," she murmured into his neck, snuggling closer. "But go ahead."

He laid his cheek to her temple, breathing in the scent of strawberries he'd grown to love so much. "I'm getting a promotion to lieutenant soon. No, it's already a done deal," he assured her when she looked up as if she would protest. "Which means I'll be supervising from behind a desk—with

Patrol at first. I will have to rotate back into SIS eventually, but it won't be for a good while."

She looked up into his eyes, her own shining. "You did this…for me?"

He nodded. "I need you in my life, Mary Alice. I'll do whatever it takes to get you and keep you there."

"Oh, Bridge. Are you sure? I know how much you like the rush and excitement of being in SIS."

A thousand sparks of hope bloomed in his heart. This didn't sound like a kiss-off. Did he really dare hope she still wanted him?

He gave her his best lopsided grin. "Guess I'll just have to get my excitement somewhere else. Got any ideas?" He gazed at her lovingly.

Wishing. Wanting.

Her expression softened and turned misty. "I might."

"Really?" He swallowed, hardly believing his luck. "Does this mean you'll give me another chance?"

"No." She shook her head, and for a horrible moment his heart stopped beating.

"I'm giving *myself* another chance," she said tenderly. "At happiness. I was such a fool to deny the best thing that's ever happened to me, to turn away the best man a woman could ever hope to want. I love you, Bridge. I'm sorry I was so blind. Can you ever forgive me?"

"Oh, God." Relief flooded his body, and he crushed her to him. "I love you, too, Mary Alice. And there's nothing to forgive. Please, just swear to me you won't think about it and change your mind later."

She raised her lips and captured his in a deep, soulful kiss. "I'll never change my mind, Russell Bridger, not if I live to be a hundred." She kissed him again, heating his blood with her certainty and the depth of desire he felt stir in her body. "You know how to count to a hundred, don't you, Lieutenant?"

A low rumble came from deep in his throat. "I don't know, Miss Mary Alice. I'm hopeless at math." He pulled her even closer.

"One of your more endearing traits," she murmured.

He chuckled as his heart melted. "I might need some serious tutoring in that department. Interested?"

She smiled as their lips met. "I might have a few nights a week to devote."

"*Nuh-uh.* I'd want you every single night."

"Oh, my," she said breathlessly, and batted her eyelashes.

"It could take a whole lifetime for me to reach a hundred. You up for that kind of commitment?"

She sighed into his chest, a contented sound, full of love and promise for the future. "Oh, yes. I wouldn't take the job for any less."

Epilogue

Bridge stood under the beribboned arch of the blossom-laden rose arbor and, grinning like a fool, placed a gold band on the hand of the woman he loved, and promised to keep her forever.

Stop! he wanted to shout to the world. *Stop and just let me savor this moment!*

He'd waited for this for so long. Mary Alice had insisted on delaying the wedding until the next spring when her roses, and the ones he'd transplanted from his dad's house, would be in full, resplendent bloom.

The day had finally arrived, and Mary Alice was radiant, beaming up at him like an angel from heaven, her pale hair glinting red in the sunlight. Her white dress floated delicately on the teasing breeze, as did the heady fragrance of hundreds of roses in full bloom. He glanced down at his side, to Mama's rose bushes, and could almost feel his mother's love pouring out from the blossoms.

His gaze wandered over the crowd of friends gathered around the arbor. His dad and Nancy stood beside them as best man and maid of honor. Bridge secretly winked to little Ivy, who swung her flower-girl basket back and forth in front of her as she watched the ceremony in awe. He spotted Mary Alice's mother dabbing her eyes in the first row, along with old Mrs. Trent and the ladies of the Historical Rose Society. Behind them were Jason Deane and Captain Trujillo and the rest of the guys from the station. There was the ever-hopeful Gray, ogling one of the teachers from Mary Alice's nursery school. The old road crew was there, too, complete with Gary and Denise and their new baby. And everywhere he looked, three year-olds ran around or squirmed in their mothers' laps.

It was great. Just the kind of wonderful, chaotic wedding day every man should have. His heart filled to bursting as he turned back to his beautiful bride.

Mary Alice slipped a ring on his finger and in a soft, clear voice made her vows to him. For some reason he suddenly couldn't focus, the gold band dissolving into a prism of soft colors. He took a shaky breath.

From somewhere far away he heard someone suggest he kiss the bride. He gathered her in his arms, and amid sighs from the friends and family surrounding them, he tenderly pressed his lips to hers. She smiled up at him, on her face a look of pure devotion.

"I love you, Mrs. Bridger," he whispered.

"And I love you, my darling Lieutenant Bridger." Her eyes reflected an endless joy. "But you know," she said, a special smile tilting her pretty lips upward. "I think we're going to have to work on your math a bit more."

"And why's that?" he said, mildly surprised at her choice of subject at a time like this. "Not that I'm complaining, mind you."

She tilted her head and looked coyly through her lashes, then grasped his hand and laid it against her flat stomach. "People will probably tease you about not being able to count to nine."

Count to—

His breath caught in his throat. Was she saying what he thought she was saying? "How far along have we gotten?"

"Just one. Maybe two. Months."

He let out a whoop and swept her up in his arms, giving her a long, joyful kiss.

"So, what do you suppose did it?" he whispered when he could think again. "The spurs?"

"Russell Bridger!" She gave him a smack on the arm and giggled. "Of course not!"

"No, you're right." He chuckled wickedly. "They just put a hole in the *sheet*, not in the—"

Family and guests descended over them both, showering them with hugs and congratulations. He felt a warm, soft hand slip into his, and heard Mary Alice's seductive voice in his ear.

"It must have been your old stop sign," she whispered. "It does need a sanding."

He looked into the laughing eyes of his new wife, and his happiness was complete.

Sanding, hell. He'd have to remember to have the damn thing bronzed, splinters and all.

About the Author

New York Times and USA Today Best Selling author Nina Bruhns pens adventurous romantic thrillers that contain a unique blend of interesting characters and settings, twisty suspense, and sizzling romance. To date, she has published over 35 award-winning novels:

3-time Daphne du Maurier Award winner

National Readers Choice Award winner

3-time RITA Award nominee

4-time RT BookReviews Reviewers Choice Award

#1 Amazon Best Seller in Romantic Suspense, Police Procedurals, Anthologies, and Movers & Shakers Top 30 Amazon Most Popular Romance Authors

Top 50 Amazon Best Seller in Thrillers, Romance, Action & Adventure, Mystery, Contemporary Romance, Thriller & Suspense, Detective, Anthologies, and Women's Fiction

Amazon Germany Top 10 in Krimis & Thriller and Polizeiromane

Amazon Japan Top 100 in Police Procedurals and Romantic Suspense

Amazon UK #1 Best Selling author in Anthologies & Collections

Read more about Nina Bruhns and her books at www.NinaBruhns.com. Sign up for her New Releases email list, and she'll let you know when each new book is published.

Facebook: facebook.com/Nina.Bruhns.author

Twitter: @NinaBruhns

Pinterest: pinterest.com/ninabruhns

Email: NinaBruhns@aol.com

Website: NinaBruhns.com

Goodreads: goodreads.com/author/show/50896.Nina_Bruhns

Amazon: amazon.com/NinaBruhns/e/B001H6GC5I